FLIGHT DOWN THE RIVER

Brigid was silent. The sun grew warmer, the Shannon turned a peaceful blue. Cormac felt a softness in his heart for the girl he was holding. A man would travel many miles to find so fierce a woman. "Biddy—" he said gently. But her eyes were closed. Sound asleep. "Behold, good wolfhound, the High King is so attractive to women that they fall asleep in his arms," he muttered to Podraig. There was no bark from the bow of the boat. Podraig, too, was asleep. If anyone was to praise the exploits of the High King he would have to do it himself. But before praise, a tough and mysterious question. Why did they want Biddy's head so badly? Why was she worth more than he?

Also by Andrew M. Greeley from Tom Doherty Associates

Nuala Anne McGrail Novels

Irish Gold
Irish Lace
Irish Whiskey
Irish Mist
Irish Eyes
Irish Love
Irish Stew!
Irish Cream
Irish Crystal
Irish Linen
Irish Tiger

Bishop Blackie Ryan Mysteries

The Bishop and the Missing L Train
The Bishop and the Beggar Girl of St. Germain
The Bishop in the West Wing
The Bishop Goes to the *University*
The Bishop in the Old Neighborhood
The Bishop at the Lake

The O'Malleys in the Twentieth Century

A Midwinter's Tale
Younger Than Springtime
A Christmas Wedding
September Song
Second Spring
Golden Years

The Senator and the Priest

All About Women
Angel Fire
Angel Light
Contract with an Angel
Faithful Attraction
The Final Planet
Furthermore!: Memories of a Parish Priest
God Game
Jesus: A Meditation on His Stories and His Relationships with Women
The Magic Cup
Star Bright!
Summer at the Lake
The Priestly Sins
White Smoke
Sacred Visions (editor with Michael Cassutt)
The Book of Love: A Treasury Inspired by the Greatest of Virtues (editor with Mary G. Durkin)
Emerald Magic: Great Tales of Irish Fantasy (editor)

The Magic Cup

Andrew M. Greeley

A TOM DOHERTY ASSOCIATES BOOK
NEW YORK

THE MAGIC CUP

Originally published in 1979 by Warner Books.

A Tor Book
Published by Tom Doherty Associates, LLC
175 Fifth Avenue
New York, NY 10010

www.tor.com

ISBN-13: 978-0-7653-5815-8
ISBN-10: 0-7653-5815-8

First Tor edition: March 2008

Printed in the United States of America

0 9 8 7 6 5 4 3 2 1

For EAMONN CASEY
(who will not mind, I hope)
in gratitude for introducing me
to the wonders of Kerry.

Time passes so gently in this country, moist
Change as slow as the cliff yielding to the sea—
Hear the trumpet from the past, silver voiced,
Its clear mark differently on you and me,
Shrewd, still close to the flock, bishop urbane—
And bittersweet sounds of the Kerry Dance,
Of hope and laughter no matter what pain
The Irish, with Jesus and Mary, caught in Romance.

When, Eamonn, you return to Inch's fair strand
And the sun explodes like thunder in the reeks,
Watch through the gray mists the sun arising:
Their weary footprints softly tracing sand
The three tired pilgrims whom all Ireland seeks—
Great Podraig, magic Biddy, and Cormac the King.

There is an Irish version of the old Celtic myth which most of us know as the Arthurian cycle—the quest for the Holy Grail.

The Irish story has a very different ending, but then the Irish have always been a strange, difficult people who think they know something no one else knows.

This is one way the Irish legend of the magic cup and the very magic princess might be told.

The Magic Cup

Chapter 1

T*hick gray clouds* trailing their black shadows across the valley floor chased the clear sky beyond the horizon. The sun flashed an occasional quick shaft of light on the singing throngs that straggled through the valley towards the green hill in the distance. Despite the thick, pungent smell of harvest in the August air, the bishop's wife shivered with cold. Fearfully, she handed the somber stranger a dish of curds.

"The sun passes quickly," she said, her wavering voice betraying the fear she felt for this red-haired man with the thick muscular arms. He could tear her apart with a single movement of those arms. She promised herself again that she would yield her life and honor only after a fierce fight. Perhaps the children could flee down the hill while she resisted. He was so strong her final battle could only last a few seconds. She drew the heavy black mantle around her pale blue tunic, hoping he did not see her slender shoulders tremble.

The stranger took the wooden bowl with elegant courtesy. For such a powerful man he had graceful, gentle-looking hands. He ate his food with surprising delicacy.

"As quickly as human life," he said gravely, sounding almost like her husband preaching a funeral sermon.

She did not know whether to sit with him on the rough, bleached bench at the entrance of their tiny hill fort or return to the house. The children were safe at the door, playing with the stranger's huge wolfhound. She stood by the bench, still shivering beneath her mantle and watching him eat as though she were a servant in attendance at a feast.

She was feeding the chickens at the wall of the hill fort when he appeared suddenly at the entrance, a tall, grim young man with huge eyebrows of flaming red, a fierce wolfhound at his side, a dangerous shillelagh gripped menacingly in his hand. He drank in the lines of her body with thirsty, piercing blue eyes. The servants were purchasing food, Enda was in Tara; she and the two little girls were completely defenseless. He had given the usual greeting, "Jesus and Mary be with this house," respectfully enough, but his knuckles were white around the handle of the cruel club.

He wished to see the good Bishop Enda. The bishop was in Tara with the Holy Abbot Colum. Might he wait for their return? It might be many hours. He had come a great distance; he would wait, if the gentle lady granted permission.

Indeed, he had come many miles. His gray pilgrim's tunic was covered by thick dust. His handsome young face was drawn tight with weariness. The bishop's wife forgot her fear long enough to remember the duty of hospitality. She wrapped herself quickly within the protective vastness of her cloak and ran to the house to fetch him food. The wolfhound inspected the frightened chickens with interest, tried to get a response from an indifferent cow, then trotted after her to the door of the house. She could feel his vicious fangs sinking into her neck. Instead the dog offered his huge head to her daughters to be petted. The younger girl pulled his big ear. The dog barked delightedly.

"Would you like a cup of mead?" she asked politely. Her heart was still beating rapidly, but confidence was flowing back into her body.

"Better that it be saved for the fair. There will not be enough to drink in all of Royal Meath for Dermot MacFergus's celebration." There was a flash of silver in his hard blue eyes, anger in his resonant voice. His feet seemed to push against the ground, as though to shove the offending earth away.

"It has been thirty years since there was a harvest festival. My husband says many are coming simply to see what such festivals are like."

His grim face turned towards her, his eyes devoured her. "One can become quite thirsty in thirty years—especially if one is Irish." His countenance was brightened by a quick, warm smile. It vanished just as quickly. He continued to stare at her intently.

"It may be many more hours before Bishop Enda and the holy abbot return. They may have to wait long before the king will see them—if he will see them at all," she said. She was afraid again. If only he would leave. Her fingers tightened on the plain silver broach at the neck of her mantle.

"I imagine that the king will see his cousin no matter

what the royal concubine Finnabair may say. The O'Neills are a determined lot, especially when they are clergy." Another hint of the smile. His smile made her want to caress the lines of weariness out of his face.

"She will destroy all Ireland with her black magic before she is finished. We Christians are no match for her." She spoke primly, struggling to keep her emotions in order.

"Does the wife of a bishop believe in fairy lands and fairy princesses, Lady Ann?" He asked ironically—this time only his eyes smiling.

So he knew her name. Her face was hot with embarrassment. "Of course, I do not, but there is something strange and unearthly about her beauty. It is also said that she really came seeking King Cormac." She felt the broach bend under the pressure of her fingers. *Oh, Enda, come home quickly. I am confused and frightened.*

He raised one of his massive eyebrows quizzically. "The monk?"

"He is not a monk. He is a scholar and a pilgrim in Rome fighting for the successor of St. Peter against the Goths. He is also the strongest warrior, the finest athlete, and the most noble poet in all Ireland. The young women grow faint at the mention of his name."

"Do the poets say he grows faint at the sight of women? I have heard no one sing of his success in love." The stranger stood up abruptly and turned to stare across from the Hill of Slaine to the Hill of Tara. He gripped his deadly club as though he were about to swing it in battle. The wolfhound turned away from the children, stopped wagging his tail, watched his master for a moment, and then, bored by a false signal, returned to the delights of having his ear pulled.

She felt compelled to defend the absent High King. "No one doubts his ability to succeed in love if he should choose." She added quickly, "May the Lord Jesus and his holy Mother protect King Cormac from the witch Finnabair, should he ever return." Thank God he was pacing up and down, no longer consuming her with his passionate eyes. She felt a firm but friendly nudge against her thigh. She gasped in dismay. The great wolfhound nudged her again and looked up at her with big, happy eyes, his mouth open in a vast affectionate grin. Despite herself, Ann patted the immense head. She grinned back and released her tight grip on the broach, letting the cloak fall open.

The stranger had turned sharply at the sound of her cry. The warm smile, the silver flash in his eyes. "You must forgive Podraig. He has a weakness for beautiful women."

Lady Ann's face flamed once more. Childbearing and the rigors of life in Ireland had only refined her brown, slender good looks. Still, even the Irish, masters of the elegant compliment, were hesitant about flattering the wife of a cleric. She rewrapped her cloak tightly.

"You call your dog after the great saint who lit yonder fire?" She did her best to cover her confusion—and her pleasure—by being shocked at the irreverence to her husband's sainted predecessor.

"Go away, Podraig," the stranger said, shoving the great gray dog gently. "You can make friends with the lovely lady after she has grown weary listening to me."

Her shaking legs could no longer support her. She collapsed to the bench, feeling grateful for its sturdy support. Podraig ignored the command. Placing his massive head on her lap, he looked up with adoration.

"My husband the bishop says that in his head King

Dermot is a Christian, but in his heart he still yearns for the old religion." She felt like she had no more strength than rainwater in a barrel.

"I would think that other parts of him might also be involved." His voice was hard. She couldn't see his eyes, which were cast downward.

"When Queen Muirne was alive he performed the old rite of inauguration—as bloody and obscene a ceremony as you will find on all the earth. Yet when Queen Ethne was here he was a devout and pious Christian who came to yonder church each Lord's Day for the Eucharist. Now that he has a pagan concubine, he proclaims a harvest festival." He sat down next to her on the bench.

Instead of being more afraid, she was sorry for his great weariness. He was so tired. The poor man had come a long way. He would never be able to sleep unless he let the tension flow out of his body. If he was going to rape her, he was going to rape her. Rapists don't talk about the Eucharist. Of course, she would not put her arm around him, as one would do with an exhausted child who was falling asleep. She banished the thought of holding him in her arms.

"Yet he has had a hard life," she said. "His three queens dead, his two sons, Colman Mar and Colman Bec killed in battle, King Cormac gone—perhaps never to return. Finnabair brings consolation to his old age. He has ruled long. My husband the bishop says he has ruled well as Irish kings go."

The blue eyes regarded her coldly for a moment. He was really quite young—in his middle twenties probably; the eyes made him look older.

"If political skills and military victory were enough, Dermot would be a great king. The king is Ireland. When he sways back and forth Ireland sways. He keeps power that way but Ireland suffers."

"Even now," she agreed dutifully, frightened by his intensity, "it is said that the crops have been poor this year because the king sleeps with a pagan woman."

"Foolish superstition!" snapped the stranger angrily. "If the crops are bad it is not because heaven is punishing us for the king's amusements; it is rather because the Irish people are confused by a king who won the great victory at Dumcreda through the help of the holy abbot and then had the foul ceremony of inauguration to keep the alliance of the pagans in the country. If the king is not clear about his beliefs, how can the people of Ireland know what they should believe?"

The bishop's wife knew that her Enda would have thought the argument too harsh, but she did not want to anger the stranger by disagreeing with him. The drops of rain, which had been falling lightly for some time, came more quickly. "The rain is worse. We should go into the house."

She gathered the two little girls together and herded them inside ahead of her and the stranger. They went past the chickens, cackling loudly to protest the rain, and entered the dark *aircha.* The stranger sat wearily on a polished wood bench by the table while she lit a candle and hurried the children into their *immdai.* She came back to the *aircha,* automatically removing the broach from her cloak. With a salmonlike leap the stranger was on his feet, a firm hand graciously lifting the cloak from her shoulders. He was very close to her, his eyes once more probing every part of her body. They were alone in a darkened house with the rain beating loudly on the thatch roof. She was conscious of the smell of the smouldering turf embers in the fireplace. She cowered back against the rough log wall, head down, feeling that she was naked before this invader.

He swung the cloak to a peg, carefully pinning the broach to it so it would not fall to the floor. He was grinning at her like a pleased little boy.

"Lady Ann, you are surely one of the most beautiful women in Ireland. You must be a terrible distraction to the good bishop in his ecclesiastical responsibilities. If I were a raiding pirate seeking new slave women, I would have carried you away on sight. But I am only a poor pilgrim, even less a threat to your lovely body than the faithful Podraig. You are safer with me in the house than if there were a bevy of holy nuns here."

She was embarrassed, humiliated, angry, and reassured. She sought refuge in his contagious laughter. What a fool she had been. Then she sank to her knees in front of him, the humiliation returning.

"I am overcome with embarrassment and fear," she said contritely, knowing that there was nothing at all to fear from this strange, attractive, pathetic man.

"In God's name, why?"

"I have treated the High King of Ireland as though he were a common traveler. I am truly sorry, royal lord. If I had known—"

"Of course, Lady Ann, you should have known. Cormac MacDermot is fool enough to travel through Ireland as a simple pilgrim with a huge stick and a wild-looking dog. He has every right to expect the reception due a king. Still, I think you must be absolved because Podraig likes you—but only on the condition that you fill this bowl with more curds."

He lifted her off her knees like a princess and handed her the bowl with the deference of the lowest of servants.

"I have not been courteous, royal lord." She couldn't look at him. Would her mad heart never stop beating?

"Then let it be written in the annals of Ireland that Ann, wife of the Bishop Enda of Slaine, was rude, hostile, and unfriendly to Cormac the High King when he came to her rath as a simple pilgrim."

She knew he was smiling his warm smile, even if she did not have the courage to look. "That's not true!" she replied hotly.

"Of course, it's not true. You invited me in, you gave me food, you offered me shelter, you petted my fierce warrior of a dog—didn't she, Podraig? You did everything one should do for a stranger. King Jesus himself would not ask for more. Nor will I."

She produced a bone for the delighted Podraig. "I have done none of the courtesies. Should I warm the water for the *fothrucud*?" she asked diffidently.

"Lady Ann, I assure you that if the holy abbot, my royal cousin Colum, should return to find me being bathed by the wife of a bishop, I would be exiled to the coldest and most rocky island of Scotland—as appealing as that courtesy might be."

Stop smiling at me that way, even if you are a king. "Even the Lord Jesus," she said meekly, "washed the feet of his apostles."

"The High King of Ireland should not argue religion with a woman, much less the wife of a bishop." He was weary and dejected again, sinking into Enda's chair at the head of their table.

She busied herself preparing for the washing of his feet, her hands still trembling and her heart still pounding. She laid out the large linen cloth in front of him, placing on it three copper basins filled with water. (Only important people such as bishops, she reflected with irony—and some pride—had copper basins.) She took two heated stones from the hearth and put each in a basin to warm the water. She arranged the ground pumice, the crushed flowers and reeds, which would be used to scrub the feet, and finally put a pile of clean linen cloths next to the basins. King Cormac watched her in silence and merely nodded his head in grave courtesy when she gave him the required flagon of mead and removed his tattered mantle.

Podraig, like a loyal and devoted servant, padded after her, always keeping his great bulk out of her way.

"I have never washed the feet of a High King before," she said, sitting on the floor in front of him. She banished brusquely from her mind the image of bathing his whole body. It would be a very beautiful body.

"Given the kinds of men who have been High King since Podraig—the saint, that is—it is perhaps just as well." The brief warmth was gone from his voice now, replaced by deep melancholy.

She removed the thonged leather sandals and gasped with horror at the sight of barely healed scars and still fresh wounds which covered the soles. "You have walked a long way, Royal Lord," she exclaimed. Her fingers tried to tenderly ease the pain away as though they had a sympathy all their own.

"From Rome." Such great sadness.

"Were there no horses in Europe and no women to wash and bind up the feet of the *Ardri* of Ireland?" She did not try to hide her tears of compassion for the poor beautiful man.

"It is good for a king to walk and to avoid the services and attentions of others." He was drifting away into grim reverie.

Gently she removed the dirt with a wet linen cloth, and began to wash his wounds with the clean water. Bigger feet than her husband's—her throat tightened at the thought of Enda. Not even a married woman should desire her husband as much as she yearned for him. He said it was not sinful, but it grew worse with the years. A passing image of his lean, strong body was sufficient to awaken her need. He was so sensible, so gentle. Soon he would return with the fiery Abbot Colum. Would the High King and his cousin quarrel? The monk was a holy man; he was also an O'Neill with the passionate temperament of his clan. He believed in his vision of a Christian Ireland with characteristic O'Neill frenzy. The O'Neills had fought among themselves before. What would Enda do if they grew angry with one another? She stopped the wandering of her thoughts and concentrated on her task.

Washing the feet of a guest was a courtesy that even women of noble background like the bishop's wife were honored to perform. Normally it was an action without sensuality, but the slightest contact with this dark, mysterious man made her blood run fast. She could feel the hard tension even in his feet, the suppressed rage which seemed to rule his body, as she very gently placed them in the warm water.

Ever so softly she cleansed his wounds. The muscles of his feet began to relax, a little peace flowed up his calves. Such strong, graceful legs—like a young birch. She should not think of the beauty of a man's legs. She never had until Enda possessed her. Now she could not help herself. Oh, what would happen to this poor man when he went to Tara? Still, she did not want to be his enemy.

"So now you think that perhaps Jesus and Mary ought

to protect Queen Finnabair from King Cormac?" he said, breaking into her thoughts.

She pulled back in horror. "My Royal Lord, you have the power to read my thoughts!"

"No, I am good at guessing." Again, there was that instant of humanity and softness in his face. He took her hands firmly in his own and drew her back to her healing work. "Gentle Lady Ann, forgive my terrible rudeness. Please do continue. My weary feet are recovering already." His fingers released her hand and intertwined beneath his chin, the weight of his head resting heavily on them. He watched her closely.

She quickly finished drying his feet. It was not merely her body that felt his gaze. She felt his eyes pry into the recesses of her soul. She tried to control her flushed countenance. She felt trapped by his gaze but also exhilarated.

She crushed the flowers on his feet, the smell of perfume filled the air. She was finished. Impulsively she bent and kissed both scarred feet tenderly. "You are welcome home, King Cormac MacDermot."

He put both hands on her head as though in benediction. The grip tightened. Warmth flowed between them. He could take her now without resistance. He would not, but he could. There would always be friendship between her and the High King. Though she did not deserve it, she delighted in his admiration and gratitude. He released her head. Could he feel the blood surging through her brain?

He helped her to stand, his long fingers firmly holding her arm. "If there was such courtesy and charm in all Ireland as I have encountered in this house today, a man would be a fool to ever leave. Your husband, the Bishop of Enda, is a most fortunate man." He spoke softly as though blessing her.

Podraig's ears raised off the floor where he lay snoozing. He barked perfunctorily.

"So the good dog Podraig announces the coming of the holy abbot," commented Cormac, the hard irony returning to his voice.

They went to the door of the house. The clouds, emptied of rain, were scurrying away as rapidly as they had come. Sunlight fell on the simple white chariot coming slowly up the Hill of Slaine. The bishop's wife felt her heart jump, as it always did when she saw the plain, shrewd face of her husband. Beside him in his chariot was a tall, straight, blue-robed figure with long and flowing gray hair.

It was Colum of Iona, the most brilliant and powerful monk of all Ireland, the unquestioned leader of Ireland's royal family.

"It is my husband the bishop and the Holy Abbot Colum," she said excitedly, hoping that her relief was not too evident.

"An honor for your house," murmured Cormac MacDermot, "far greater than having a mere High King come to call."

Chapter 2

The *bishop's wife* restlessly opened the shutter to the tiny window of her bedchamber. The full moon of harvest-tide turned the mist on the Hill of Slaine a pale silver. She could hear in the distance snatches of song from Tara on the still night air. They were songs of the harvest god Lug. It was August; the days were still long in Ireland. Only a few hours of real night settled on the earth before the gray of morning returned to the bishop's compound. Unusually cool night air came through the open window. Shivering, the Lady Ann wrapped a blanket around her body over the thin sleeping-linen. She would not sleep until her husband returned. He had accompanied the holy abbot to the road to meet the abbot's nephew and aide, Baithene. King Cormac was gone to the stone church to spend his last night in prayer before returning to Tara.

Ann was more afraid than she had ever been since she and Enda left Britain to come to the Hill of Slaine. It was a nameless fear, unlike the ones she knew with Cormac earlier in the day. To be a woman was to risk violation at the hands of any drunken brute who did not fear the reprisal of your family; to be confused by the attention of an attractive man was the price of being a woman with deep passions. These fears were part of daily life.

She turned restlessly in her bed. If only Enda would return. She needed his protection and love. What if anything happened to him? She chased the thought away. It was unbearable to think of herself defenseless in this pagan country. Now she was too hot; she shoved the blanket away and felt the cool breeze touch her lightly.

The fears of this Lugnasa Eve were ghostly, unreal, undefinable. A threat of disaster hovered in the air like the germs of a plague preparing to strike. There were demons loose in Ireland—witchcraft, curses, plots both human and diabolic. She put aside the linen, let the night air caress her breasts. She wanted to belong to peaceful pursuits—the breeding and raising of children, the giving and receiving of love. She wanted to be free of the pall of ominous politics that, like a huge thunderhead, hung over Slaine and Tara.

She clung to the rough wood of her bed with the same intensity with which she had clung to her broach earlier in the day. If anything happened to Enda, would Cormac protect her? Of what value would the protection of that mad boy be—half monk, half king—confused, tired, unhappy? The breeze momentarily was painfully cold. She was too tense to pull the blanket back. What happened to those who trusted Cormac MacDermot?

The rhythm of the wild music across the valley began to

pound in her blood. It touched deep inside her a desire to yield to its primitive excitement. She twisted restlessly, as though in a paroxysm of love. She was a Christian matron, pious and reverent. Would the pagan within her never be still? She tried to shut out the noise of the revelry and the picture of her screaming passionately with the rest by remembering the somber conversation at her table.

She heard more about the crisis in Tara than any British woman would ever hear about politics. In the Romanized culture of her native land, men would not think of discussing matters of state in the presence of women. In Ireland a woman's right to listen and participate were taken for granted.

She closed the shutter softly. It was still cool, but she left the upper part of her body uncovered as she twisted back into her bed. The air against her skin was so peaceful. She might be less concerned if the men did not take her presence for granted. She would be better off to know nothing of the plots in Tara, not to have witnessed the tension between the *Tanaise,* the "expected" High King, and his powerful monastic cousin from Iona.

They had greeted each other politely, clasping hands like Irish warriors. The great Colum towered over his cousin. When Enda conducted them into the *aircha* she felt that two handsome, impatient bulls had entered her house, one with short red hair and a grim young face, the other with a thin countenance set in a frame of long, graying blond hair and lined by the rigors of monastery life, the hardships of travel, and the responsibilities of immense power.

"The Bishop of Rome sends his blessings to the great Abbot of Iona," said Cormac, irony tainting the solemnity of his message, as he released his cousin's hand.

"And how fares it with the successor to the Fisherman?" replied the abbot in his rich, booming voice, his shepherd's staff extended in the solemn ceremony, his eyes glittering even in the dim light of the room.

"It fares as well as can be expected with Goths ravaging Italy every year. Your brother in Rome worries about other fisherfolk, those of Ireland, holy cousin, who will not celebrate Easter at the same time as the church of Rome."

Cormac settled back in Enda's ornately carved chair and clasped his hands behind his head. He was baiting the abbot and enjoying it.

"Our way is more ancient," said Colum, his broad face flushing angrily. All through his life Colum had fought against the O'Neill temper. Now, toward the end of his middle years, the holy man was reported to have it well under control. This cousin knew how to torment him. The more angry Colum became, striding up and down by the fire, the more urbane the High King pretended to be. For the first time Ann disliked him.

The High King shrugged indifferently. "The Bishop of Rome has the strange notion that he holds the keys of the Fisherman, that the center of Christianity is Rome, not Iona. Doubtless he is mistaken."

The abbot pounded the floor of the house with his staff as if it were a battle-axe.

Enda, always the smooth diplomat, quickly intervened. "There is room in the Christian church for only one faith but many customs. The time of Easter is a custom. Sit down, noble guests, so that my wife and I may offer you the supper that your long journeys have earned you both."

Oh, Enda, you are so wonderful. Only I know that you are as passionate as they.

Suddenly aware of her presence, the two men bowed courteously. Enda had been clever.

"Jesus and Mary, be with this house," said the abbot gravely, piety and courtesy temporarily restraining his anger.

"And all who live in it," added the High King, rising from the chair that was not his and bowing to her with exaggerated deference.

"Jesus, Mary, and Patrick, be with our honored guests," she managed to reply, hoping that she sounded like a mother reproving two foolish little boys.

During the meal they talked of Rome and Europe, where the invasion of the Goths was destroying the remnants of the Roman Empire. Only at the end of the meal, as they munched on the apples she put before them, did their talk turn to Ireland.

"It will be a long, dark night in Europe, I fear," said her husband solemnly, his hands flat and steady on the oak table she so lovingly polished every day. Dear man, he sometimes sounded pompous. That was part of being a bishop.

"When it is at its darkest the light of faith will shine forth from Ireland and illumine the world," said Colum, his face glowing with excitement. "Already our monasteries are appearing in Britain and Gaul. Someday there will be Irish monks praying to God even in Italy." He extended his hands in a graceful, sweeping gesture as though embracing the world. No wonder so many had followed him. His enthusiasm filled the room like the heat of a fire. How like Cormac's were his long, tapering fingers.

"Then the Christian people of Italy will wonder, as do the Christian people in Gaul, about monks who come from a land which is still pagan." Cormac clenched his goblet like a weapon for combat. Why was the fool so angry? She felt even more impatient with him.

The flat light of the long August twilight sifted through the narrow windows of their log house, casting twisted shadows on the faces of the three men seated around the rough-hewn table. The soft, dank smell of harvest-time hung in the air. Ann poured some of their precious wine into the expected High King's flagon. The words came before she thought to stop them. "The Christian people in Gaul are wrong, King Cormac. There are many Christians on this beautiful green island." Again the humiliating warmth in her face.

"You see, holy abbot, all is not lost. With lovely women like the Lady Ann on our side, we will surely triumph over the Druids." His voice, almost tender at first, hardened into its usual irony. "Then your monks can replace the Druids and rule Ireland."

Monk or not, Colum of Iona was too much a descendant of Neill of the Nine Hostages to let a compliment go by unmatched. "If all the women of Ireland were as virtuous as the bishop's good wife, royal cousin, there would be no fear or hunger in the whole land." He bowed his head respectfully in her direction, his silken voice for a moment that of the smooth courtier.

"If all the priests were as dedicated and devout as her husband," Cormac joined the game, "we would not need monasteries to fight human sinfulness." His tone was even more courtly.

"And if the Irish talked less and drank less, there would be more peace on this wild island," she spat out angrily. Her fists clenched tightly, her voice shrill, she knew that her eyes were shining dangerously and that her skin had turned crimson. *Dear God, what have I done?*

The three men stared at her in disbelief. Though she had taken only a half goblet of wine, she was talking as if she were drunk. She plunged on into the depths of the ocean. "King Dermot is dying, poor man; he will not speak to his cousin the Abbot of Iona; a pagan witch is ruling in Tara, the harvest was bad, there are wars and cattle raids all over the country, and the descendants of Neill of the Nine Hostages play foolish word games with one another." She wished they would go home and she could be in her husband's arms. Why wouldn't the ground devour her and cover her embarrassment?

"She may be Maeve reborn," commented the High King dryly, recovering his tongue and a trace of a smile.

"Given her virtue it would be more likely holy Brigid," responded the abbot in a choked voice, as though he were trying to restrain laughter.

"Surely your woman has already become an Irish mother," said Cormac to her dumbfounded husband. "Now, please, gentle hostess and sweet lady," he raised his voice, sensing that she was close to another outburst, "do not be angry at us again. In our own mad O'Neill way the holy abbot and I are fond of one another. We have a painful matter to settle. We play our silly games to work up the courage to face our quarrel. You give us reason to seek the answers we must." It was the warm, powerful voice of a king talking to an admired and respected counselor. She would have fled from the room in shame if it had not been for the unabashed admiration on her husband's face. Thank God, the two mad O'Neills quickly forgot her presence.

"You will go to Tara in the morning?" The abbot's voice was soft, definite. He leaned across the table towards Cormac, his long body straining to reach the sick heart of the young man. "The Lady Ann speaks for the whole of Ireland. We need a king. You are the Expected One."

"An accident of birth, good cousin. King Jesus did not give me patience with fools nor hunger for battle nor love for power. You are the abbot, and you think of kingdoms and wars and power; I am the king, and I think only of solitude and peace." He buried his head in his hands, his energy drained away; he was limp, diminished. She wanted to hug him with sympathy.

"When you have solitude you are more restless than when you are with people. What do you seek in life, Cormac MacDermot?" The abbot's temper was rising again.

"King Jesus." The words were torn from twisted lips, a simple reply that caused Ann to tremble. The Jesus she knew did not demand such terrible seriousness.

"You will only find him after this life. You will only earn the right to live with him in the Promised Land to the West when you have served him as *Ardri* of Tara." The abbot was out of his chair, staff in hand, standing dramatically at the head of the table.

It was Cormac's turn to pace before the fireplace. Again, his body was filled with the tension and energy of barely controlled passion. Ann no longer wanted to hug him. The fires in him would destroy anyone who got too close.

"So, abbot cousin, you know what King Jesus wishes? He wants me to preside over an island with as many kings as there are hills? And most of them little better than armed cattle thieves and rapists? He wants me to be a ceremonial king who sleeps with the goddess Maeve to bring fertility to Ireland? He wants me to bring peace and order to this mad land in the only way a High King can—

with his blood and his right arm? He wants me to marry some noble Irish slut, make her pregnant, and keep her sober enough to bring an heir to the O'Neill line—that sacred family founded by a pirate and made up of the worst criminals Ireland has seen since Finn MacCool himself? Strange, good cousin, I do not find that life for me in the Gospels."

Cormac spoke as though he were addressing a crowd of hundreds. His graceful hand cut through the air like a sword of a polished fighter.

The abbot answered calmly. "He wants you to make Ireland Christian."

Cormac stopped pacing and swung around to face the abbot. "What is a Christian in this country?" The stroking sword of his hand was now harsh, deadly. His body was coiled for battle, his face a cold white, eyes angry slits. "Half the people who celebrate the festival of Lug across the valley cannot distinguish him from King Jesus. Your monks and those of Kiernan at Clonmacnoise make pictures of King Jesus in which he looks just like Lug. You claim that the stone phalluses all around the country are really crosses. Your Christian Brigid is the saint of spring; her shrine is at Kildare and her day is celebrated at Inbolc—just like the pagan Brigid. Most Irish think she is Mother Mary reborn. You want me to fight the white-haired harlot who is besotting my father's old age for a Christianity where Jesus is Lug and Mary is Brigid?"

Cormac stood straight and strong by the fire, his eyes blazing like a burning ember, caught up in the power of his own words. The bishop's wife was horrified by his blasphemy and amazed to see in Enda's tired face a hint of appreciation. The tart, thick smell of the turf with which Ann had just restocked the fireplace filled the room. She poured more wine for her husband and Cormac, milk for the abbot.

"You forget that we say Brigid's cross represents Christ the light of the world," said Colum of Iona calmly, resuming his seat at the table and sipping the fresh milk. "That would add to the power of your speech."

The fire went out of Cormac. "I was not making a speech," he muttered. He slumped into his chair—spent, beaten.

"It is time, Cormac, it is time." The abbot spoke more gently, resting his hand on the younger man's shoulder. "We have done great things since the sainted Podraig built yonder church. We must finish the work. This may be our last chance. If the Goths should invade Ireland—"

Cormac MacDermot merely shrugged.

Poor King Dermot, thought the bishop's wife. The great king who had set the first sacred stones at Clonmacnoise was dying now, seeking love from a spy because he did not have the love of a son. Little love any human could expect from a son like this.

So it seemed to have been decided. The last glow of twilight settled into the short darkness of night. The O'Neills, taking leave of their hostess with grave courtesy, departed into the night, one for Iona and the other for holy Patrick's church.

Why was she frightened, Ann asked herself, as she shivered on her hard bed? Was it the love and hate of those two half-mad men? Was it the mention of invasion by Goths? The magic of Finnabair? The threat of famine over the country? Cormac's blasphemy? Was it the harsh attractiveness of that haunted man? There would be difficult days—the sort her parents had known before the peace in west Britain that Arthur won. She wanted her little girls to escape such terrors. Yet there was no protection for them in a bishop's ring fort.

Enda would know. Would he never return? The abbot did not really approve of a married priest, much less a married bishop. He treated the bishops in his monasteries like common monks. Enda stood for the Roman church with its neat, orderly divisions like those in Britain with a diocese in each city. There were no cities in Ireland, only forts on hills; here was no neatness and little order. Enda himself had said that the Roman way meant little. Real power would more and more be with the abbots. Ireland's church would be ruled by the Pope of Iona, as he called him. Yet between Enda and the abbot there was respect and admiration, however much the priests from their two regimes might quarrel with one another.

Enda finally returned weary and quiet. Her heart jumped, as it always did when he returned. Modestly she pulled the linen to her neck. What would Enda think if he saw her waiting in bed half naked?

He hung his mantle on the wall by her head, opened the shutters slightly to look across the valley toward the lights of Tara. The moon etched the tired lines on his face. He glanced down at her.

"Still awake?" He saw her need for love.

"Yes." She was surprised by the anxiety in her voice.

He sat on the bed and took her hand. There was the firmness of need in his touch. "Frightening men, aren't they? From anger to laughter to piety to anger again as quickly as you can turn a mill wheel." He began to gently caress her face. Worry lifted its cold grip from her. It was sinful to permit a man's touch to have so much power over you.

"But he is a handsome man, isn't he?" Enda went on, his fingers lightly touching her neck, still thinking of the king though his sturdy body was demanding other activity.

Ann hoped he could not see her flush in the moonlight or feel the blood rushing to her face. "He is a strange, haunted man. I felt so sorry for him. I liked him; I was afraid of him," she said honestly enough. "Oh, Enda, what will he do in Tara?" Her voice broke with concern for the High King, for Ireland, and for her family.

"Only God knows, dear one. I fear he will be no match for Finnabair. The nobles will think him hard and arrogant. Cormac MacDermot is seeking something. Until he finds it there will be no peace in Ireland— Ah, you look so lovely in the moonlight. I fear no bishop should have a wife like you." He cast aside his tunic, a pitiless and determined lover thirsting for a conquest.

He gently pulled back the cover and opened the sleep-linen. He took her firmly in his arms. Her body awaited him eagerly. His hands began their subtle exploration; she tingled with delight. Her own hands, hungrily digging into his muscles, sought the sweetness of his flesh. His skin was soft, smooth, lovely.

"Perhaps Cormac MacDermot should have a wife." Her voice was already hoarse with awakened desire.

"He would have to be very fortunate—as I am—in his choice. The woman who marries Cormac MacDermot will need magic more powerful than Finnabair's." His words became breathless as he began to take possession of her. Enda's own magic, so familiar and so new, deprived Ann of her power of speech. Her only response was a whimpering sigh.

Later, as she drifted into sleep, she wondered if it were

really true that the shadow of the sacred king cured infertility. Would there soon be the longed-for new life within her again? She knew that Cormac MacDermot would have dismissed such thought as foolish pagan superstition.

Chapter 3

The *slave girl* Brigid looked up anxiously from her work on the bank of the River Nith. Tara glittered in the morning sunlight, bedecked for the fair like a harlot waiting for a score of lovers. She had taken the queen's white dress to a place on the Nith between the second and third walls so that she would not be seen. It was humiliating to be washing a dress on the first day of the festival. It was also dangerous. A slave girl of so little importance that she could be put to work on the morning of *Tailtiu* was fair game for anyone who wished to begin the day's lusty entertainments early. She must be careful. She must always be careful. She pounded the cleaning stone angrily on the harlot's dress.

There were no clouds in the sky. The wooden stockades gleamed almost white in the sunlight. Near her were the somber, dank fairy well of Nemnach and the enchanted stone house of Mairisiu, sacred places that most of the inhabitants of Tara avoided. They did not forget the fate that had befallen the slave girls of an earlier King Cormac. Her two predecessors would protect her, Brigid told herself. There was no danger of the fairy king lusting after her. She pounded the soiled dress ever more fiercely with her rock. The fool queen should take more care when she drank wine. The ground was hard on her knees. It didn't matter.

Though it was still early in the day, Tara was already alive. The *rath* of kings, glimmering brightly in the reflected light of colored banners, was filled with people—poets to sing songs, lesser kings seeking allies, cattle merchants bartering their herds, magicians performing their tricks, the hurling team from Cashel swaggering in confident expectation of victory, litigants seeking judgment—as though poor old Dermot were capable of deciding anything—even a group of sterile women hoping to become fertile in the shadow of the king. Brigid pounded the rock against the soft cloth again, wishing the cruel Queen Finnabair were inside it. She would have cursed the queen but cursing was dangerous. She could not afford the risk.

Beyond the house of the king was the great assembly hall where the banquets would be served for the next seven nights. Ireland's most gallant warriors would insult one another over the piece of the steer to which each would lay claim or the place at the table which each thought was his right. There would be many fewer warriors when the festival was over. Fools, Brigid told herself. Why couldn't one of them accidentally put his sword to that haughty witch?

Anxiously she looked over her shoulder. She was still

alone. A slave girl could afford no illusions. She was worth much less than the four head of cattle for which a *cuhmal* could be bought. A wandering noble or even a common lout could amuse himself with her with no one to protest. Finnabair could put a knife in her; there would be no complaint. She was King Cormac's slave only because in his vague memory a doddering old man remembered he had promised his dying wife he would heep her for Cormac's return. Sometimes Dermot remembered his promise, sometimes he did not. Being bondwoman to the absent *Tanaise*—who did not know himself that she was his, since he was long gone before his mother died—was not much protection at Tara, where it was said that Cormac MacDermot would never return.

Her knees were hurting. She had nice legs—the only part of her that might attract a man. She must protect her knees. They were pretty too. She put a thick cloth underneath them, then virtuously pushed it away. What mattered the tiny knees of a foolish slave girl? She angrily threw the cloth toward the river, hesitated for a moment, got up to retrieve it, and put it on the ground where she would kneel. "You're a foolish, vain woman, Biddy," she told herself. She kept the cloth under her just the same.

The stream that flowed from the well ran down the side of Tara's vast hill like a band of melted silver in the morning sunlight by the Fortress Maeve and into the valley opposite Slaine. Horses' hooves sounded on the road. Quickly she hid behind the three magic stones. She suspiciously watched the riders in their splendid purple tunics and milk white mantles. Racers, she thought. Every farmer in Ireland who had a horse about whose speed he boasted in drunken argument would come to prove it in a race. There would be wagers and fighting and more bloodshed, and, of course, more drink. By nightfall, Brigid knew, she would be the only sober person in all Tara—probably the only one who hadn't lost a bet. She didn't believe in betting—not that there was much choice; she had nothing with which to wager. The other slave girls did not like her because she was so stern—no drink, no gambling, no frolicking with servant boys, no joking. They said she acted like a nun.

What a pig Finnabair was—spilling wine carelessly on this lovely dress, then sending her out in the chill morning air to clean it. She was as drunk as any warrior last night, flaunting her body, letting that senile fool fondle her in public. When she finally returned to her chamber she beat Brigid in a drunken rage. It pleased her to beat someone as she scraped the great slabs of ugly *ruam* off her face.

Brigid frowned. She wondered whether she would ever give herself to a man. The thought of coupling was disgusting. Someday she might love a man; she could hardly imagine its happening, much less a man loving her back. Someday, any day, a man could take her; that was merely something to be endured. Yet if he were King Cormac—would she find him disgusting? Could he make her want to belong to him? She pounded the rock again. Foolish and dangerous dreams. But such sweet dreams. How would he touch her? What would he make her do?

The vile dress was clean at last. She spread it out on the flat rock next to the stream, carefully placing a large cloth beneath it. It would require hours to dry—time to think and dream, free from the noisy foolishness of the festival and the sound of pipes and drums that shattered the morning silence.

Her thin shoulders hurt from last night's beating. Did

Finnabair still fear the memory of the last queen? Was it fear that made her so hateful? If so, then the witch must have weaknesses no one knew. Craftily Brigid tried to imagine what they might be, how she could exploit them.

King Cormac might return. Brigid smiled. He was not yet thirty years old; already he was a legend in the whole of Ireland. Finnabair had good reason to fear the Christian champion should he come back. Would he remember Brigid? Probably not. She had been a child he rarely bothered to notice. There was nothing about her to merit notice.

She had thought about how to get into the king's service when he returned. There were times when King Dermot could be reached, particularly when Finnabair was sleeping. There were ways of seeing that she slept longer than usual. The problem would be how to deal with Cormac MacDermot after she began to serve him. She remembered him well. She imagined him running down the hurling field, his marvelous legs pounding the turf like a galloping stallion, his face flushed with the love of the game, his stick swinging gracefully over his head, as his arm muscles rippled under his sweating skin. Others were stronger but none so agile, so quick to seize the tiniest opening for a score. Now she pictured him kissing her after the game, the strong smell of a perspiring male absorbing her, his fingers pressing her tiny body against his own. Later in his bedchamber he would begin to kiss her slowly at first, then insistently.

There was a noise—someone coming. She gripped the cleaning rock. They would pay a price—no, there was not another living being in sight, only the sound of the festival in the distance.

He was such a strange man, so kind and gentle to

servants, so suspicious and hostile to friends. His moods changed from stormy to melancholy to wistful to recklessly funny as quickly as the Irish weather changed. Women worshipped his handsome, vigorous body; he was alternately charming to them and unaware of their existence.

Someday he would belong to her. She would make the clouds flee from his soul. There would only be sunshine and laughter. An old seeress had told her as a little girl she would someday be Queen of Ireland. She knew it was true even before the old woman's withered lips had pronounced the prophecy. If she was to be queen, it had to be as Cormac's wife. Such dreams were absurd, she told herself sternly, pounding with renewed vigor on the soiled dress. She could not afford silly fantasies. But the dreams were with her day and night. Sometimes it seemed that a beautiful woman came to tell her that the dream was true. She could not be sure whether it was when she was awake or sleeping.

There was a noise behind her again. She jumped with fright. It was only a small rabbit—as afraid as she was. The animal raced madly for the wall. She had the plain all to herself again. She laughed bitterly. A worthless slave girl cleaning a harlot's dress and dreaming that she would be Queen of Ireland.

The sun rose higher in the sky, the wind freshened. She had intended to bathe later when the sun warmed the water, but smells of roasting meat reminded her that she was hungry. She gritted her teeth at the thought of the first sharpness of the icy waters, but it would be many days before she had another chance. Carefully she scanned the lonely plain around her. No one in sight. Her body wasn't much to look at. She wanted no one to see her naked.

Unknotting the rough cord *crios,* she slipped out of her tattered gray tunic, looked with disgust at her thin little body, and plunged bravely into the water.

It was colder than she expected. Her slight frame shook violently, the pebbles on the bottom hurt her feet. One had to get used to pain. Shivering, she climbed back onto the bank, washed her own tunic in the clear stream waters and then spread it next to the queen's dress—a poor mate for so rich a robe. As she huddled under her patched black mantle the chill slowly ebbed as the sun-absorbing material warmed her and made her sleepy. Again she looked around. Still no one in sight. It would be risky to sleep; it was always risky to sleep.

The girl touched her throat with some of Finnabair's scent, shamelessly stolen. She had given up hope of ever looking much like a woman. Everyone else had grown up physically; she resigned herself to a pretty face, large eyes, trim legs on which she could run like a frightened doe, and a body like a small boy's. So be it. Less likely to attract some drunken warrior.

In the distance the sounds of voices, songs, music, and neighing horses blended together. They were starting the fertility dances now, she thought, imagining the ancient rite of naked bodies. She stretched out on the soft grass, her eyelids heavy with lost sleep of the night before. There would be at least another hour before she was missed.

She felt herself melting into the warm sun and blue sky. The hard green turf beneath her was becoming soft, the harsh festival music turned into gentle strings. Someone was humming. She was dressed in the richest of saffron tunics, laden with gold jewelry. She was a bride on a wedding bed. The beautiful woman was standing over her smiling complacently. "Did I tell you that you would be Queen of Ireland? Will you take care of him for me?" Was it Queen Ethne? No, it was someone else, someone even more beautiful. Then her man came, only it was not a man but a wild stallion, his hoofs pounding the ground. One of the hoofs pounded into her stomach. There was a searing pain.

Brigid awoke. There was still a pain in her stomach. Hunger. A horse in her dream and terrible fear. No, the horse was real, very near, just down the stream, and she naked beneath her old cloak. She grasped for her cleaning stone, could not find it.

Too late to hide. The rider would see her, the dresses on the rocks. What could she do? She lay still, frozen with terror.

The rider galloped by. He took no notice of her. One of Dermot's personal guards, riding as if there was news of great importance. An invasion? No, not on festival day. Then she saw a figure walking down the path behind the rider, his eyes fixed on the top of the hill where Tara stood. He walked slowly, dressed in pilgrim's brown with a shillelagh clutched in his hand. Beside him strode a huge wolfhound. She saw the red hair and hard, angry face. Was she still asleep? It was Cormac! Even the slow, painful walk did not disguise his confident athlete's authority. No wonder the guard galloped with such speed. The *Tanaise* was returning to keep Lug's festival with King Dermot and Queen Finnabair. Brigid's heart jumped with exultation. High King Cormac was back.

He had not seen her. Scrambling to her feet, she moved quickly. Such a fool to return now. He looked old, tired, weary, sick at heart. She felt a great tenderness for him. "Dear God," she prayed, "whoever and whatever you are, give me the wit and skill with words I need. I have nothing else. I will take care of him for you."

Deep in the soul of Brigid the slave girl a tiny voice whispered, "You are a fool, Biddy, you have fallen in love with the High King of Ireland."

She would not listen. She rolled Finnabair's dress into a neat bundle, tucked it under her arm and began to run recklessly up the hill of Tara with all the speed of which she was so proud. She cared not whether anyone noticed her. There was so little time. She wanted to sing.

Chapter 4

The spirit of Cormac MacDermot was as heavy as a rain cloud before a storm. Writing poetry for the night's banquet depressed him more than the meeting with his father. He threw his writing quill away in disgust. Lugnasa was a festival of harvest, a feast of fruit, of apples, pears, and berries. Unlike the grim feast of Samain three months away, it was a time of lightness and gaiety. His poems were that way—light and merry. They lay before him accusingly on the polished oak table. What a hypocrite he was, he thought with self-disgust. He could write songs to win the evening's prize when his mind was battered by thoughts of the fearsome demons of death. Angrily he brushed them aside, knocking some of the sheets to the floor. He sipped wine from the golden goblet on the table, then drained the cup in one reckless gulp.

All day he had walked through Tara as in a dream. The

people he saw—Murtaugh, King Dermot his father, the glorious Finnabair—were mysterious ethereal folk who slipped through a half-remembered dream. Tara was not real; it was only the eggshell-thin background for his dreams. Everything was unreal, floating on a smooth golden sea, drifting toward the Many-Colored Land—

He stood up, tightened his *crios,* rearranging the sharp knife he now carried in his belt. Despite his depression and gloom there was a faint haze of something else. Opportunity? something seen fleetingly like a touch of mist on a sunny morning. Was there something he was not supposed to miss? "King Jesus," he prayed ardently, "if there is opportunity here in Tara, don't let me miss it." Darkness descended again. He was only deceiving himself. The last opportunity was lost long ago.

Cormac poured another goblet of wine. He sipped it carefully this time. Good, he thought to himself. Some things were still fine in this sacred center of Ireland. So was the artwork on the chalice. Maybe Colum was right, he mused.

He picked up the quill and leaves of verse from the floor and neatly rearranged his table. Maybe he should be king. Could anyone but a king care so passionately about the land? Perhaps it was his destiny to lust after the mystic Maeve, the mother earth who was Ireland. King Jesus knows there is no one else on this hill who cares for the poor land. He groaned softly. A terrible fate to be so wedded to the land. Better the green countryside of Ireland than the white witch who replaced it in his father's affections—poor senile old fool.

He sat down again dejectedly. His headache was worse, aggravated by the disorderly noises of the festival.

Where had this golden, jeweled goblet come from? He

sipped its contents again. Someone had seen to it that the chamber in the banquet hall reserved for the Expected King was prepared for his return. Blackberries, cold lamb, cheese, and wine filled the table. A blazing saffron *leine* graced his bed, a sparkling green *brat* and *crios* hung on the wall peg with golden *torcs* and *lunulae* resting on the floor next to the *leine.* An elaborate jeweled broach was provided to fasten the *brat.* He would be an impressive High King tonight. The room was spotlessly clean and fragrant with the scent of yellow roses; the great oak beams were dusted and polished; the copper bathing tub glowed dully in the reflection of his candle. Had Finnabair seen to this part of the reception? There was no mistaking the look she gave him when she caught his eyes.

He pressed his fingers against his aching head. He needed time to think. He had been trying to think since Ravenna. Tara was a distracting dream, because he was focused inward on his tormenting thoughts. But he was groping in the dark, unable even to give a name to the demons in his spirit. What was it about which he had to think? The black writing quill broke in his tense fingers. He tossed it aside and absently took the heavy knife from his belt to keep the pages of verse on the table from being blown away by the wind.

The image of Dermot and Finnabair would not leave his mind. What an ugly end for a great king. What would his own end be like?

Dermot's sins had caught up with him. Too much food, too much drink, too many women. Gross in body, his dirty white hair hanging over his face, he talked like a man who was drunk, his slurring words revealing a brain dimmer than his tongue. He did not recognize his son and heir when Cormac entered the door of his house. He wheezed and wiped his nose.

"Who is it there?" he demanded querulously. "Finnabair, is this some young upstart come to make trouble on Lug's feast? If he's come from Colum, send him back. I don't want any simpering monks to spoil my festival. Lug is going to give me new life, just as you said he would. Colum wants me to die a quiet Christian death, curse him."

This was only the bare shadow of the man whom the great Kiernan proclaimed king on the shores of the Shannon, a ghost of the father Cormac had admired. Approaching death had done this to Dermot MacFergus. Staring at him in grim silence, Cormac wondered fearfully what death would do to him. "King Jesus, protect me," he prayed. "Take me now if I am to die the way of my father."

"It is your son Cormac the Expected. He has come to help you celebrate the festival," said the full-bodied young woman who stood by the king's bed, holding his hand, her voice as thick and rich as a goblet of mead. White hair, green eyes, red *leine,* golden rings and bracelets—she was all they had said she was. Cormac felt lust stir within him. He had not had a woman in a long time. Every movement of her subtle body was an invitation. "Welcome, King Cormac," she continued warmly. "Your father rejoices, as does all Tara, on your return." She had seen his lust and responded.

"Cormac, is that you, boy?" sputtered the old man, saliva dribbling down his chin. "Thought you would never come back. Off in Rome, eh? Too good for us, eh? Colum send you here to convert me on my death bed? I'll surprise him. Won't die yet, will I, Finnabair my love? Lot of life still left. Speak up, boy, haven't you anything to say for yourself?" Dermot narrowed his eyes, trying without success to focus on his son.

Cormac's heart tightened with grief. If only there were something— He moved closer to his father. A picture of the slender limbs of the bishop's proper but passionate wife flashed through his head. "Honor and praise to you, King Dermot. I have come back because there was nothing left for me in Ravenna. I yearned for the soft hills and green fields of Ireland. I desired to look once more into the wise eyes of Tara's king." But in fact his eyes were eagerly consuming the body of the witch Finnabair.

"Humph—always had a way with words. Everything a man would want in a son except— You like my Finnabair, boy? Don't get any ideas about her. She's mine, do you hear? I'm going to live to enjoy her for a lot longer." His thin claw tightened around the girl's waist.

Cormac said evenly, "The splendors of Queen Finnabair's loveliness dim the eyes of a poor pilgrim. Truly, only a king could adequately love such beauty." It was sufficiently ambiguous to satisfy both truth and the old man's jealousy.

Who was she? What power had sent her? Cashel? Armagh? Druids? An alliance of chieftains and lesser kings? The northern O'Neills seeking revenge for Dumcreda? Could a body that perfect be merely human? Was she really a witch from the Many-Colored Land?

For much of the day he had walked through the precincts of Tara. Chieftains, nobles, freemen, tenants, slaves swarmed over the hill arguing, fighting, ogling the naked women in the fertility dances, admiring the magicians, waiting for the excitement of the races. The sky was clear, the sun warm; the smell of human sweat mixed with the stench of animal manure and the aroma of roasting pigs and steers to produce a strong, earthy odor. Mead and cheap wine flowed like a mountain stream in springtime. The crowds were frantic in their gaiety, as though they knew the harvest they celebrated was bad, the fruits they devoured not plentiful. It would be a hard winter in Ireland.

He was too preoccupied to think of the famine or to notice the festival activities save through a thick haze, a haze filled with pictures of the drooling lips and clawlike hand of Dermot, the full breasts of Finnabair, and the imagined slender legs of Lady Ann. His head began to ache. If only he could think clearly.

Lugnasa was a prayer that the winter ordeal to come would be bearable, a hope that the celebrants would survive the season which started tomorrow, a season of scraping for the last few bits of food necessary to keep animals and humans alive until Inbolc, six months away, when spring returned. The festival was a drunken binge to kill the pain of fear. There was not a person in Ireland who did not worry anxiously about whether he would be alive when the goddess—or saint—Brigid proclaimed the end of winter.

He had to think clearly. His headache was growing worse. He wanted no part of a woman. Yet his need for one was intense. Everyone knew the *Tanaise* was back. He was cheered wherever he went—but from a distance. The greetings from chieftains and kings were cautious. They feared his temper, he thought, and wondered whether they dared draw swords with him at the banquet. They could rest easy; he no longer cared where he sat or what piece of meat he received. Impatiently he waved aside the cheering throngs. Baffled, they soon left him alone.

On the far side of Tara, in the flat, green field between

the Rath Grainne and the triple mound of Ness where people were already gathering for the races, he encountered Murtaugh MacMurtaugh, his father's steward. The thick brown hair and forked beard were turning white, the strong shoulders slightly bowed now, but the quick warm smile was still wide on the open, ugly face. "The *Tanaise* has returned," said Murtaugh in that mixture of irony and cautious joy which in Ireland passed for a warm welcome.

"To see if the steward is still doing his work well." Cormac laughed vigorously, grabbing the strong rough hand in his own.

"Ah, the steward has little power anymore, King Cormac, as your quick eyes have doubtless noticed. All is in order in Tara." This time there was no joy blended with the irony. Murtaugh looked suddenly older. He stroked his beard in dejection.

"Bad times when a king grows old." His own good spirits quickly died. He felt as dejected as the steward looked. Still he lusted for Finnabair.

The steward's face creased in a grim frown. "She is a woman of much power, Cormac. There is none who does not fear her. I think she comes from hell, by Podraig and Brigid I do." His hand rested defensively on the handle of his sword.

Murtaugh could do battle till the death with earthly powers, but with powers from the Many-Colored Land—

"Such beauty from hell?" asked Cormac sarcastically.

"Beware of her. It is said that she has really come for you." The steward intoned his solemn warning ominously.

Cormac permitted himself a slight, cynical smile. "We shall see, Murtaugh MacMurtaugh."

He did not stay for the races. With head throbbing and

imagination raging he sought out the banquet hall to prepare his poetry for the evening's contest. If he was to further Colum's plan for recapturing Tara from Finnabair, tonight he would have to be Cormac MacDermot the greatest poet in all Ireland. Ireland was on such evil times, there were few poets. Shallow and clever rhymesters earned their livings flattering the powerful kings. Not so in the old days. If he understood Colum, it would not be so when the monasteries ruled all of Ireland. He wondered if his cousin ever permitted himself the worldliness of writing poetry. No, only the worldliness of politics. He thought of a funny poem about Colum writing poetry, found a new writing quill, set down the verse, and laughed loudly. He scrawled out the lines. What was there to laugh about?

The great oblong banquet hall, the newest building in Tara, shared the top of the hill with the king's rath. By the standards of Rome and Ravenna it was nothing more than a very large wooden building, painted white to glisten in the sunlight. Still, it was the largest and most spectacular building Ireland had ever seen. It had four quadrants, each representing one of the four kingdoms of Ireland. The center, which was the eating chamber itself, represented his own Royal Meath, the center of the center, the Hill of Tara. At the north end of this central chamber were the twelve couches where the king would recline with the other heroes of Ireland.

Why did everything the Irish built end up looking like a barn for their cattle? The hall inside was unlit and smelled of fresh paint—a dark, gloomy place when not lighted by thousands of candles. Hundreds of servants bustled about preparing for the banquet of Lug. One greeted him respectfully and offered to lead him to his chamber in the north section. Cormac was surprised that a room was assigned to him. More astonishing were the thick new hangings that marked the door. Only after hours of working with his songs did it occur to him that someone had prepared the room for his use, including writing materials on the table—someone who knew his angry fingers broke many writing plumes.

He thought of opening the shutters on the tiny window to let in the sunlight but decided against it. The gloom of candle flame fit his dark mood more than the implacable August sun. What fool had bothered to make him welcome? Another puzzle to make his head hurt even more.

The draperies parted. Three servants entered with buckets of steaming water for his bathtub. Unlike ordinary folk, the High King had his bath water heated over a fire instead of raised to proper temperature by hot stones from the fireplace. He was to bathe before the banquet whether he wanted to or not. He thought briefly of the bishop's wife and the gentleness with which she had washed his feet. How good she would taste at the end of a long day.

A very small servant, hardly more than a child, seemed to be in charge of the silent group who filled his tub as though he were not in the room. Cormac wondered idly whether it was a boy or a girl. The short hair said boy; the pretty face and vast wide blue eyes gave a hint of the feminine. Podraig, who had been snoozing in the corner, settled the matter. Sniffing cautiously at the small servant, he nudged it in the belly with his huge friendly nose. "Go away, silly dog," said the child impatiently, its face grimly solemn. Podraig only wagged his tail.

"My lady should be flattered," Cormac offered, rising with a gallant bow. "Podraig shows interest only in the most beautiful of women."

"Then Podraig is losing his sight, even as the High King Cormac," said the girl. Her tart response was uttered in a soft voice which reminded him of the tinkling bells at mass.

The wolfhound was not to be rebuffed. He put his big paws on her thin shoulders and offered to lick her face. The girl succumbed, as did all women, to Podraig's charms. She put her arms around his head and playfully rocked him back and forth. No trace of a change of expression came to her rigid face. "Silly, silly dog," she said affectionately.

"Am I to be grateful to you, dear lady, for preparing my chamber on such short warning?" he asked, smiling despite his headache. The child was so grimly solemn.

"Why else does the High King have a bondwoman unless she prepares for his return?" She ignored his effort at playful gallantry and watched intently as the water was poured into the tub.

"You are my bondwoman, child?" he demanded, now angry at her veiled impertinence.

"Worth four head of cattle on the market, noble lord." The bells in her voice were unperturbed.

"Yet so small a bondwoman would not win me four head of cattle." Instantly he regretted the cruelty of his joke.

"Is it not said that for all his talents King Cormac does not merit the market price for *Tanaises?*" she shot back at him unhesitatingly, like a bowman shooting in battle.

A quick flash of fury boiled through his blood. He gripped the knife on the table. "You have a sharp tongue, slave girl," he shouted.

"If it displeases my lord, he can always cut it out with his knife," she replied, unconcernedly laying out towels on the floor next to the tub.

"Is Cormac MacDermot a man to do such a thing?" he demanded, rearranging the towels.

"A man can do what he wants with his slave girl." She pointedly put the cloths back in order.

He took her frail shoulders in his hands and shook her furiously. "You did not answer me. Am I a man who is cruel to servants?" Realizing what he was doing, he released her and shoved his hands beneath his belt to contain their restless movement. The other servants discreetly departed for more water. Podraig stood close to the girl.

"It is not said of him that he is cruel, but men change as they grow old," she responded coolly. "Instead of cutting off a worthless slave woman's tongue, he might merely shake her to death as a hound does a rabbit."

He laughed softly and sat back in his chair. "You should be doing the poetry tonight instead of me. Come here, clever wench, how is it that you belong to me?" She stood in front of him, eyes down respectfully but showing no fear.

"When your mother, the queen, was dying she made King Dermot promise to save me for you until you returned. Do you wish to bathe now?" The servants had returned with the last buckets of water. The copper tub was filled to the top with steaming warmth.

He remembered an unsmiling and annoying child who ran at his mother's skirts. One day, driven beyond all patience by her, he had dunked her in the icy waters of the Boyne. She had refused to cry. Good God, what was her name?

He took the small chin in his hand and tilted her head back to examine the depth of her immense blue eyes. He felt anguish, as though someone had pierced his body with a sword. This poor creature depended totally on him for her existence. He could snuff her out like a troublesome bug. Yet no human should have such power.

"What am I to do with you, Lady Brigid?" he asked, shaken. He tightened his grip on her stubborn chin. Thank heaven he remembered the wench's name.

"You might sell me for one head of cattle or cut me into small pieces to feed to your horses, or even drown me in the holy Boyne. Will you bathe now?" She tried to ignore the fierce hold he had on her face—there was pain in those vast silver blue eyes.

So she hadn't forgotten either. "Instead, I shall afflict you with my poetry." His headache was easing. He released her chin, feeling another acute stab of anguish as he saw the red marks his fingers had left.

"It is as my lord wishes." She folded her hands and lowered her eyes like a nun at prayer.

Gently he pushed her towards the table. "Sit down, woman, I can't read to an audience that is standing."

She sat docilely in his chair. He opened the shutters and stood by the window so that he was illumined by the sharp sunlight. Posing for a poetry recitation for a slave girl? *King Jesus, I have become perverted.* He read the hymn to the feast anyway. Indeed, he read it with all the drama he would spend on a queen.

Tara, site of generous Fair,
Smooth the lawn for coursing there;
Hosts who sought its trysting-place
Conquered in its brilliant race.

On those high-beloved grounds
Many are the burial-mounds,
Where, with fame that never dies,
Many a king and noble lies.

Queens and kings and deeds of shame—
For those wailing, hither came
To the face of Tara old
Crowds at harvest, so 'tis told.

Heaven and earth, sea, moon, and sun,
Jetsam, fruits by tillage won,
Mouths, ears, eyes, feet, goods in fee,
Hands, and tongues of soldiery.

Faces stern that never yield,
Trappings such as warriors wield,
Dew, the forests, verdure bright,
Flowing tide, ebb, day and night—

These the pledges: that the Fair
Every third year gathered there,
By no strife disturbed, should be
Held in solemn harmony.

When the harvest month began
After lapse of three years' span,
Daily seeking victors' praise
Riders raced through seven days.

Settlement of tax and due,
Legal cases to review,
Laws to publish and declare—
This the business of the Fair.

Men and women here must be
Bound by strictest purity:

Nor in wise unseemly, rude,
May they, each on each, intrude.

Here is music—trumpet, horn,
Drum and pipe the Fair adorn:
Here is poetry—the bard
Seeks and gains his due reward.

Here romance—exhaustless theme!
Legends, vague as in a dream:
Here is wisdom—proverbs sage,
Satires, lore of seer and mage.

Here is history—tales of old,
Ever new, though often told,
Annals, conquests, wooings, strife,
Love and hatred, death and life.

But what noisy rabble's there,
On the border of the Fair?—
Vagabonds with drums and bones,
Shrieking to their bagpipe-drones—

The poem went on for many more stanzas while the girl sat in expressionless silence. She showed no reaction at all when he finished. No queen would dare respond so unenthusiastically to him. "So, dear Biddy, you have nothing to say?" he asked impatiently, remembering now that she did not like to be called Biddy.

"You have come a long way and you are tired." Her response was flat and devastating.

"You do not like my Lugnasa hymn?" He felt the anger surging within him again.

"If my lord wishes me to like it, then I will like it. If my lord is so foolish as to care what I think, I think it is much like other festival poems—better, perhaps, than most but not original." She spoke dispassionately—like a monk in a classroom analyzing the weakness of bad verse.

"So, child, you are an expert on song?" He adjusted the dagger at his belt.

"I am only a stupid bondwoman, noble king. I will be a useless bondwoman if I do not bathe you before the waters grow even colder. You must look your best for Queen Finnabair." She filled his goblet with wine.

Cormac was embarrassed. To be bathed by the soft hands of the bishop's wife would have been a delight, but this solemn-faced child stirred up feelings of modesty he had not known since he left the monastery. "It will not be necessary, good Brigid. I am quite capable of preparing myself for the witch queen." He brusquely dismissed her. The wench had made him blush.

"You wish me to leave, King Cormac?" She picked up her shabby cloak.

"I see that you are as sensitive and intelligent as you are hardworking, slave child." He began to shuffle through his pages of verse as though the girl no longer existed.

"Do you wish me to find a more beautiful slave girl to bathe you?" she said implacably.

Curse the child. He had hurt her again. "I fear the gentle wolfhound would not accept a rival of yours. Now leave before I begin to think again about the Boyne." He unknotted the *crios* and rearranged the towels for the second time.

She turned at the curtain. "I will wake you at dawn, noble king."

"At the risk of your life you will. It will be a long banquet. An old man needs his sleep if he is to do battle with Cashel on the hurling field."

She hesitated accusingly. "You will not walk the ramparts of Tara at sunrise?"

The girl was a devil. Of course he should do that. If the king could not do it, the king-to-be should. Why hadn't he thought of it? "I am not sure, Biddy, which of us is the slave. Wake me at first light. Is there anything else I should be told?" His obedient deference was not altogether feigned, for this afternoon he had met his match.

"The bath water grows cold, O kingly poet." Her head was tilted back, the stubborn jaw victoriously scoring its point.

"Not as cold as the Boyne." He grinned and stepped toward the escaping figure, his laugh following her through the heavy curtain into the outer hall.

The water was in fact still quite hot. It soothed the *Tanaise*'s weary body, temporarily eased his melancholy, even lifted his spirits. "We have found one ally in Tara, have we not, good Podraig?" he asked his dog. The wolfhound barked assent.

"In truth, mighty dog, I think we both should fear her tongue more than the magic of Queen Finnabair." He sipped wine from his goblet, now very cautiously.

Podraig thumped the floor with his tail.

Chapter 5

Cormac heard a sharp cry from a woman in pleasure. Once more the banquet hall of Tara was a temple of Venus. He cautiously moved his arm. It hurt less now, but that might be only the result of the wine. He loosened the *crios* around his blue *leine* and removed the golden buckle. Biddy had insisted that he wear the saffron again but he refused to let the meddlesome child have her way.

He had drunk too much. It was unwise to be drunk on the night of the banquet of Erihu, the goddess of sexual passion after whom this insane land was named. Judging by the stifled cries to be heard throughout the building, she was receiving much honor this night. He imagined what the pleasure cry of the bishop's wife would be like. Why could he not get that intense, frightened woman out of his mind? Oh, God, I must have a woman—almost any woman would do.

The day had been hot and heavy. It would rain before the sun rose again. In the distance were the drums of thunder. Lightning flickered through the window shutters, the dense air of the banquet hall throbbed as if the building itself were sexually aroused. He twisted uncomfortably in his chair. He should go to bed; he was too tired for a woman. He hurt too much. Finnabair would not come tonight. He slipped towards sleep, his fantasies picturing the screams of the Lady Ann as he tore her garments away. She was a devout Christian matron. It was sacrilegious to permit such dreams about her.

He could not sleep. He pushed hard at the mind pictures of Ann, sat up in bed as though to shove them away. The candlelight blurred in front of him, turning his chamber into a misty bog. His body tormented him. Foot races, horse races, and, today, hurling. He was still champion of Ireland. Meath had routed Cashel, but he was bruised and cut and aching. A game that equipped Irishmen with a stick and license to use it invited disaster.

Every time he closed his eyes he became dizzy and his stomach turned uneasily. Would the effect of the wine never wear off? He had drunk beyond all reasonable limits to kill the pain. He rose from his bed to fetch a half-filled goblet from the table. Maybe more wine would put him to sleep.

He also drank to forget Finnabair. He hungered for her—green eyes, sinuous body, lingering smile. For too long he had been celibate.

Moving painfully back to his bed, he sat down on it. Two more female shrieks. The witches enjoyed it. No woman would stay in the hall tonight if she didn't want to be taken. They were worse than the men; they were less drunk and more deliberate.

The Mediterranean world knew orgies, but not the long periods of continence that the Celts alternated with their frenzied festivals. A people of extremes—not enough sex, then too much. He was no different, he thought, pushing his fists against his forehead. He had denied his human urges beyond all reason; now he was out of his mind with passion. He must have the woman. He must touch that soft flesh and— He drained the wine goblet and threw it violently against the wall. It clattered to the floor.

Lightning flashed, thunder sounded closer. The storm was outside him and inside too, a storm of hunger. He could tell the difference between a harlot's games and a woman's longing. She wanted him. Seducing the *Tanaise* might be part of Finnabair's work in Tara; it was work she would enjoy. If she would only come, if he could only crush that diabolically lovely body in his arms.

There were few in Tara who would defend her. The champions on his father's council—Rory, Donal, Brian, Failen—were contemptuous behind her back while obsequiously flattering to her face. An occasional official like Murtaugh or the old warrior Tuathal dared to ignore her biting wit. Her magic was not altogether from the devil. She knew how to control and manipulate men.

What were her goals? Tara was weak and corrupt now. Was that it? Was it being softened for an invasion? From where? The men of Cashel seemed to fear her as much as the others. The few Leinstermen who came to the feast made the sign of the cross whenever her name was mentioned. In his foggy and drugged brain he was suspicious that she was the kind of trick his cousin Rory of Armagh, Prince of Ulster, would use to avenge the humiliation of Dumcreda. Rory was a Christian, but he would not be above employing a pagan witch to even the score with Dermot—and with the Abbot of Iona.

That pale yellow hair and those deep flashing eyes! Even in Ravenna there were none like her. She demanded to be held and loved by a strong man. She was always near him during the days of the festival. The poor old king slept most of the time where they had propped him up at the banquet table or laid him on a litter in the fields. She gave Cormac the prize at the end of the poetry contention, her green eyes shining with admiration. She applauded his racing victories, presented him with the goblet at the end of the race around the outer stockade. She led the cheering for him in the great hurling victory that afternoon, her face flushed and magnificent with excitement. Could one so innocently lovely possibly be evil?

Tonight at Erihu's banquet she reclined seductively next to him, between the *Tanaise* and the *Ardri.* The old man was soon asleep, so all her attention was focused on Cormac. She dressed like Etain at the well—a green *leine* trimmed with gold, rich purple *brat* bound by a jeweled gold *fibula.* Her white hair was braided into two golden lock rings. No man under heaven, he told himself, could fail to want her. There was promise in her every movement.

A stirring at his curtain brought him to instant attention. It was only the nettlesome slave girl Biddy.

"No stable boy to frolic with on Erihu's night, slave child?" he asked cruelly.

"My noble lord mocks me. I have come to see whether the wound in your shoulder still bleeds." She stood quietly next to his chair, her eyes fixed on the floor.

No one in the history of Ireland, he thought, was so devoutly served as he was by Biddy. Food, drink, clothes, bandages for his injuries—all were there before he thought of needing them. With all the attention came advice and insult. He had grown weary of her tongue. Cutting it out might not be a bad idea.

She stood meekly by the bed. "May I look at the wound, King Cormac?" she asked with infinite respect.

"Would it do any good for me to say no?" He sighed and loosened his tunic.

Very gently her fingers explored the bandage. "Whatever other harm you did at the banquet tonight, you did no more harm to this." She touched him so delicately that he felt only a flicker of pain.

"Your words are always harsh, good Lady Brigid, but your fingers are gentle." He sighed again. If only women could not talk. Their bodies were traps, their tongues the weapons with which they killed you once you were caught.

"Then my fingers betray me." Her eyes never left the ground.

"I have not heard your criticism of the hurling match," he said angrily, wanting to bait her into a battle.

She was silent.

"Come now, bothersome slave girl, you are wise in everything else. Do I have to command you to speak?" He grabbed her thin wrist roughly.

"It was a mighty victory for Royal Meath," she said unenthusiastically.

"Yes?" He tightened his grip, knowing that he was hurting her, defying her to set her tongue against his power.

"But in your younger days, you surely would not have permitted their last two goals." She drove her sword home despite the pain in her voice.

He pulled back his other hand to hit her. She did not

flinch. "I have never beaten a woman, Biddy," he said wearily. The ache in his shoulder forced him to drop his arm. "I will not do so now."

"I am yours to beat, noble lord," she said submissively and rubbed the red mark made by his fingers.

He lay back on the bed, his anger dying. Why did he let her bait him? He said tiredly, "What harm did I do at the banquet tonight?" trying to probe her mind as delicately as she probed his wounds.

"I have told you already, mighty king." Still the submissive slave—her only armor, poor child.

"Am I not following your advice to be friendly with the members of the council and the champions and the lesser kings?" He pounded the bed in frustration with his clenched fist.

She was silent, positioned by the door, looking eager to escape. The light from her candle was reflected in the blue mirrors of her wide eyes.

"I am not a Christian, my lord, but was not King Jesus kind and gentle with people, particularly the weak and the confused?" Her voice was sharp, her tiny body suddenly tense with anger.

His voice was deadly calm. "A pagan slave child dares to tell the High King of Ireland how to be a Christian?"

"King Jesus would not approve of an arrogant, proud, angry man who feels sorry for himself and hates everyone else. You do not serve King Jesus at all, only your own pride!" She screamed furiously at him, carried along on her own anger like a log on a flooding river.

The pain of his wretched body, his aching head, the lust for Finnabair, anger at himself, all blended into mindless rage. He jumped from his bed, grabbed the unresisting slave girl and dumped her into the cold waters of his tub. "Vile slave!" he shouted. "I would not foul the sacred Boyne with your miserable body!"

He shoved her under the water, yelling, "So now plead for your worthless life! Ask mercy of the High King lest your tongue be finally silenced!" He was breathing heavily. He let her face emerge for a moment's gasp of air. She spluttered and coughed but did not plead. Cruelly he pushed her under again. Good. She would drown. No, he would not kill a slave, he would drown her only in ridicule. Standing her up in the tub he tore her shabby gray *leine* from her body.

She was rigid in his hands, terror showing for the first time in her eyes, a fawn preparing to die. Cormac MacDermot's head spun. She was no longer a child but a girl blossoming into womanhood. The drab *leine* hid a body in which loveliness was beginning to bloom. For an instant of raw terror, lust for her flamed like a bonfire. Ravage, punish, destroy this girl-woman. Spend your passion on her. Her body is a budding delight. Rip it to pieces, enjoy its suffering, exult in its death agony, show her what it means to be an instrument in the hands of a mighty king. Then tenderness calmed him. He lifted the shivering girl out of the tub. She was still stiff with fright. He drew a big towel close around her frail body. How could anyone hurt such a delicate innocent?

"I'm sorry, Biddy," he choked.

"My lord can do with me what he wants." Her teeth were chattering, her voice a whisper.

"In a year or two, Brigid, you will be one of the most beautiful women in Ireland," he said, his throat tight with conflicting emotions.

"My lord mocks me." She was shaking like a young tree in an ocean storm. He was shaking too.

"I do not. I am sorry I have treated a young woman like a child." *Please forgive me, little one. I did not mean to hurt you. You are so lovely.*

He was still supporting her. His head was clear. Somewhere in the back of his mind there was forming a contrast between Biddy and Finnabair. He dismissed the images.

"The waters of the Boyne were much colder." He accepted his contrition.

Cormac wrapped a blanket around her. She stood less rigidly now. Podraig entered the room and began to nuzzle the wet slave girl. A white hand and a tiny naked shoulder emerged from beneath her coverings to pat the dog. He resisted an urge to reverently kiss that pale shoulder. He took his arms away from her.

He felt as though he were a man about to die, passing in accusing review of himself. "Podraig will take you back to your bed, Biddy; it is not safe for lovely women to be walking by themselves in Tara on this night, especially in such attractive robes." He sought relief from his confusion in uncertain comic gallantry.

With a sound something like a sigh she picked up her soaking dress. Girl and dog went out through the drapery into the night. This time she had no parting barb to hurl at him. Nor did she look back.

Podraig was back shortly. He contentedly curled up in the corner of the room. Cormac envied the dog the simplicity of his mating behavior. "Found yourself a she-dog tonight, did you not, great wolfhound? Well, I am waiting for one, too. But mine may never come."

So like a fragile wildflower at the side of a forest path, the kind of blossom which made him want to kneel to thank King Jesus for making the world a lovely, fragile place. Such flowers were to be treasured rather than trod upon. *King Jesus, must I worry about treasuring this tiny budding human with the thorny tongue? Are there not enough problems? Can you not at least let me enjoy Finnabair this one night without heaping yet more burdens on my back? Cannot I be a pagan for a few brief hours?*

Twisting uncomfortably in his bed, he thought once again of Tara, his lust momentarily allayed.

The slave girl was right—no, he had better think of her as the slave woman. If he were to play Colum's game to the end, he should make friends and win allies, not hold himself back, not hide behind an aloof reserve. Why couldn't he do it? What was it he lacked?

Young Rory MacFelan wanted to be friendly. A tall, handsome young king from the coast, the fair-haired boy did not hide his pleasure at being on the same hurling team with the legendary Cormac MacDermot. Rory's smile came quickly, his temper slowly—the perfect ally. Cormac kept him at a distance. How many other men had he known like Rory, who were now buried in the hills of Italy?

At Erihu's banquet Rory had approached him early with a pretty, very frightened girl. Cormac could not remember her name, though she had been presented to him early in the festival.

"You will grant us pardon to leave the dinner, King Cormac?" the young man asked, embarrassed by the worship of Erihu that was already taking place in the dim corners of the hall. "This is not a proper place for a Christian virgin. I would get her safely back to her father's tent."

"Her virtue is safe in this hall as long as I am High King," Cormac replied curtly and then added, "as long as she wishes to be safe." He permitted an edge of skepticism in his voice.

"Truly, King Cormac. But for a young girl it is shocking—and in truth, it is not a proper Christian feast," responded Rory, his eyes pleading with the king for understanding.

"Tara is not a proper Christian place, Rory MacFelan. One cannot honor the god Lug in a monastery, can one?" Contemptuously he turned his back on them.

Rory left with his black-haired, black-eyed virgin in hand. In the dark night on the hillside on the way back to her father's tent she would be kissed passionately—probably for the first time.

She would enjoy it, too. When a man and woman come together it matters not whether they are Christian or pagan, they are only animals.

Podraig stirred restlessly. Cormac open his eyes. There was someone in the room. His own candle had burned out, so the room was dark. The person at the doorway carried two candles. A low growl sounded from Podraig.

It was as though a garden of flowers had entered his room. She wore only the green *leine,* which hung unbelted and loose. No jewelry, no hair ornaments, no *ruam* on her face.

"Have you fallen asleep waiting for me, Cormac MacDermot?" she asked reprovingly. "I am disappointed in you. My charms do not have the power they once had." She swayed provokingly to the edge of his bed. Podraig, disdaining to take human coupling seriously, settled back to sleep.

"It was a very long day, Queen Finnabair." His head throbbed again, his hands were trembling. "It is the greatest of pleasures to wait for you, fair-haired woman."

"Ah, there is Cormac the poet again. You are so good at many things—song, sport, battle. I wonder how good you are on Erihu's bed." There was tease and challenge in her mocking voice. Slowly she pulled back his wrinkled *leine.* "You have a presentable enough body—what can you do with it, grim-faced High King?"

Naked before her taunting eyes, Cormac felt all the lust of the day return now, as primal and irresistible as the Shannon flowing to the sea. "I can give a good enough account of myself if need be, pagan queen," he said through clenched teeth.

She sat down next to him on the bed and began to stroke his chest. His hunger for her quickened fiercely. She began to kiss his chest. He was sinking into the bog of sweet desire which comes just before conquest of a woman.

"You are shy and timid, King Cormac; your Christian women know nothing about pleasure. Do not be afraid of me; I want only to make you happy."

She began slowly to lower the *leine* from her shoulders, letting it fall to her slender waist. "Am I not worth waiting for, great poet? Will you now sing my praises?"

There was eagerness in her hot green eyes—and fear too. In the tenseness of her aroused body was a frightened plea that he not hurt her. Cormac was now nothing more than his own passion, pounding for release. He took her in his arms and savagely kissed her. The only thing that mattered was to possess that glorious white body. He pulled off the rest of her *leine* and sank his fingers into her breasts. She was yielding herself totally. In a few moments—

The drapery parted and the slave girl Brigid entered the chamber, candle in hand.

"I have brought you warm milk to ease your sleep,

noble master," she began, as calmly as though the sun was at its zenith in the sky.

Finnabair was furious. Rising from the bed, she seized Cormac's shillelagh and viciously struck the bondwoman, knocking her to the ground. "Curse you, slave! you have tried my patience for the last time. I will beat your worthless life out of you. How dare you disturb me!" Her rage was like that of a trapped and wounded bear.

She lifted the club to strike again. Cormac twisted it out of her hand. Had she struck Brigid again the wolfhound would have torn out her throat. As it was, Podraig merely knocked the naked queen to the ground and pinned her there with his great paws, growling deeply.

Cormac struggled to pull the reluctant hound off the queen's body. He dragged the naked harlot to her feet. "Listen to me, you ugly witch," he snarled. "Do you dare even to touch my bondwoman again it will not be the wolfhound to tear you to pieces. Get out of here! I want none of your evil charms."

Filled with disgust for her and for himself, he rudely shoved the trembling queen through the curtains into the darkened corridor. Contemptuously he threw her *leine* after her. "Cover your nakedness when you walk the halls of Tara, royal slut!" he shouted. Later, he knew, she would be furious; now she was terrified. Podraig's fangs at her throat would not be easily forgotten.

Brigid lay motionless on the floor, covered with warm milk that had spilled out of the broken pitcher. A thin stream of blood trickled down the side of her face. "You humiliated her needlessly, fierce master," she said. She would not look at him. He remembered his nakedness and quickly wrapped the *leine* around his waist.

"I want no more sermons from you tonight, slave girl. You have saved me from the wiles of Queen Finnabair. Is that not enough?" He was still shouting. He lifted her from the floor with the same roughness with which he had treated the harlot. He wanted to be rid of all women.

Brigid, holding onto the great dog for support, rose unsteadily to her feet. "I do not know what you mean, terrible lord."

She was lying, damn her, and both of them knew it. "You never brought me warm milk in the middle of the night before. You knew Finnabair was here; you have succeeded in turning my night of passion into comedy. Now get out! Leave me to ponder my stupidity alone."

Biddy had learned something about his anger this night. She did not try to parry his thrust. She knew now when to leave him alone. She stumbled out as Finnabair had done, trembling and frightened. The wolfhound accompanied her. Again she did not look back.

Cormac MacDermot slumped to his bed. No more lust tonight. It was one way to be cured—to make a fool of yourself. What a stupid dolt he was. He should have nothing to do with women. Better he had stayed with the holy Kiernan at Clonmacnoise. *Oh, wise cousin Colum, the great king who will save Ireland for King Jesus has made a clown of himself not once but twice this night. Far better that you had sent wolfhound Podraig to Tara by himself. The High King Cormac is rude with men and ignorant with women; you should lock him up in the darkest hole on your grim Iona.*

He lay back and moved restlessly for a time. Would sleep never come? A smile tugged at his lips. "I have brought you warm milk," she had said. He laughed so loudly that Podraig wakened from his rest and stared at him. The child had an uncanny sense of timing. Just the right moment. "All right, Podraig, I'm going to sleep now." The dog settled back. Cormac's heavy eyes finally closed.

Outside, the rain beat against the wooden roof of the great assembly hall. The turf of Tara would be wet and muddy tomorrow.

Chapter 6

A *cold autumn* wind swept in from the western sea, covering all of Ireland with soft rain and mist. The sacred waters of the Boyne and the Shannon rose beyond their banks and flooded the country and its people. The turf fire in the hut of Flan the Teller of Tales smelled of the soft rain. So did the fur *brat* and hood of Cormac MacDermot as he huddled with Flan at the door of the hut and looked out through the fast-moving fog that covered the rolling Meath countryside.

The haggard old storyteller sipped his mead sloppily and turned his silver head to the king. His voice droned on mechanically. "So, King Cormac, everything runs in a cycle. Another white-haired queen has come to Tara, another king is made foolish by her wiles, another *Tanaise* must lose at chess to her and go forth to seek another Delvcaem to drive the witch-queen from Tara."

Startled, Cormac looked up from the smouldering fire into which he had been gazing. He knew the story of King Art MacConn, of course. Pagan nonsense. There were no parallels between Becuma and Finnabair, himself and King Art. Yet if Flan was telling the story to him, he was telling it to everyone. Were others waiting for the fatal chess game between him and the witch? The winter feast of Samain was drawing near when the souls of the dead and all the spirits from hell were loose on the land. The superstitious Irish would believe anything at this time of the year.

He was groping in a fog at Tara as thick as that outside of Flan's cave. It was as though he were watching himself in one of the plays the traveling Greek actors used to perform at Ravenna. Tara was an unreal backdrop, the people in it as unsubstantial as the winter mists. Sometimes he could play the game of being king; most of the time he was deep in his own thoughts, thoughts so obscure and twisted that he himself could not give them a name.

He stood up and walked to the cave entrance, drawing heavily from his own cup of mead. "Tell me the story again, O teller of tales. At least it says I will win over the evil queen."

The old man looked at him shrewdly. "The wheel always turns, King Cormac, but it does not always turn in the same direction," he said.

"Still, tell me again of Art MacConn and the Princess Fair Breast," Cormac insisted. Perhaps in that story there would be the secret key which would unlock the chamber of mystery into which he was trying to break.

The old man began with all the preliminary details of

an oft told and well-remembered tale. Then came the fateful chess game. A light began to gleam in the old man's almost sightless eyes.

"A hard game that was," he said, his face glowing like one of the embers in his fire, "and at times each of the combatants sat for an hour staring at the board before the next move was made, and at times they looked from the board and for hours stared on the sky as though seeking in heaven for advice. But Becuma's foster-sister, Aine, came from the Shi, and, unseen by any, she interfered with Art's play, so that suddenly, when he looked again on the board, his face went pale, for he saw that the game was lost.

" 'I didn't move that piece,' said he sternly.

" 'Nor did I,' Becuma replied, and she called on the on-lookers to confirm her statement.

"She was smiling to herself secretly, for she had seen what the mortal eyes around could not see.

" 'I think the game is mine,' she insisted softly.

" 'I think that your friends in Faery have cheated,' he replied, 'but the game is yours if you are content to win it that way.'

" 'I bind you,' said Becuma, 'to eat no food in Ireland until you have found Delvcaem, the daughter of Morgan.'

" 'Where do I look for her?' said Art in despair.

" 'She is in one of the islands of the sea,' Becuma replied, 'that is all I will tell you,' and she looked at him maliciously, joyously, contentedly, for she thought he would never return from that journey, and that Morgan would see to it.

"Should I go on, O High King?" asked the tale teller dubiously.

"Yes, go on." Cormac ground out his words like a stone crushing grain.

And so the old man went on with his tale.

Art, as his father had done before him, set out for the Many-Colored Land, but it was from Inver Colpa he embarked and not from Ben Edair.

At a certain time he passed from the rough, green ridges of the sea to enchanted waters, and he roamed from island to island asking all people how he might come to Delvcaem, the daughter of Morgan. But he got no news from any one, until he reached an island that was fragrant with wild apples, gay with flowers, and joyous with the song of birds and the deep, mellow drumming of the bees. In this island he was met by a lady, Credè, the Truly Beautiful, and when they had exchanged kisses, he told her who he was and on what errand he was bent.

"We have been expecting you," said Credè, "but alas, poor soul, it is a hard, and a long, bad way that you must go; for there is sea and land, danger and difficulty between you and the daughter of Morgan."

"Yet I must go there," he answered.

"There is a wild, dark ocean to be crossed. There is a dense wood where every thorn on every tree is sharp as a spear-point and is curved and clutching. There is a deep gulf to be gone through," she said, "a place of silence and terror, full of dumb, venomous monsters. There is an immense oak forest—dark, dense, thorny, a place to be strayed in, a place to be utterly bewildered and lost in. There is a vast, dark

wilderness, and therein is a dark house, lonely and full of echoes, and in it there are seven gloomy hags, who are warned already of your coming and are waiting to plunge you in a bath of molten lead."

"It is not a choice journey," said Art, "but I have no choice and must go."

"Should you pass those hags," she continued, "and no one has yet passed them, you must meet Ailill of the Black Teeth, the son of Morgan Tender Blossom, and who could pass that gigantic and terrible fighter."

"It is not easy to find the daughter of Morgan," said Art in a melancholy voice.

"It is not easy," Credè replied eagerly, "and if you will take my advice—"

"Advise me," he broke in, "for in truth there is no man standing in such need of counsel as I do."

"I would advise you," said Credè in a low voice, "to seek no more for the sweet daughter of Morgan, but to stay in this place where all that is lovely is at your service."

"But, but—" cried Art in astonishment.

"Am I not as sweet as the daughter of Morgan?" she demanded, and she stood before him queenly and pleadingly, and her eyes took his with imperious tenderness.

"By my hand," he answered, "you are sweeter and lovelier than any being under the sun, but—"

"And with me," she said, "you will forget Ireland."

"I am under bonds," cried Art, "I have passed my word, and I would not forget Ireland or cut myself from it for all the kingdoms of the Many-Colored Land."

Credè urged no more at that time, but as they were parting she whispered, "There are two girls, sisters of my own, in Morgan's palace. They will come to you with a cup in either hand; one cup will be filled with wine and one with poison. Drink from the right-hand cup, O my dear."

Art stepped into his coracle, and then, wringing her hands, she made yet an attempt to dissuade him from that drear journey.

"Do not leave me," she urged. "Do not affront these dangers. Around the palace of Morgan there is a palisade of copper spikes, and on the top of each spike the head of a man grins and shrivels. There is one spike only which bears no head, and it is for your head that spike is waiting. Do not go there, my love."

"I must go indeed," said Art earnestly.

"There is yet a danger," she called. "Beware of Delvcaem's mother, Dog Head, daughter of the King of the Dog Heads. Beware of her."

"Indeed," said Art to himself, "there is so much to beware of that I will beware of nothing. I will go about my business," he said to the waves, "and I will let those beings and monsters and the people of the Dog Heads go about their business."

He went forward in his light bark, and at some moment found that he had parted from those seas and was adrift on vaster and more turbulent billows. From those dark green surges there gaped at him monstrous and cavernous jaws; and round, wicked, red-rimmed, bulging eyes stared fixedly at the boat. A ridge of inky water rushed foaming mountainously on his board, and behind that ridge came a vast warty head that gurgled and groaned. But at these vile creatures he thrust with his lengthy spear or stabbed at closer reach with a dagger.

He was not spared one of the terrors which had been foretold. Thus, in the dark, thick oak forest he slew the seven hags and buried them in the molten lead which they had heated for him. He climbed an icy mountain, the cold breath of which seemed to slip into his body and chip off inside of his bones, and there, until he mastered the sort of climbing on ice, for each step that he took upwards he slipped back ten steps. His heart almost gave way before he learned to climb that venomous hill. In a forked glen into which he slipped at nightfall he was surrounded by giant toads, who spat poison, and were icy as the land they lived in, and were cold and foul and savage. At Sliav Saev he encountered the long-maned lions who lie in wait for the beasts of the world, growling woefully as they squat above their prey and crunch those terrified bones. He came on Ailill of the Black Teeth sitting on the bridge that spanned a torrent, and the grim giant was grinding his teeth on a pillar stone. Art drew nigh unobserved and brought him low.

It was not for nothing that these difficulties and dangers were in his path. These things and creatures were the invention of Dog Head, the wife of Morgan, for it had become known to her that she would die on the day her daughter was wooed. Therefore none of the dangers encountered by Art were real, but were magical chimeras conjured against him by the great witch.

Affronting all, conquering all, he came in time to Morrigan's dun, a place so lovely that after the miseries through which he had struggled he almost wept to see beauty again.

Delvcaem knew that he was coming. She was waiting for him, yearning for him. To her mind Art was not only love, he was freedom, for the poor girl was a captive in her father's home. A great pillar a hundred feet high had been built on the roof of Morgan's palace, and on the top of this pillar a tiny room had been constructed, and in this room Delvcaem was a prisoner.

She was lovelier in shape than any other princess of the Many-Colored Land. She was wiser than all the other women of that land, and she was skillful in music, embroidery, and chastity, and in all else that pertained to the knowledge of a queen.

Although Delvcaem's mother wished nothing but ill to Art, she yet treated him with the courtesy proper in a queen on the one hand and fitting towards the son of the King of Ireland on the other. Therefore, when Art entered the palace he was met and kissed, and he was bathed and clothed and fed. Two young girls came to him then, having a cup in each of their hands, and presented him with kingly drink, but, remembering the warning which Credè had given him, he drank only from the right-hand cup and escaped the poison.

Next he was visited by Delvcaem's mother, Dog Head, daughter of the King of the Dog Heads, and Morgan's queen. She was dressed in full armor, and she challenged Art to fight with her.

It was a woeful combat, for there was no craft or sagacity unknown to her, and Art would infallibly have perished by her hand but that her days were numbered, her star was out, and her time had come. It was her head that rolled on the ground when the combat was over, and it was her head that grinned and shrivelled on the vacant spike which she had reserved for Art's.

Then Art liberated Delvcaem from her prison at the top of the pillar and they were affianced together. But the ceremony had scarcely been completed when the tread of a single man caused the palace to quake and seemed to jar the world.

It was Morgan returning to the palace.

The gloomy king challenged him to combat also, and in his honor Art put on the battle harness which he had brought from Ireland. He wore a breastplate and helmet of gold, a mantle of blue satin swung from his shoulders, his left hand was thrust into the grips of a purple shield, deeply bossed with silver, and in the other hand he held the wide-grooved, blue-hilted sword which had rung so often in fights and combats, and joyous feats and exercises.

Up to this time the trials through which he had passed had seemed so great that they could not easily be added to. But if all those trials had been gathered into one vast calamity they would not equal one half of the rage and catastrophe of his war with Morgan.

For what he could not effect by arms Morgan would endeavor by guile, so that while Art drove at him or parried a crafty blow, the shape of Morgan changed before his eyes, and the monstrous king was having at him in another form, and from a new direction.

It was well for the son of the Ardri that he had been beloved by the poets and magicians of his land, and that they had taught him all that was known of shape-changing and words of power.

He had need of all these.

At times, for the weapon must change with the enemy, they fought with their foreheads as two giant stags, and the crash of their monstrous onslaught rolled and lingered on the air long after their skulls had parted. Then as two lions, long-clawed, deep-mouthed, snarling, with rigid mane, with red-eyed glare, with flashing, sharp-white fangs, they prowled lithely about each other seeking an opening. And then, as two green-ridged, white-topped, broad-swung, overwhelming, vehement billows of the deep, they met and crashed and sank into and rolled away from each other; and the noise of these two waves was as the roar of all ocean when the howl of the tempest is drowned in the league-long fury of the surge.

But when the wife's time has come the husband is doomed. He is required elsewhere by his beloved, and Morgan went to rejoin his queen in the world that comes after the Many-Colored Land, and his victor shore that knowledgeable head away from its giant shoulders.

Art did not tarry in the Many-Colored Land, for he had nothing further to seek there. He gathered the things which pleased him best from among the treasures of its grisly king, and with Delvcaem by his side they stepped into the coracle.

Then, setting their minds on Ireland, they went there as it were in a flash.

The waves of all the worlds seemed to whirl past them in one huge green cataract. The sound of all these oceans boomed in their ears for one eternal instant. Nothing was for that moment but a vast roar and pour of waters. Thence they swung into a silence equally vast, and so sudden that it was as thunderous in the comparison as was the elemental rage they quitted. For a time they sat panting, staring at each other, holding each other, lest not only their lives but their very souls should be swirled away in the gusty passage of world within world; and then, looking abroad, they saw the small, bright waves creaming by the rocks of Ben Edair and they blessed the power that had guided and protected them, and they blessed the comely land of Ir.

On reaching Tara, Delvcaem, who was more powerful in art and magic than Becuma, ordered the latter to go away, and she did so.

She left the king's side. She came from the midst of the counselors and magicians. She did not bid farewell to anyone. She did not say good-bye to the king as she set out for Ben Edair.

Where she could go to no man knew, for she had been banished from the Many-Colored Land and could not return there. She was forbidden entry to the Shi by Angus Og, and she could not remain in Ireland. She went to Sasana and she became a queen in that country, and it was she who fostered the rage against the Holy Land which has not ceased to this day.

So the tale was told. The old man extended the cup in his bearlike paw. He must have been a great warrior once. Cormac filled it with mead.

"There are other versions of the story, great Flan." He was standing at the door frame gazing into the fog.

"Every tale can be told in many ways," murmured the old man imperturbably.

Cormac turned back into the hut. "In some the queen is named Morgan, not the king; in others King Art must also bring back the magic cup from which he drinks the wine." He sounded to himself like a scholar at Clonmacnoise—a pompous one at that.

"In all it is only through much suffering and struggle does he win the prize," responded the storyteller solemnly, his nearly blind gray eyes fixed on Cormac.

"Indeed, wise old man, the hero must always suffer; otherwise, why would there be stories? Still, King Art, who was the father of another Cormac, who was the father of the great Neill, has long since gone to the Land of Promise in the West. So has his magic queen Fair Breast. There is no Morgan, no Delvcaem, no magic cup today." He drained the last drop of his own mead and hit the side of the cave with his gloved hand.

"In the Many-Colored Land there is always a Morgan, always a Delvcaem, always a magic cup," said the old man mysteriously.

"Always a chess game between a young king and a white-haired woman?" Cormac asked sarcastically and poured some more mead. Anything to stay warm.

The teller of tales shrugged his shoulders and put a lump of turf into the fire. "You will have to go forth to the Many-Colored Land eventually, King Cormac. It is so written. You will play the chess game with Becuma—Finnabair—eventually, whether you want to or not." The words of prophecy were spoken without emotion.

The poor man was so old that he could no longer distinguish between the real world in which humans lived, suffered, worked, died and the dreamworld of stories. If the people of Tara were listening to him—he was the most famous storyteller in Royal Meath, after all—they probably had come to believe Cormac was Art MacConn returned. Even the Christian half of Ireland believed in the return of souls from a former time. Taletellers told tales, superstitious people believed them. Evil ones like Finnabair would know what use to make of them. No wonder Rory MacFelan had advised him to visit the storyteller Flan.

The fog was less dense. Abruptly Cormac got up, gave the old man a gold coin, shook his gnarled hand, and strode out somewhat unsteadily to his wet horse. He was more confused than ever, drifting now like an empty curragh on a stormy sea.

On the way back to Tara he would stop at the rath of Lorcan the wealthy farmer, whose daughter had so bemused the poor MacFelan. Rory would be there.

Despite his *brat* and hood, Cormac was wet to the bone when he rode into the walled *rath* of Lorcan. The horse of Rory MacFelan was already there. Rory still ignored Cormac's peculiarities—though the black-eyed virgin seemed to dislike him intensely. What was the girl's name? He never could remember it. He should have asked Biddy before riding out in the rain. Rory had not noticed that he called her "daughter of Lorcan," but the girl did not like it.

They sat at the door of one of the neat stone and thatch outbuildings, just inside the stockade of Lorcan's rath, holding hands and gazing into one another's eyes. What did lovers find to talk about, he wondered. Rory was pleased, as he always was to see the *Tanaise*. He rose and extended his hand. Cormac, alighting from his horse with the practiced ease that befits a king, grasped Rory's hand with more warmth than he had intended. He must have drunk too much mead.

The girl was less delighted. Modest Christian maiden

she might be, but there was a look of toughness about her shapely body. She was still a virgin, he was sure, though not because of any reluctance on her part to give herself to the young king. If there was any hesitation, it was on Rory's side, poor fellow. She would make him a loyal wife; he would be a kind and gentle husband. For a moment Cormac pitied his own loneliness. It would be good to come home to a black-haired wench like the daughter of Lorcan. The nights would not be damp with her in your bed. He dismissed the thought. The girl must have seen the flash of lust in his eyes because she averted her face.

"So you have seen the storyteller Flan?" asked Rory guardedly.

"I have seen him, gentle Rory, and have heard again the tale of Art MacConn and his magic princess—without the magic cup, however, which I think is an essential part of the story."

He sat down on the bench with the young lovers, attracted by their glow. He must either cast in his lot with Rory and the young kings against Finnabair or eventually be driven from Tara. He knew that as well as he had ever known anything. But the fog in his head was so thick he could not decide. The risk of letting these young folk begin to love him was frightening—but why should it be so? At this moment they warmed him more than the mead.

"Are not the cup and the princess the same thing, Cormac? They are both sacred vessels to bring life to the king and to Ireland."

"I had not thought of that. You are right, good friend." His head was dizzy. He must be more careful with mead.

The reference to vessels brought a faint blush to the face of the daughter of Lorcan.

Cormac thought that as a poet he should have seen the

symbol. He wanted to laugh. He must steady himself. "Flan hinted that all Tara thinks I'm the king in the story and am fated to go into exile."

Neither Rory nor his woman seemed surprised. Silently she brought Cormac a goblet of milk and a piece of cheese. She even smiled at him—a lovely, radiant smile. He had called her man "good friend"; she forgave him everything. Fortunate Rory MacFelan to have a woman who loved him as much as he loved her. He closed his eyes and his head whirled from the effects of the mead. Quickly he opened them. Did they know he was drunk?

"Finnabair would use the story against me if she could." He sank his teeth into the tart, strong cheese.

"You bring conflict to Tara, Expected One. Many would be glad to see you go. They have grown used to Finnabair and the collapse of order. The story is a danger for you." Rory's young face was clouded with worry. The girl wrapped her mantle more tightly around her fresh young body.

No, they didn't know he was drunk. They had come to expect that he would act strangely. Why not act even more strangely?

"Do not play chess with her, good king," said the daughter of Lorcan in the longest sentence she had yet spoken.

"Do you think I would lose, lovely lady?" He sipped his milk and smiled sweetly for her.

She turned crimson. "She is a witch, King Cormac—we would not want to lose you." Her black eyes were warm with affectionate concern.

How quickly a few costless kind words won friends. "If there were a real Princess Delvcaem somewhere in the Many-Colored Land—" he mused.

"They say," the daughter of Lorcan spoke timidly, perhaps afraid that the High King would laugh at her, "that he who seeks the magic cup seeks the perfect woman." Gracefully she put another slab of cheese into his empty hand.

"Wondrous, lovely lady," Cormac laughed drunkenly. "If that were true the search would be over, for then surely the magic cup would be in this very hill fort of Lorcan." He delicately touched her long black hair. Good God, will Rory be offended?

Instead the young king was delighted. "Pity the poor man who finds the perfect woman and must live with her for the rest of his life."

They all laughed—even the virgin, despite her scarlet face.

"Especially if the perfect woman is Irish," she retorted.

The girl had courage.

"Alas, for Cormac Dermot the search for the perfect woman cannot end in Lorcan's rath," he said, now caught up in the spirit of the drunkenness he had brought to the rain hill. "Someone of more courage than he has already laid seige to that stronghold."

He downed the cup of milk in one swallow, choking on it. "He must search elsewhere for the Princess Delvcaem," he sputtered through the milk on his lips. *Oh, my God, they must know I'm drunk. They seem to like me this way.*

"In God's name, my friend, you do not believe the stories?" Rory looked frightened.

Cormac wondered if he did. Was there somewhere a magic princess waiting for him? She would change him, transform him so that he would always be gentle, as loving as these two young people who sat with him so companionably on the rain-soaked bench in the rath of Lorcan.

He nibbled at the cheese. Why did he have to leave? "The king must travel to strange lands and suffer much before he can rule in Tara."

The mead seemed to be wearing off. The fog was seeping into his head again.

"Have you not traveled enough and suffered enough already?" Rory laid his hand on Cormac's arm protectively.

He never wanted to leave these friends. But he would only bring them suffering and death. He grasped the hand of Rory, kissed the forehead of the marvelous virgin more ineffectively than he had intended and rode off into the mists toward Tara. Would to King Jesus that there were a magic princess for him somewhere.

That night he did not eat at King Dermot's table in Tara but alone in his bedchamber. Brigid brought him a cold slice of meat, berries, and a goblet of wine for evening fare. She placed them before him on the table as quietly as a bird gliding across the sky. His head was aching from the mead.

"Did the teller of tales amuse my noble king?" she asked with mock diffidence.

One hid nothing from her. "He did." Did she know about the visit to the Rath Lorcan?

"You remembered that Lorcan's daughter is called Fionna?" she persisted implacably.

"I did," he lied. He pushed his meal aside. His stomach was tight. Too much mead, he wondered, or too much affection?

She had taken her usual position by the draperies at the door, hands behind her back, head and shoulders bowed—the obedient slave. "You will lose if you play chess with Finnabair."

The second woman today to worry about him. *If the mead hadn't worn off, Biddy, I'd be sloppily kissing you too.* "Better in chess than in bed, is it not, all-knowing bondwoman?" he asked curtly.

She silently turned to leave. Podraig intercepted her for his ration of affection.

"Is there a magic princess waiting for me somewhere, Lady Brigid?" It was a pathetic plea. He was ashamed of himself. Still, he rose from the table and joined her at the doorway.

Rarely did he catch her by surprise. She paused, then said, "The beloved of King Rory must have been very beautiful today." She sighed.

Damn the woman, she saw too much.

She went on. "You will only find the magic princess and her magic cup when you search for her inside yourself."

The child—damn it, the woman—was wise beyond her years. "I can search for nothing in Tara's halls, Biddy." Why must he sound so miserable?

Her wide solemn eyes turned on him with sadness. "Where will you search, then, O tormented MacDermot?" She spoke with gentle pity and then removed the wine from his table.

Brigid's compassion was more devastating than her irony. After she left, her forehead still unkissed, he opened the shutters to look out into the thick fog which had rolled up to Tara, covering everything like a soaking wet linen cloth. A smell of burning turf hung in the moist air. If only King Jesus would grant that out in the fog there might be a magic princess, imprisoned by a cruel king, waiting for him to come to her with freedom and love.

Chapter 7

The rain poured out of the gray late afternoon skies, a fit setting for the departure of a failure. He had come back from Ravenna and the papal court at Lugnasa not six months ago; it was not even Inbolc yet. Harvest-time over and Cormac MacDermot did not last till spring—a quick-dying late autumn blossom. He mourned his passing as he would mourn the passing of such a flower.

Hunching his shoulders against the stinging wind, he rode by the Rath Maeve where King Dermot's hired soldiers lived. They would not be sorry to see him leave, though few in Tara liked or trusted Queen Finnabair. Except for those who gained by disorder, they had welcomed his return as the salvation of Ireland from the pagan witch. His taciturn arrogance had offended even the professional soldiers eventually, and they had the most reason to admire him. His feelings of sorrow for himself grew deeper. He was mired in such feelings just as his chariot wheels were often mired in Tara's thick, cold mud. He enjoyed the mire.

He had been outwitted by the queen in that foolish chess game; she imposed her solemn *geis* on him to find the magic cup and bring back to Tara as his bride the Princess Delvcaem. She had ordered him into permanent exile. There were ways of getting out of a *geis*—kings did it every day—with public opinion on their side. For Cormac there was no support. The golden-haired woman had timed her vengeance well. She knew there would be not a single voice raised in all of Tara in favor of the grim-faced heir to the kingship. He had rejected her; she took her revenge. Now Tara was hers.

Cormac rode by the second rampart, not looking at the great earth wall which was topped by a high log stockade, a massive ditch of water in front. Tara was impregnable. It had never been taken. For centuries it had never even been attacked. A High King was beaten only because he rode out of Tara to do battle or because power was seized from within. Tara's walls were useless against Finnabair, who worked her wiles within men's hearts. Some day those who were happy to see him go would yearn for his return. It would then be too late. He reveled in his own sadness.

He was dry beneath his hooded black fur cloak. The wolfhound Podraig, always by his side, enjoyed the rain. Podraig enjoyed everything. He should be High King of Ireland. People liked him.

He steadied the horses who slipped in the mud. He did not want to be king. Pride was a shield beneath which hid fear. He was afraid to be king, afraid to lead men into battle, to make decisions that could cost the lives of women and children.

There were so many things he did not understand, so many mysteries. Why did God permit killing and death? Why did the innocent suffer? Why did his mother die just when the poor old king needed her? Why was Finnabair, that witch with the wondrous powers, permitted to enchant King Dermot? Cormac had yearned to be a monk so that he could spend his whole life pondering such questions. His teacher Kiernan was right; he did not have the patience to be a monk among other monks. He should remove himself totally from human company and become a hermit on some mountaintop like the holy man Kevin.

Was the tale about Kevin true? Had he really drowned his sweetheart when she dared to visit him at his mountain retreat? Cormac smiled wryly. He was no better than Kevin. King Jesus liked people. Cormac knew that he should too. Yet he found the faithful hound Podraig more attractive as a companion than any human. He would not miss Tara; he would miss no one here. Cormac MacDermot needed no one, loved no one, and was loved by no one. So be it.

He had failed. As *Tanaise* he should protect Ireland from evil demons like the witch Finnabair. Enda the bishop had warned him of his increasing danger; Brigid, his servant girl, gave him daily accounts of the mounting number of his enemies; Colum, whose *geis* forbade him to come within the ramparts of Tara *(what a typical Irish absurdity—a holy abbot subject to pagan superstition!)*, told him that no magic of Finnabair could defeat him so easily as his own grim pride. Well, it was another successful prophecy for the holy abbot, whom the discreet Enda had doubtless already summoned from Iona to confront this new crisis—the final crisis, Cormac recognized.

The pagan O'Neills win the fight against the Christians; Ireland sinks back to the unredeemed and hopeless heathen times.

His horses were slowed by the heavy mud. What would it be like outside beyond the third rampart after these five straight days of rain? There was no hurry; he was going nowhere. He turned to take his last look at Tara against the darkening sky. The great banquet hall built by his father and the adjoining older structure stood sharply against the sky. He would not see them again.

The rain-soaked fields between the second and third ramparts were empty. Doubtless there were some sentries somewhere, peering into the mists as night closed, but he could not see them. He was alone with two horses and Podraig. The burdens lightened on his shoulders. He would survive Colum's noisy disappointment, Enda's silent reproach, the Lady Ann's sad brown eyes. He would be free of Tara and the High Kingship forever. If Ireland was ever to be Christian, let it find some other leader; it would not be Cormac MacDermot.

Podraig bounded ahead of the chariot, barking with delight. His dog barked that way only for beautiful women—though he growled at Finnabair, and the devil knew how lovely she was.

A figure appeared at the entrance of the third ring, standing not underneath the watchtower but in the driving rain. Podraig was frisking delightedly around her. It must be a woman; the light was too dim to tell for sure. As Cormac approached he could see the slight figure of the slave girl Brigid.

Soaking wet, she stood in the rain without cloak or shoes, waiting. Her short hair plastered against her head, dull brown gown clinging to her trim girlish legs, she did not look like the undernourished lad he almost took her for when he rode into Tara. Six months had established her femininity beyond doubt. Poor Biddy. She would be pretty for a few years and then ruined and cast aside by some lout whose fancy she caught. Ugly servant girls had a better chance to survive among the good Christians of Tara.

He fought back further temptation to sentiment. Pulling in the reins, he looked down at her coldly. "What brings you, Lady Brigid, to the third ring on this wet night? You wish to cut short your life by becoming ill? Does your pagan namesake keep the sun shining in your heart while the rain pounds your brain?" His voice was harsh, the proper tone for a king with a bondwoman not worth the market price.

The tiny, squinting face was somber in the failing light. Rainwater washing down it made her look like a grotesque river elf. "No more than does the Christian saint who bears the same name," she retorted, her old impertinence brought back by the rain.

Anxious to be out of Tara, he said roughly, "Go home, Biddy, and dry out. I am leaving Tara."

"To search for the magic cup and the Princess Delvcaem to bring home as your bride." The drenched face solemnly peered up at him in his chariot.

"You cannot come with me, Biddy," he said curtly.

"It is for my noble master to say. I am not afraid." Her total dependence on him cut again at his soul with a sword of anguish.

"Biddy, child, I don't think you're afraid of anything in Ireland. Where I am going you cannot come." There were other things he wanted to say to her. Poet or no, they would not come. Brusquely he turned away and signaled his horses forward.

As the chariot moved on, Podraig stood by the limp and forlorn slave girl. It was unlike him not to leap ahead of his master, eager for what was to come. The dog barked loudly, interspersing his protests with wails that reminded Cormac of the legends about the banshee's cry.

Cormac took his whip from the side of the chariot. Wolfhounds were taught to be obedient. He hesitated. It was a very strange wail. Was there danger for him if he left the soggy slave girl behind? Stopping the chariot, Cormac turned, and in his most solemn tone of command ordered, "Come, Podraig!"

He rode on, confident that the dog would know he was serious. Podraig did not come. Cormac hesitated. Perhaps there was something to learn from Biddy before he rode away from Tara forever. He turned the chariot around.

Biddy had not moved. Her head was downcast, she ignored the barking wolfhound and seemed not to hear Cormac's returning.

"What will happen to you, woman, after I am gone?"

She did not look up. "Do you think Queen Finnabair will forget that I saw her humiliation? Do you think Cormac's slave would be permitted to remind people of him after he is gone? Do you think I will live even one night?" She paused. "Oh, she has special pain for me to make my dying hard." Her voice was flat, without emotion.

"Do you seek death, Biddy?"

"Does a doe chased by the hounds want to die? Is she not too frightened to know or care?"

Could anyone possibly appeal for life more softly? "You could not hope for long life. You must know, Biddy, that death will take you soon." He spoke cruelly to kill his own battling emotions.

"As always, my noble master is wise." She accepted

the sentence of death with resigned obedience, her eyes turning downward toward the water at her feet.

She was a minor and trivial bit of human dust, possessing only the damp brown dress she wore and the slight, weak body that shivered in the cold rain. Is the doe that falls victim to the hounds fortunate to be spared the pangs of winter hunger and the sickness of old age? He looked at the slight shoulders, growing indistinct in the encroaching darkness, and made up his mind.

He picked her up and swung her onto the chariot beside him. There was almost no weight to her. "There is not much to you, Biddy, you are as light as a sparrow," he said gruffly.

"There is at least a loyal heart for your service, noble master." She spoke with the dedication of a nun taking a vow.

Something sharp stung King Cormac's eyes, which he brushed at impatiently. He stretched his cloak around her to protect her from the rain. The beat of her heart against his body melted him. She shivered.

"We will get you quickly to Slaine. The bishop's good wife will have a warm bed and dry clothes for you. If King Cormac has a kingdom of only one person, he must guard it well." Protectively his fingers tightened against her ribs. He was shivering too.

The wolfhound Podraig trotted happily beside the chariot, oblivious to the rain and the cold.

Chapter 8

The *bishop's wife* pushed her broom angrily against an offending lump of mud. It was impossible to keep a house clean with so many visitors. The rain was over, the day had dawned bright and blue. The visitors were about to leave. Fury was building within her. Men were so stupid. Why couldn't any of them see the solution to Cormac's problem?

"Still sweeping, woman?" Enda snapped nervously at her as he entered the house. Even his gentle disposition had been strained by the presence of the visitors.

She threw the broom against the wall and burst into tears. "You're like the rooster in the chicken house at laying time. Must you be responsible for every madman in the O'Neill clan?"

He jumped with dismay, opened his mouth to reply in kind, then hugged her fiercely. He would have dragged her off to bed in the middle of the day even though she was five months pregnant, but Brigid came through the door with the two children. The slave girl looked surprised. "I will give them their noonday food," she said tentatively, placing a bowl of freshly whipped butter on the table.

"Thank you, child," replied Enda smoothly. "The Lady Ann and I will make sure that all the supplies are ready for your journey." He pulled Ann outside of the house. "You're right, dear one," he whispered, still holding her tightly. "Everything you are thinking is right. They are both mad. We will be well rid of them. The girl is a jewel, Cormac is a blind fool. His search is absurd. I should do something, but I can't. If anyone is to save him it must be that tiny slave. We must pray for her." His voice trailed off.

Ann was sobbing again, angry at everyone—everyone but Brigid.

When they first arrived and Cormac silently handed the soaking girl over to her care, Ann thought she might be Cormac's lover. Was it not strange for the king to take a mistress so young? Now she knew that whatever the bond between them might be, it was not the sort that made them bed partners. Cormac treated her with grave respect, occasionally returning her caustic irony with a sharp remark of his own, which was, in fact, the only time he roused from his lethargy. The girl was obviously more of a woman than Cormac was willing to see. Brigid seemed content that it should be that way.

Brigid's embarrassment when Ann peeled off her tattered and soaking tunic was evidence enough that she was not Cormac's mistress. Most slave girls lose their modesty quickly; this one had not. She was a lovely little thing, her body rounding rapidly towards a beauty that would soon make men's throats dry with longing. Ann rubbed her wet skin with a towel. The child knew she was being inspected and cowered protectively behind huddled shoulders and crossed arms. She was ashamed of herself because she did not know what the older woman thought of her.

Ann spoke directly and bluntly, "You have a lovely body, good slave girl. Soon you will be a very beautiful woman."

Brigid considered this thoughtfully. "Is it truly so?" she asked uncertainly. "I—I have heard this once before. I cannot tell." But she uncrossed her arms and straightened her shoulders.

Poor child. "It is truly so. I only hope my daughters approach womanhood with so much promise of grace." She wrapped a dry towel around the child and forced a cup of warm mead laced with honey into her tiny hand.

Brigid shook her head slowly. "I never thought that it would be so. I do not doubt you, Lady Ann. It is hard for me to understand—" and with a big leap over chasms of distrust and fear, "I—I would like to be as beautiful as you." The words poured out like water boiling over a kettle.

Ann could not help herself. She hugged the slave girl and began to cry. Brigid did not weep but she hugged back. "Some of us have been blessed by the good God, Brigid. Our grace comes slowly but it endures long. You and I are like that."

The slave's eyes sparkled. She sipped the mead, flushing with its warmth and sweetness. She let the towel fall from her shoulders, secure in Ann's affection, and smiled. It was the only time she smiled during her stay at the house. She would not smile at Cormac. Brigid was a fool, too, thought Ann, her anger rising again. This time she included the lovely girl in it. *Smile at him once a day, you little idiot, and you'll be Queen of Ireland in a week.*

She prayed to Mother Mary that the fool MacDermot would recognize the value of his bondwoman. She released her fierce grip on Enda's hand and returned to the house. Someone had to be cheerful. That afternoon, though, she was weary with the burden of her coming child. She sang and played the harp to bring some cheer to the cold hearts of their melancholy guests.

The decision to go on the foolish pilgrimage had been made the day before after a long, stormy battle of recriminations between the abbot, who had finally come, exhausted from his journey through the rain, and the gloomy, guilty expected King.

"To think I prayed it would not be lust that trapped you." Colum's anger was spent at last. He was slumped in a chair looking very old.

A light flickered in Cormac's sad eyes. "That prayer at least was heard," he muttered sorrowfully, leaning against the wall at the same place Ann had stood when she thought he would violate her. Memories of that sweet terror did not lessen her fury at Cormac's foolishness.

"There was no support at all for you in Tara? Surely such pagan nonsense about *geis* could not drive out a High King?" He leaned forward eagerly, striving to understand what had gone wrong with his careful plans.

"Cousin, I suspect there were other reasons for Art, the son of Conn, leaving too. The *geis* happens to be a fortunate excuse. Should I come back tomorrow with Delvcaem and the magic cup, they wouldn't want me in Tara. Finnabair is supreme. It is better to have no king than to have one who disapproves of what is happening."

Self-pity was replacing anger. She despised that in him even more.

"Especially when that king offends even those who

want to be his friends," said the fearless Brigid, sounding like the bell that summoned the faithful to mass.

For the first time the Abbot of Iona noticed the tiny figure on the other side of the crackling fire. His shrewd blue eyes widened with interest. "Who are you, young woman?" he asked with gentle courtesy—an O'Neill even in time of crisis.

"I am Brigid, the king's bondwoman, holy abbot." She paused for a moment, undecided, then rushed on. "Your cousin is a harsh man. Tara is not ready for a new king—even a smiling, laughing one. Much less could it accept a haughty king who promises only gloom and death. King Cormac cares for no one. If he had not left Tara when he did, he would have been killed by those who came to fear his black mood. He loves no one and is loved by no one."

She moved from the wall to the center of the room, pointing her tiny finger at Cormac like an abbess accusing a postulant of fornication. Cormac sat silent, staring into the fireplace, oblivious to her courage.

"Yet," said Colum, meekly defending his cousin, "he does inspire you to the devotion of blunt and honest talk?"

"Good abbot," she turned on him, "do I look like a bondwoman who can offer anything else? I have not been baptized; still I know of King Jesus. I know he taught kindness and joy, forgiveness and peace. I see none of these among the Irish who claim to be his followers—including their kings and abbots." She was as lovely as Queen Maeve preparing for battle. Still, Cormac would not look at her.

Brigid knew how to humble the O'Neill clan, the bishop's wife thought.

"We try our best, Brigid, my child," the abbot answered

wearily. "King Jesus, fortunately for us, forgives us our mistakes. I perceive that you would not." He spread his hands in appeal, a courtier-missionary pleading for understanding from a queen.

"I saved her life," muttered Cormac glumly into the fire.

"Twice," said Brigid. "—the way you would save the life of an ant or a sparrow, the life of an inferior creature unworthy of your notice." Her bell-like voice was ringing out clearly, as though it were sweeping across the countryside.

"You are more than an ant or a sparrow to me, Biddy."

At least the fool had looked away from the fire and said something kind.

"Surely not as much as a wolfhound." The dog, who tried his best to divide his time evenly between Ann and Brigid, at that moment had his ungainly head in the slave girl's lap and was gazing contentedly at the Abbot of Iona.

That great churchman threw back his gray-blond head and laughed loudly. "Ah, Brigid, my child, to be loved by Cormac MacDermot more than the hound Podraig would put one beyond the ranks of mere mortals."

The abbot and the slave girl had determined by some mysterious communication that they liked and trusted one another.

"But what is to be done?" asked Enda irritably. He had grown desperate from trying to moderate the O'Neill battle, poor man.

"My lord Enda," said Brigid. "Cormac MacDermot and I must go in search of the magic cup and the magic princess." She turned to the abbot. "If your cousin in Armagh can play the game of waiting, good abbot, so can your cousin the High King. Poor King Dermot still lives. The harvest was bad, but there is no famine in the land. It will have to get much worse on yonder hill before King Cormac will be welcome. In the meantime, let him search for the magic cup; the legend will grow. If he fights now, he loses; if he waits—" The girl's words flowed like melting butter.

She spoke like a general planning a battle. Ann shivered. There was something of a witch in Brigid.

Cormac roused himself from the fire and rearranged his belt, a sign that he was trying to come alive. *About time, you lump of turf.* "Finnabair must expect me to return to Italy. As long as I'm in Ireland she will not sleep easily. No one in Meath needs to be told how the story of Art MacConn ended!"

It was the most practical speech Cormac had made yet. This dark, agonized man hoped desperately to find the magic cup and the princess who went with it. The search, not the waiting, would hold his attention. "Oh, my God," Ann thought, "he really is going to look for the magic cup. They're all insane."

"It is said that in the west of Ireland," her husband said, as mad as the rest of them, "beyond the kingdom of Munster, out on the wild rocks, there are many peoples with strange customs—hereditary pirates who keep alive old customs and beliefs—older even than the Druids."

"The monks beyond the Shannon have told me," added Colum enthusiastically, "that the pirate queen Morrigan still rules on some of the islands off the coast." He rose from his chair, excited.

Cormac was filled with restless energy. His hand was on his knife. He strode to the open doorway through which the blue sky appeared like a pane of glass. He seemed to want to be out of the door at once. To the abbot he said, "Your mad friend Brendan speaks of sailing to the Land of Promise?"

"Poor old man. He's the best sailor in Ireland, and he cannot accept that the land to the west is not in this world. But beyond Brendan's monastery there are peculiar peoples and happenings. God knows what you will find out there, Cormac."

The wild O'Neill gleam was now in both their eyes.

"Mother Mary, protect us," prayed the Lady Ann. The poor old Abbot Brendan was less mad than any of those in her house.

The abbot continued, "You should visit the hermit Kevin at Glendalough. He knows more about the world out beyond than anyone else. It is said that he never leaves his hermitage—but still he *knows.*"

"I thought he was dead." Cormac's interest was like a fever. His hands were clenched, his eyes bright, his thick arms coiled for battle.

"He starts those rumors for the fun of laughing at them—like the story of the drowned Kathleen— Oh, yes, good cousin, you will enjoy visiting Kevin." Colum was himself once more—intense, vigorous, commanding.

The two descendants of Neill of the Nine Hostages had crossed the subtle line separating sophisticated men of the world from wide-eyed dreamers. Both Cormac and Colum, true to their Irish heritage, had begun to believe in the search for the magic cup. They paced up and down like hurling players before a match.

Enda spoke again. "The girl Brigid will stay with us."

Although the bishop's wife loved her man with passionate devotion, now his placid common sense was beyond all bearing. How could he have so missed the point?

Had he been in Ireland so long that he did not understand that the search was not only insane but pointless if Brigid did not go?

"I am the king's bondwoman. I must go with him," Brigid said firmly, ending the discussion.

There was no protest from Colum, who approved of her influence on his gloomy cousin. Cormac had doubtless learned not to argue with her.

"But—" said Enda, trying to be sensible, poor, dear, beautiful, silly man.

"Gentle husband," Ann interrupted him softly, "if Brigid does not go along, I fear that King Cormac will forget to eat."

There was laughter from everyone but Brigid, who never laughed when Cormac was present. The confused Enda caught his wife's eye. "Of course," he said, "and one does need to eat if one is searching for a magic cup."

The night after the pilgrims left, as he held her in his strong arms, she was glad she had Enda to protect her. She could not tell him she thought Cormac and Brigid would never again climb the steep road to the top of the Hill of Slaine.

Chapter 9

A *huge, black-bearded* monster, the holy hermit Kevin, was trying to drown her in the river. She had not meant to tempt him. Why would he not let her breathe? No, it was not Kevin, it was Cormac. She was not Kathleen but Brigid. But why was he trying to drown her? "Please don't—!" The waters swirled around, her lungs filled.

Brigid woke up coughing, her body in a cold sweat despite the stuffy air of the tiny wattle-and-thatch hut in which she and the High King had taken refuge. She choked back the sound, fearing to wake the others. Lying perfectly still, she tried to sort out the terrors of the dream from the terrors of the waking world. Despite the frigid dampness, sweat continued to pour from her body.

This smelly little hut where she and Cormac sought refuge from the cold winter rain was evil. She could feel it in her heart, in her bones, in the pit of her stomach.

There was danger in the early morning hours before the long night turned into the brief, gray day. All times of change were filled with terror, especially the changing of the seasons—the most dangerous transition in the whole year. Horrible forces would be loose in the world as winter turned to spring. It was not a time to be awake in early morning on the side of a windswept, rain-soaked mountain.

She was afraid to sleep because her dreams were so terrible; yet if she did not sleep, the next day would be even worse. She had barely been able to move at the end of yesterday. Would she be able to get up when the pale gray light summoned them to begin their pilgrimage again? Finnabair, soldiers, evil spirits, forest demons, her own sickness, the unsmiling inhabitants of the hut—horrors everywhere.

She rolled over restlessly on the cold dirt floor. The fire glowed faintly. The old man was snoring. Three humps, which lay just out of reach of her hand, were the old woman and two brutish young men. She could not see Podraig; perhaps he had gone out into the rain. The wolfhound did not like the dank little hut and its shifty-eyed inhabitants. He seemed to know that it was no place for a High King—even one hunted down by enemies. She did not want to stay the night. Cormac had insisted that they needed one night out of the cold winter rain. He meant that she needed a dry night if she were to go on.

The people who lived in the hut were surly. The obligation of hospitality was grudgingly given; their small eyes glittered at the sight of the gold with which Cormac paid them. Tomorrow she would mock him about his dangerous generosity. He would only smile. Her tongue angered him no longer. To Brigid, he was the worst danger of all.

It had begun the day after they left Slaine, before they were forced to abandon their chariot and supplies to hide from Finnabair's pursuing horsemen. The sun shone brightly then, the last day they saw much of it in weeks of wandering and hiding. Their clothes were clean, their hearts eager for the journey. Cormac sang songs of hope as the horses trudged down the road toward the Wicklow Mountains to the south. Brigid, who had never been more than a few miles from Tara, found her heart beating fiercely at the thought of excitement and adventure with the High King.

Cormac stopped singing suddenly. "I must say something to you, Lady Brigid," he said solemnly, halting the horses. He wet his lips with his tongue, a most unusual action.

"What else can a bondwoman do but listen when her master speaks?" Such a tart response usually kept him on the defensive.

"You are more than a rabbit or even Podraig to me," he murmured softly.

Her heart beat as though she had run up the whole Hill of Tara. "Cannot a small bondwoman be easily replaced? Where is there another Podraig?" Did he hear the tremble in her voice?

He would not be turned from what bothered him. "I cannot think of you as a slave, Biddy. You are too old to be my daughter and too young to be my wife or mistress."

He was getting angry. Careful, Biddy— "If it is what King Cormac says, it must be true; it is not said that—"

His hand clamped her mouth shut, but he did not hurt her as he had at other times when he seized her. His beautiful arms were so strong, his graceful fingers so tender— She thought that her heart would burst with sweetness.

"Nor would any wife or daughter speak so harshly to me. So, Biddy, since I will not have you as a slave and I cannot have you as a wife, you will be my foster daughter. That is finished."

All very clear and decisive. He sounded confident again. He had done his duty, poor, silly man. "May not a master call his slave whatever he wishes?" she said impudently when he took his hand off her mouth, hoping that her voice sounded flat and servile.

Cormac's face tightened with anger. He did not reply because just then he saw the horsemen coming down the valley after them. They hid in a grove of trees. The pursuers came dangerously close. Brigid was numb with fright as they rode by. Ten men against one were odds too great even for Cormac and Podraig. What would she do in such a fight? She took the king's knife from his belt, thrilling at its thin, sharp feel in her hand.

"Dermot's personal guard," said Cormac. "Finnabair must want us not only out of Tara but dead. Biddy, what are you doing with my knife?"

"May not even a slave girl die bravely?" Her teeth were chattering.

Cormac laughed approvingly. His anger at her refusing to accept the role of foster daughter was forgotten.

It was as a foster daughter he insisted on treating her. She was carried across streams, given the best piece of meat when they ate, addressed with ceremonious respect. She retaliated by becoming an even more docile slave. Food and drink were ready when he was hungry and thirsty, dry bracken was spread for his bed, his feet were carefully washed at the end of the day.

One night before they lost their chariot in the rain-swollen Liffey, Cormac insisted on washing her feet. She was too tired to find the words to prevent him. Her head became dizzy every time he picked her up to cross an obstacle. When he kissed her feet she came close to collapse with a mixture of terror and delight.

"They are very cold, Biddy," he said, gently wrapping her feet in a dry cloth.

"Is not the day cold, cruel lord?" she stammered.

"Cruel, Biddy?" She had stopped him again.

"If you treat me so graciously, will I not forget what I am and begin to think I—I am someone important?"

He pulled back from her, rebuffed and baffled. She must keep him that way. If she were not so wet and tired, perhaps she could cope with him and with her own unruly emotions. She had been amused when the good bishop's wife told her about the "enslaving gaze" of the High King. It was an odd superstition from such a pious Christian matron. Now she knew what Ann meant. Those eyes, filled with secret pain, probed the smallest part of the soul. He had let his hair and beard grow long, abandoning the Ravenna style at last. The long, curly red locks made him even more beautiful. When he carried her across a brook his touch was so gentle. Her feelings grew more difficult to restrain with each passing day. If only he were not so strong and handsome, if only she did not love him so much.

She was worn out from the difficulties of their journey. She had come to help him; now she was a burden he had to worry about; he had to protect her from the rain and the cold. Surely he would have turned to fight their pursuers if she had not been with him. They would not dare to kill the High King. The dangers of this smelly hut in which they were spending the night were dangers he and Podraig were enduring for her.

She rolled over again, anxiously listening carefully. Was there movement in the hut? Where was Podraig? Would the rain never stop? What was that noise? Should she wake Cormac?

It was her fault they had lost the chariot with most of their supplies. The pursuing horsemen finally caught them in an open meadow on the banks of the Liffey. With drawn swords they advanced in a converging semicircle toward their quarry. Cormac drew his own sword; she clutched his knife—it was hers now—strapped to her thigh, much to his amusement. Then he decided to risk crossing the shallow ford. The rains had made the waters deep. The horses fought against the current, the chariot swayed as its wheels bumped the rocks on the river bottom. They might have made it if she had not lost her hold on the side of the chariot. Deftly he reached back to grab her; the horses yanked the reins out of his hand. The chariot and all its supplies tilted into the stream.

Cormac quickly cut the harness from the horses so they could escape. He grabbed her around the waist and shoved her toward the bank. Then he waded back into the river, sword in hand, to grab some of their sacks of food. The horsemen on the other bank hesitated, knowing they would have to cross in single file to face the High King's sword one by one.

The chill of the water took away her breath. She lost her footing and began to slip under. She felt the touch of death. Podraig, who had already climbed up on the bank, jumped back in. She grabbed the hound's huge neck and dragged herself up on the muddy bank—wet, cold, and frightened.

"Come and fight, you sons of hell!" thundered Cormac, his face flaming with anger. It was the first time she had seen the battle lust on him. The gentle Podraig, who had just saved her life, caught his master's mood. He howled wildly and bared his teeth. Finnabair's soldiers stayed on the opposite bank, watching intently. Then they turned and rode off into the mists. The battle heat was still on Cormac. "You live, woman?" he said harshly.

"Thanks to you and good Podraig, mighty lord." She was too weak to rise from the ground.

He softened. "Did you just thank me, Biddy?"

"You and Podraig."

He stood over her, hands on his hips, still the manly warrior after battle. "It is a wonder, Biddy, that Podraig tolerates either of us. Come, we must find shelter. They will be back." He slung the sack of soggy meal over his shoulder and picked her up in his arms, a second soggy bundle.

"I can walk," she screamed at him angrily.

He put her down, she took two steps and fell in the mud. Without a word he picked her up again. Despite her humiliation, she felt her heart pick up its beat. He was a beast. How dare he smile at her?

They found a small farm rath. The suspicious tenant and his wife let them dry out and spend the night in an outbuilding. Cormac slept with his sword unsheathed by his side, how soundly Biddy did not know because she was asleep as soon as she lay down on the rush-strewn floor. When the dull light of another rainy dawn awakened her, both Cormac and Podraig were already peering into the mists, waiting for battle. With a quick smile he took her hand. She was too afraid to pull it away. He held her fingers as though he were a mother holding a baby.

The horsemen never appeared. "They may have told the witch woman we died in the river," Cormac mused thoughtfully. "But why would she bother to pursue us in the first place? There are many things about this journey I do not understand."

"Is that possible, great king?"

He did not notice her irony. His face was locked in a puzzled frown.

She freed her hand. He did not notice that either.

"Well, we must go on. The magic cup awaits us." He strode decisively ahead with the hurley player's walk. She had to run to keep up.

South of the Liffey, the hills were steeper and the forests thicker. Their progress was slow because of the mud and the rain. Cormac insisted that she rest often. He did his best to provide shelter each night, if only some long branches angled against a large oak. Always he guarded a glowing ember from the fire of the night before. If it should lose its glow, there would be no warmth or dryness for them at all.

Few animals were to be seen in the forests. Unlike foolish humans, they would not venture from their winter shelters. It seemed she would never be dry and warm again. The rain soaked through their fur cloaks; their inner garments were always damp and sticky. They were not walking but swimming through a sea. When it was not raining, moisture fell from the soggy tree branches and seeped up from the muddy forest floor. She was afraid that she would become sick from the wet and the cold; then she hoped she would sicken and die quickly. Anything would be better than the rain, the wind, the mud, and the mists.

They said little to one another, conserving their energy for the task of slogging through the enveloping wetness. Even the wolfhound lost some of his zest. They stumbled on toward the mountains and Glendalough where the mysterious hermit Kevin might—or might not—tell them how to find the magic cup.

"You are a good traveler, Mistress Brigid," Cormac said to her as they huddled around a tiny fire one dark, cold night.

"If a master wishes to mock his bondwoman, may he not do so?" She rubbed her numb hands close to the fire. It hurt her lips to talk.

He sighed. "I will never mock you, Biddy. To be a good traveler is to stay alive and keep going." He added another stick to the flames.

She felt tears in her eyes and lowered her head. "How long will I be able to do either, kind master?" Her voice broke. In another moment she would throw herself into his arms.

"After we find this mad hermit—if we find him—the Abbot Kiernan will protect us at Clonmacnoise until we are ready to go on." His voice hesitated at the mention of Kiernan.

She was safe again. Why was he afraid to face his old teacher? She did not want to know how far it was from Glendalough to Clonmacnoise.

They were only a day or two away from Glendalough when Cormac had insisted on seeking a night's rest in this vile hunters' hovel. She was near collapse; despite her protests about the dangers of trusting the grotesque people who lived here, they stayed. Cormac was next to her, breathing softly and regularly in sleep. Why should the beast be able to sleep so easily? She touched his broad, strong back. Poor dear man. She wished she were a magic princess who could make his suffering go away forever.

Fantasies about Cormac flooded her imagination like the

raging Boyne flooded its valleys at springtime. His strong arms were holding her so she could not move, his hands relentlessly explored her body, his lips demanding response. He would pin her to the ground, tear off her robe, set her aflame with hunger, and then—she fought the fantasies off. They were terrible, fearsome, disgusting—and delightful.

She would touch him tenderly, kiss him softly. All the tenseness would flow out of him. His naked body had looked so beautiful that night she saved him from Finnabair. She would give him pleasure to make him forget that slut. Again she tried to go to sleep.

A huge, dirty paw clamped down on her mouth, another twisted her arm. Someone else moved toward the sleeping king. Desperately she grasped the knife she wore on her thigh under her *leine* with her free hand. She pulled it free and struck blindly at the huge shape over her. A sharp cry of pain sounded in the hut; she felt warm liquid spurting on her face. She struck again and again, twisting and pulling free and plunging it in again. The hands that held her loosened their grip.

The hut came alive with sound and movement. Was that her voice screaming? Bodies tumbled by her. Podraig's guttural snarling was all around. "Please, good hound, remember who I am," she pleaded. There were agonized screams and dull groans—terrible sounds of death and dying in the darkness. Then a flash of flame illuminated the scene as someone put a piece of burning wood to the thatch roof.

"Biddy!" Cormac was shouting desperately. She tried to answer, but her voice would not work. The fire spread; the blazing hut was now brighter than daylight.

The dead body of one of the young men pinned her to the floor. She was covered with his blood. The other youth was headless, limbs still twitching, his head lying nearby already on fire. The older man and the woman were also dead, their throats ripped open. Podraig's mouth was dripping blood, his teeth a shining red. There was blood on Cormac's sword, blood all over her, blood everywhere.

Brigid was sick. Her body twisted with the force of her stomach trying to tear itself out of her body. Cormac pulled the corpse off her, scooped her up in his arms and dashed from the flaming hovel. Podraig bounded after them.

The hut was engulfed with fire. Cormac cradled her in his arms, gently stroking her hair as she vomited again and again. The image of the dead bodies was before her eyes, the feel of the hot, sticky blood still fresh on her skin. Cormac held her tightly and said words she could not understand—peaceful, reassuring sounds that slowly brought a weak calm to her racked and exhausted body.

Finally, she found her voice. "I will clean your garments when it is light, gentle king," she said hoarsely.

"We will not worry about that, Biddy. When a slave girl saves the life of a king, she is permitted a brief respite from her duties."

How dare he laugh at me, the brute? "It was so ugly. I never knew— Those poor people." She was still weeping. Would she ever be able to stop?

"They would have killed us, Biddy." He tried to sound calm.

"Truly. But is it wrong to feel sadness that they would be driven to such murder and die the way they wanted us to die?"

He stopped stroking her hair. "Most people would not think that way, Biddy." After a long pause he added, "You are a remarkable woman, good foster child." He began stroking her hair again.

She wanted to say something sharp in return. There were no words. Fatigue spread through her aching body. With the strong arms of the High King around her, Biddy fell asleep. She woke to find herself wrapped in his cloak. The sun was out, high in the sky. Smouldering ashes where the hut used to stand smoked in the clear air. Her cloak and *leine* were hanging from a tree limb drying in the sun. A warm fire burned beside her; on the other side lay a gentle Podraig, dozing. Cormac leaned against a tree, one hand on his hip, watching her with an amused gleam in his eye.

It was a good sleep. The horrors of the night were a distant dream. She felt strength seeping back into her, then sudden shame. He had cleaned the sickness and blood off her naked body.

"You slept long, brave maiden." He was playing the courtier with her again.

What should she say? She reached fearfully for words, just as she had for Podraig's neck in the Liffey.

"King Jesus has taken pity on us and sent the sun. We have nothing but salt meat with which to eat our meal of thanksgiving, though. I suppose that you are now so hungry, you will not mind." He cut a small piece of meat and put in her mouth. "Chew very slowly, small one. I do not want you sick again."

Now he was the kindly old father with the foster child. She preferred the courtier. "If a worthless slave girl is treated so nobly every time she is sick, why should she not be sick often?" she said unsteadily.

The son of Dermot smiled his amusement. He was very handsome. What had he thought of her poor skinny little body? Had he noticed the changes? Did he like her breasts now?

"Am I to be limited to but one piece of beef?" she asked.

In the late afternoon with the glow of sunset on them they began once more to climb toward the top of the Wicklow Mountains, overlooking the great valley of Glendalough.

Chapter 10

T*he glare of* sun on water made Cormac squint. The three pilgrims skirted the tree-lined shores of a small lake whose wavelets glittered brightly in the chill sunlight like jewels on the stem of a chalice. Cormac and Biddy had stout walking sticks, new sandals, and warm clothes. They had expected little physical help from the strange hermit Kevin and had received much.

It was easier after they climbed slowly down from the Wicklow Mountains. Ireland's spring was struggling to be born. Nights were cold; days were bright and clear. Podraig and Brigid frolicked merrily through the days and shivered at night. Neither of them could resist the fascination of the lakes and rivers, the meadows and the early wildflowers. Though the slave girl seldom permitted delight to show on her face, she reported the wonders of her explorations and discoveries with the glee of a small child.

She was a wildflower herself—the bloom returning with the first touch of spring sunlight. Recklessly brave in time of danger, she had pushed her tiny body to its limits during the difficult climb up to Glendalough, stubbornly refusing to admit her own exhaustion. They could have traveled more rapidly without her; still, she was a pretty little thing. It was good to have someone to talk with by the fire at night.

What would Kiernan think of his traveling to Clonmacnoise with a bondwoman? Other members of the O'Neill clan had arrived with women at what they considered their private monastery. They had not been students of Kiernan as Cormac had. The affable, shrewd abbot could see through him as no one else in Ireland. What would he think of Cormac's return, of the failures at Tara, of the search for Delvcaem? Cormac punched the ground with his walking stick. Kiernan would not reprimand him. He never did. That made his quiet comments even more painful.

Perhaps it would be better to abandon the pilgrimage and stay at Clonmacnoise. There would be folk on the other side of the river who would take care of Brigid. She would be angry, he knew. What did he care for a slave girl's anger? She and Podraig were running to catch up with him. She ran well—like a boy. He had to make her look less like one before they got to Clonmacnoise. He didn't want Kiernan's first impression to be that he— Underneath her *leine* she was now indisputably a woman; but her short hair, drab gown, and slender body could leave you in doubt. An image of her body as he bathed it after the attack in the hunters' hut raced through his mind. He quickly pushed it away. She and Podraig ran up to him breathlessly, her shoulders heaving with excitement.

The girl's recuperative powers were astonishing. She was sick and battered when they came to Glendalough. After a few days of Kathleen's gentle ministrations she had all her energy and enthusiasm back.

Older women seemed to like her—first his mother, then Ann the wife of Enda, now the mysterious Kathleen. He noticed they did not treat her like a child—a younger sister, perhaps.

"What did you think of the holy hermit and holy hermitess, wise and prudent Brigid?" He quietly asked his slave turned foster daughter, using the same tone which holy Kiernan used when demanding an explanation for a text from scripture.

Brigid flipped a stone into the lake and watched its circles widen.

"Is it not clear that Kathleen loves him?" she responded disapprovingly.

"How could all those stories about his trying to drown her ever spread through Ireland?" He dug his staff into the thick soil and climbed over a huge tree root by the shore.

"Oh, they are true, learned king. She told me that when she first came to be with him, he did try to kill her. Then God revealed to him how they could live together in holy chastity and help each other to spend lives of prayer." She tossed her head in a defiant gesture she seemed to have acquired at Glendalough.

"Do you believe that, child?" he asked patronizingly, and extended his hand to help her over the root.

"I believe the Lady Kathleen, my lord." She stepped daintily to the other side of the root, as elegant as a princess, her white ankles reproving him for doubting the honor of the Lady Kathleen.

"A man could live in chastity with a woman so beautiful for—it must be thirty years?" There was an edge of crudity in his voice which he instantly regretted. He did not wish to offend her modesty. He remembered her blooming breasts the night she had saved his life; he had washed the blood off them very quickly while she slept, respecting her modesty even when she was unconscious. He had resisted the temptation to kiss them reverently. His tenderness for the girl was becoming an infection he must watch.

"You are the one, royal son of Dermot, who believes in the power of the grace of King Jesus," she observed quietly. The sunlight danced in her eyes as in the waters of the lake. Her hand rested confidently on the thick tree trunk.

The girl had a way of turning his faith against him. "Men and women are not made of stone, Biddy," he insisted firmly. Why did he always sound so pompous when he was losing to her?

She turned and walked pertly ahead of him down the tiny beach on the shore of the lake. "Do we not travel together without sinning, brave master?" A barely audible whisper but another saucy toss of the head.

Cormac felt stunned, as though one of the great pine trees had fallen on him. "That's different—I mean—" He was stammering. Without realizing it, he picked up the pace of their walk. Briskly he forged ahead of her.

"I am not as beautiful as the good Kathleen." She had lagged behind him, so he could no longer see her face. There was no doubting her triumph.

"I am wise enough not to try to compare the beauty of women. I meant that we were not childhood sweethearts; we will not live across a valley from each other in two caves and meet once a week for the next thirty years." He was even farther ahead of her now, stumbling out of his own trap.

"No, good king. I'm sure you would not live in a cave for thirty years."

Her impudent voice was a sword hitting home. Damn her. Traveling with her was like a hurling match against a skilled defensive player who always keeps you off balance. At Clonmacnoise the holy Kiernan could protect her should any of Finnabair's riders come seeking her head. He and Podraig would go on to the west in search of the magic cup. He must resist the impulse to throw her impudent little body in the lake. She was a nuisance and a distraction. He should have left her at Glendalough.

As they waited for the first light of Inbolc to rise over the valleys, Kevin spoke in disconnected sentences about the sun, the moon, and the stars. The Irish, he insisted, the flickering fire shining in his wild eyes, were the first in Europe to understand the movement of the heavenly bodies. They had taught their philosophy to the Greeks.

Cormac questioned him urgently. "Is the magic cup to be found? Does Queen Morrigan still reign in the islands to the west? Is the Princess Delvcaem still captive?"

The fire wavered in early spring breezes, casting bizaare, elongated shadows on the walls of the small cave.

"Does the fire still burn on Brigid's day? Will the sun shine for three months? Did the Lord Jesus rise from the dead?" The holy man made his quirky laugh sound, his eyes flashing with an enigmatic light. "No search is foolish, O High King. You will surely find what you seek in the islands of the west."

"The magic cup and the Princess Delvcaem?" He pounded the floor of the cave with an eager fist.

"You will find what you seek when you find that which it is you seek." He giggled—most unlike a wise and holy hermit. His eyes danced impishly.

There was an answering giggle from Brigid.

"Hush, child," said Kathleen, very gently.

The hermit turned slowly towards Brigid, a strange glow in his eyes. "Does the small pagan find my prophecy unpleasing?" His voice was suddenly gentle and playful.

"Will we all not be happy when we find that which it is we seek?" said Brigid, unabashed, playing with a vast ear of the sleeping wolfhound.

She looks very pretty, Cormac thought.

Silence hung in the air of the narrow cave. The light of the fire glowed on its walls.

"She is of both the old Ireland and the new, Kathleen," the old man said, as though he were announcing an important oracle.

Cormac felt his heart beat with an odd sort of pride. Biddy was a match for anyone.

The first light of the dawn of Inbolc slanted across the eastern sky at the other end of the glen. Kevin rose from the floor. He was more than two yards tall.

"King Cormac will yet rule in Tara," he said finally. "The child of both Brigids will not be forgotten."

It was spoken as a solemn benediction. They went out of the cave into the dazzling light of the rising sun. Spring had come to Ireland.

Cormac was glad to escape from Glendalough. They ate the Lord's Supper in the stone church in the valley, then walked along the swift, bubbling river, through the valleys and by the forested lakes toward the plain of the Shannon and Clonmacnoise. The mountains, their odd love, and the terrible silence of the caves had made the two hermits a little mad. Their enigmatic expressions and mysterious words suggested a wildness like a fierce winter thunderstorm. He no longer cared about Kevin's predictions; he would carry his quest to the end no matter what the hermit said.

Clonmacnoise would be much better. Holy Kiernan was a sane and solid man—no wild caves, no strange women companions, no ambiguous predictions from the Abbot of Clonmacnoise.

"Soon we will see the great Abbot Kiernan," he said firmly to Biddy, regaining some of his self-confidence.

"I wish to meet his famous dun cow," she shot back.

Pure stubborn spitefulness. He felt his jaw tighten. The little witch was baiting him again. "Only in Ireland, I suppose, are holy men made famous by their cattle."

"Yet would it not be more disturbing to you, O Christian king, if he had a companion like Kathleen instead of a dun cow?" There was a defiant glow in her eye and a provocative lilt in her voice. The bells were playing a mocking tune today. She climbed over another big tree root—this time with no need of his help.

"I think, solemn-faced traveler, that I should have left you in the mountains of Wicklow with those two crazy folk." He sighed in mock weariness.

It was time, he decided, that they stop for a noonday meal. They sat in a small clearing on the side of the lake in the bright sunlight, which was not yet obscured by the shadows of the pine trees. The meadow beyond had the good rich smell of Irish soil, pleasant and reassuring to a man who was a king of farmers.

The sun promised warmth and the spring to come. Biddy had been easily worn by the dampness of the wet season. She needed spring's restoration, poor child. He prayed over the bread and cheese they were to eat. The hermits had given them good food and would not take Cormac's gold in return. He would have enough to buy horses and new supplies when they got to the plain and still have most of his gold left. He could have caught a trout in the lake, but he was in a hurry to reach Clonmacnoise.

"Do you not pray to anyone for your food, tiny pagan?" He began to chew a thick slab of cheese.

"Would God listen to me when a High King is praying?" she asked ironically.

She moved away the snoot of Podraig, who was nuzzling her side. "Go away, you silly dog," she commanded with mock impatience.

Podraig accepted that as a compliment. Even the dog seemed more concerned about a bondwoman than the High King.

Against the background of the gleaming blue lake, the curve of her body was still defiant. A provoking Biddy, he told himself, was a pretty Biddy.

Turning toward the waters of the lake in which she could see her own reflection, she took her knife and began to cut away some of her hair. It had grown longer—and turned more blond—as they had traveled.

"Stop that, Biddy. I do not wish you to cut your hair," he said imperiously.

She whirled on him, surprise, anger, defiance in her face and her voice. "Even a slave girl may do what she pleases with her hair!" She spit out the words furiously.

"Not if I say she cannot." He was angry too.

Her big blue eyes smouldered. "You will have to beat me to make me obey, harsh king," she screamed at him.

Across the small fire, he grabbed the hand that held the

knife and tried to snatch the blade away. She clung to it as though her fingers were a vise. Wild with anger, he pulled her to her feet, spun her around, and pried the fingers away. Only when he had her arm twisted behind her back did she drop the knife. It fell silently on the grass.

"Brave, mighty king," she hissed, her body taut, her chest moving up and down rapidly. The tiny arm he held behind her back was as smooth as fine linen, her absurdly slender waist a graceful sword in his hand. Tenderness contended with fury inside him. The tableau of their struggle reflected in the placid waters of the lake tore at his heart.

"You feign meekness, wretched slave, but you do whatever suits your pleasure," he barked at her. Tenderness won. He still held her, but without force.

She resisted no longer. "Now I am a slave again," she said weakly.

A score for her. "Neither slave nor daughter would be so disobedient," he said sadly.

"Why does the great High King of Ireland care what I do with my miserable hair?"

Was she really close to tears? He must remember that she was still the smallest of girl children, despite her tongue and her fresh, new breasts.

Tenderness tamed his fury. A pathetic little arm really—but nice to hold. He would hold it for another moment. Podraig did not like the struggle. His two friends should not be quarreling. He barked loudly.

"Beat me, courageous warrior, force your will on me," Brigid taunted him.

He let her go. "I don't think Podraig would let me, Biddy. I am outnumbered," he sighed.

"When you are asleep I will take the knife again and

cut my miserable hair. Then what will you do?" Spiteful fury once again and a very vigorous toss of that defiant head.

"It is not miserable hair. I will tie you by your toes from a tree." He laughed. That was the only effective weapon against the witch.

He sat on the log again, picking up his slab of cheese. Podraig stopped barking and ran back and forth between them, trying to reconcile his fellow pilgrims.

"Would it suit my excellent foster daughter to listen to my reasons for wanting to see her hair grow long, as a girl's hair should?" he asked quietly.

She settled down across the fire from him, Podraig's head nestled in her lap.

"High Kings do not have to give explanations," she responded bitterly. She looked out over the lake, breathing rapidly.

"Yes, they do, provoking wench. Soon we will come to Clonmacnoise where it will be seen by all that King Cormac has a—traveling companion."

At the word "companion," Biddy closed her eyes. Her face turned a deep red.

"If—if it appears that the companion is a boy—then certain bad thoughts will arise about King Cormac. If it is a girl—a pretty girl—then the thoughts will be much less bad." He was stumbling badly, looking for a way out of the forest of his own words.

"I am not a pretty girl," she said softly, bowing her head in shame.

"At Clonmacnoise others will be the judge of that. Besides, when we approach the raths of the Shannon I shall buy you gowns that will settle the matter." Good God, he sounded like a proud father—or a placating husband.

She opened her eyes. "I need no such gowns."

The eagerness in those big blue lakes told him she would wear the gowns with vain delight. Wicked Biddy.

"Now you are being not only stubborn, which I expect, but unintelligent, which I do not expect. I need you to be in splendid gowns." He took her hand to help her to her feet. Gracefully she accepted his assistance.

She picked up the knife from where it had fallen in their struggle on the grassy floor of the meadow. In the background a foolish robin had begun to sing. Tucking the knife back in her girdle, she said docilely, "It will be as you command, shrewd master."

Did she actually like the idea of being taken as the mistress of the High King? Vain, silly child. But what will you look like in a splendid gown?

Her vanity returned when he found a large, well-stocked farm where there were many *leines* for sale and some elegant *brats*. He bought her two gowns trimmed in gold, one a deep red and the other a light blue. A shining saffron cloak with a hood blended with both of them, as did the saffron belt which she tied tightly around her slender waist. They even had a bronze ringlet for her hair. It was not long enough yet, but Cormac had learned to hold his tongue with this willful child. She looked especially defiant when she fastened the ringlet to her hair. An impish gleam flickered across the lakes of her eyes.

"Do I cause pleasure in the eyes of my master?" she asked sarcastically, twirling the red *leine* before him.

"It will no longer be doubted that it is a girl with whom King Cormac travels. The poets will sing songs of his good taste in foster daughters." He laughed lightly. She was not offended. The witch thinks that it may be true.

The women of the rath pleased her by insisting that the

robe had been made just for her. She sat on her horse with graceful pride as they began their journey across the soft meadows leading to the Shannon.

"So, wretched slave," Cormac said, goading her gently as they rode along, "I dare not take you too close to the monastery. You will bring bad thoughts to the heads of the holy monks." The boar was seeking the lance again.

"If such as I cause them bad thoughts, son of Dermot, they ought not to be in the monastery," she replied airily, her nose tilted high in the air.

The lance had gone unerringly to its target. Yet foolish Biddy, the High King thought. One dress and some cheap jewelry—already you think you are a queen. He would not dispute with her about the temptations of monks. She had begun to tempt him, damn her. He tightened his grip on the horse's reins.

The sun was sinking in the west, turning the still brown fields the color of the golden trim of Biddy's gown. As it disappeared, they rode up the last line of low hills and saw curving sharply into the distance the deep red waters of the Shannon. Beyond they saw the wattle huts, the log houses, the small stone churches, and the earthen walls of the sprawling monastery and school of Clonmacnoise.

On the other side of the river, riding away into the darkness were a group of horsemen. Even from this distance Cormac thought they looked ominously like members of the royal guard from Tara.

Chapter 11

"Oh, *you will* certainly find pirates in the islands to the west, Cormac, my boy," said the Abbot Kiernan merrily. "They will have stolen treasure in which there may be some legendary cup. So if they don't kill you and put your head on a stave in front of their rath, you will come back to Tara with your magic cup." He dug his staff into the soft earth of Clonmacnoise as though it were the stave for Cormac's head.

Kiernan was troubled when he came down the path to Cormac's cell. Talk about the magic cup seemed to have temporarily restored his good humor. Sitting on a worn stone bench, the two of them watched the Shannon roll by beneath a sky packed with fluffy gray and white clouds.

The little balding Kiernan, with his shrewd, sparkling eyes, was a peasant, a man of the land. He ruled the vast monastic precincts of his abbey like a large farm. The thousands of ascetics, married monks who were part of the monastic community, foster children, penitents (in fact prisoners), and students who flocked to the banks of the great river were all treated as respected clients and tenants. In a land where almost everyone was a farmer—including kings and poets—only a farmer could govern the largest settlement in the country. If any of the monks and students thought differently, there was always the dun cow grazing placidly at the entrance of Kiernan's hut or ambling after him around the monastery grounds. Just now she was viewing Podraig with bovine disdain.

"The magic princess?" Cormac asked indifferently. He leaned negligently against the door of the beehive-shaped rock hut in which he had lived as a student. How good it would be to stay here, to sink into the peaceful, reassuring routine of monastery life again.

"Unless they have given up the practice of having daughters, there will be a girl who will be happy to claim that she is Delvcaem. She will be a savage, Cormac, and will probably cut your throat some night while you sleep." He laughed merrily again. Instead of being disappointed in his old pupil, he seemed immoderately amused.

Why seek the magic cup when he could stay with such a good and sensible friend? Kiernan was wise; the pursuit of the magic cup was childish folly. How had he ever come to think otherwise?

The abbot poked his stick into the ground again and absently felt the dirt. His gray eyes narrowed. "I wonder why you seek a princess. It is said that you already have one with you." His eyes shone brightly at the trap he had sprung.

Biddy had been left in the straggling hamlet on the other side of the river where, with their families, lived those called lay monks, who tilled the monastery fields. The students who were not monks would surely have noticed the red-gowned, yellow-haired girl who was said to be the king's companion.

"Brigid is not a princess and she is not magic, reverend teacher," he argued defensively, his face warm with embarrassment. "She is only a foster child left to me by Queen Ethne. Finnabair hated her so that she had to leave Tara with me."

He rose from the stone bench on which they were sitting.

The abbot seemed unsatisfied. "They say she is very lovely," he mused absently.

So Biddy had been talking with the students. Wench. Probably arguing with them and insulting them. "She has a quick head and a quicker tongue," he said hotly. "You are suggesting, holy abbot, that she should be Queen of Tara?" He turned to face the monk, hands on hips.

The little farmer laughed merrily again, smoothing the wrinkles in his dark blue robe. "Always the hidden anger, eh, Cormac? No, I'm wondering why your father's harlot would send soldiers seeking to kill a harmless foster child. Troops of the king's guard searching for a harmless little bondwoman? Very odd. It is a great trouble to work so hard for vengeance against a mere child." Kiernan's gray eyes probed the king's. No laughter now.

So that was what was on his mind when he came hesitantly on the path to the king's hut. Cormac looked down the bank of the river. Clonmacnoise was a sprawling collection of huts, houses, stone cells, and small churches. At the edge of the monastic stockade was the guest house, and beyond it stretched the monastery lands, fields worked this lovely spring afternoon by the *manaig,* the married monks whose families had been attached to the monastery since its beginning. Beyond them were the outer walls of the monastery. In the other direction was the schoolhouse, the now empty grain stores, and the stone bell tower. Most of the monks were working outside in the warmth of the day and the light smell of spring in the air, copying manuscripts, poring over books, carving statues and crosses, listening to instruction, bending over a painting, a poem. Soon it would be dark; they would return to their prayers and meditations.

He loved the calm order of Clonmacnoise. He wanted to give up his crazy pilgrimage and stay. He had almost decided to. Would he now have to go because of the wretched girl? "She will be safe here, won't she?" he asked uneasily. "They would not attack Clonmacnoise. Were you not the first to proclaim my father king long ago?" He hoped he had misunderstood the implications of the monk's words. Would he be driven out of Clonmacnoise?

"Would they not? Those who were here showed no reverence for holy places. Your father is no longer the man who helped set the first stones of Clonmacnoise. Yet if a foster child of the High King is left with us, we will try to protect her."

Kiernan, too, rose from the bench—slowly, the drain of his responsibilities drawing the vitality out of his body.

Cormac watched the blue waters of Ireland's sacred river flowing calmly toward the great ocean over the horizon. The abbot would take Biddy under his protection even though it meant putting his flock in danger. He was making no promises that his protection would be very helpful.

"Holy abbot," he sighed as though he were the most

long-suffering of men, "if Biddy were in this monastery for more than a day you would find that the monks would listen to her instead of you; yonder dun cow would become her devoted servant, and you would be a useless decoration readily dispensed with when she did not need you." He jabbed his sword hand into the air as if he were addressing an assembly of kings and stared balefully at the sacred Shannon.

The abbot thought it very funny. "Then it is good she is not permitted here. But surely," he added, with a characteristic hunch of his shrewd shoulders, "the kind of—er—foster daughter Cormac MacDermot would bring to Clonmacnoise—"

"How does one find these pirate islands in the west?" Cormac abruptly changed the subject, reaching into his belt for the knife which was not there.

It was the abbot's turn to sigh. "If you have anything worth stealing, they will find you. You should walk or ride no longer. We will find you a comfortable boat. Go down the Shannon toward Clonfert. My holy brother Brendan knows the west well after all his voyages. I'm sure he could find any number of pirate islands for you to search. He is over eighty now and still dreams of sailing to the Land of Promise, poor man." He twisted his thick oak staff nervously. He did not want to drive the High King away, yet he had no choice.

Cormac gazed towards the line of gray clouds pushing their gnarled hands over the western horizon. "Brendan will help me find the magic cup?" he asked dubiously, trying to recapture the magic of the pilgrimage.

"A man who searches for the kingdom of heaven cannot be bothered with goblets and princesses and High Kings. He will give you directions to the pirate islands if

I write him to do so." Kiernan's shoulders slumped. He looked old and tired.

A bell tolled. It was time for prayer, then the supper of bread, bacon, cheese, and milk or mead, depending on how ascetic one was. The abbot and Cormac clasped hands. There was sorrow in the older man's eyes. "Would that you could stay here in peace." He began to walk down the path towards the river, Cormac at his side. "After all, they may not return—but I had to tell you."

Cormac put his arm around his teacher. "Holy abbot and good friend, it is the will of God that I must leave. Neither you nor I can change that. I do not want to run. You do not want me to leave even though it is not safe to stay. God knows best. We are still friends. Someday I will return."

The warmth in his voice revived Kiernan's spirits. "So now the student teaches the teacher and the layman preaches to the monk." The merry laugh was back, the eyes twinkling again. His pace down the gravel path quickened. "You will be a great king, Cormac."

How often, wondered Cormac bitterly, blinking in a sudden flash of sunlight, did he say the same thing to my father? But it is not Kiernan's fault my father made him a false prophet.

He thought briefly of going back across the river to tell Biddy that they would soon have to depart the peace and security of Clonmacnoise for the obscure regions of the west. No, there were too many wild tales about his relationship with her already.

The next morning it rained early, then the clouds were swept away by a cold, fresh wind. Ireland was beginning to turn its natural green. Cormac emerged from his stone hut and watched the bustle of small skiffs slicing back and forth across the river. The cold wind stung his face. It felt good. He stretched his arms, drinking in the morning's clean air. Spring's birth was hard in Ireland. The wind coming up the Shannon whipped its water into small waves against the current. There must have been a mighty storm on the ocean, the kind sailors like the Abbot Brendan took for granted but which terrified a land-bound man. It was time to leave after all. Perhaps the O'Donnals in Kerry would protect Biddy. Finnabair would not dare to attack those hardy west-of-Ireland kings.

Kiernan and the inevitable dun cow approached down the little path that passed in front of his hut. "Jesus and Mary be with you, great High King." The abbot moved slowly, his huge brow clouded, his shoulders sagging again. "They are a day's journey away. They will be here tomorrow at midday. We will protect our guests as best we can, Cormac—" His plain, open face was lined with worry.

"How many are there?" Cormac asked briskly. He wanted to fight.

"Many. Perhaps forty," replied the abbot grimly.

Forty men—half the king's guard. All to take Biddy's tiny head? So he would have to run. Another humiliation. He shrugged. "There is no need, loyal Kiernan. We must leave for the west. The day will come when this threat to your great monastery will be punished."

"We seek not punishment, son of Dermot, only peace." He shook his bald head sadly.

"There will be no peace in Ireland so long as Clonmacnoise can be threatened by a royal harlot," snapped Cormac, his fury rising. "This day will not be forgotten." If he was doomed to be cast down into hell, he would bring others with him.

He quickly poled a skiff over to the other side. Biddy was in front of the ferryman's small whitewashed house.

She wore her precious blue gown and was bent over a book. Her hair was like dull gold in the pale morning light. During the two weeks at Clonmacnoise she had tried with the help of the ferryman's wife to learn to read. The air was fragrant with the sweetness of spring roses. It was too early for roses. *So Brigid—now it's scent. Each day more vanity—no time to talk of it now though. Someday soon I will have to spank you for your impudence.* He told her they had to leave at once.

"I will put on my pilgrim's gown." She closed the book, rose quickly and turned towards the cottage.

"No, Brigid. You will leave Clonmacnoise dressed as the foster daughter of a king." Again he felt an impulse to kiss her forehead. *So long since you have smelled scent on a woman, Cormac?*

She did not ask why they had to leave. Back at the rough landing Kiernan already had a curragh ready for them heavily laden with food and supplies, including his sword, a spear, a shield, and a new poet's harp.

"We do not leave Clonmacnoise empty-handed, I see," said Cormac wryly.

"In Ireland no one should go hungry, Christian king," replied Kiernan sorrowfully, knowing that his pupil was fleeing like a hunted stag.

"We shall remember your generosity, good friend." He put his hands warmly on the monk's shoulders in the ancient farewell of Celtic warriors.

There was pain in the abbot's voice. "You will sit in the back with the paddle and merely steer the boat. The good Shannon at least will work for you." The poor old man was close to tears.

Cormac tossed the neatly tied bundle, which was Biddy's little collection of gowns, into the leather boat.

"Peace to you and all this holy monastery, Kiernan," he said with the confident serenity that befits a king.

"May God and King Jesus and the Holy One and Mother Mary go with you to bring you back to Tara, O High King of Ireland," he intoned solemnly.

Biddy was on her knees on the landing, her head bent, her yellow hair spread like flowers on the blue sea of her gown. "Would it be wrong, great abbot, to give a small blessing to a pagan?"

Kiernan seemed to notice the blond head and the blue gown for the first time. His face lit up, his pudgy, brown-flecked fingers delicately touched the golden flowers. "May all those who protect King Cormac also bless and protect this devoted foster daughter, and may Podraig and Brigid truly bring this child of Ireland home to peace and happiness." The monk was in tears. At least he knew now that Biddy was no more than a foster child.

Cormac did not delay. The Shannon would be speedier than horses once they got to the oak forests to the west. The king's guard would not dare search in those haunted regions. He needed a day to reach safety. Deftly he lifted Biddy into the bow of the boat. She was not as light as the day they rode out of Tara. The wolfhound Podraig jumped lightly into the midsection. Shoving the craft toward the middle of the current, Cormac leaped into the stern. With a quick, skillful twist of the paddle he turned the curragh toward the great ocean to the west.

On the near bank blue-robed Kiernan raised his hand in melancholy benediction. On the far bank stood the monks of Clonmacnoise. As the three pilgrims moved down the river, the monks sang the *Salve Regina.* Their praise of Mother Mary bounced back off the fiercely blue Irish sky, a sky that matched the monastic robes of the men of Clonmacnoise. Cormac felt a catch in his throat as he waved them a last farewell. He was being driven from the place he loved most, a hunted, harried outcast. Tears came to his eyes, tears for his own misery.

"Do you not wonder why we leave so suddenly, silent pilgrim?" he asked Biddy as the turn in the river hid Clonmacnoise.

"Does my master think I am so stupid not to realize that Finnabair still pursues us?" Biddy responded irritably, not looking round. "She has no respect for the holy ground of the monastery."

"All-wise Biddy, why is it your head she seeks instead of mine?" He dug the paddle in the water to steer away from the bank.

"My head? How can that be?" she exclaimed, turning towards him, her face frozen in surprise.

"She must think you are more of a threat to her in Tara than the *Tanaise.* Maybe she is right." He shrugged his shoulders and was surprised at the tenseness in them.

"You should have left me behind, High King. Of what use to Ireland is my foolish head?" she asked sorrowfully.

Cormac was silent for a moment, occupied with correcting the drift of the boat to keep it in midstream. The river bubbled musically against the hull. In the distance a cow announced that it was milking time.

"Finnabair thinks your pretty skull is worth much trouble to separate from the rest of you; it must be of great value indeed. I should let it go easily? Also, stern-faced pilgrim, that head carries on it the blessing of holy Kiernan."

Biddy put her arm around Podraig's huge neck. "He is a nice man," she said complacently, with a slight toss of the now sanctified head.

Chapter 12

The soft white moon looked down in gentle reproach at the bondwoman Brigid as she walked disconsolately along the reedy banks of the sacred river Shannon. Moonlight splashed the waters of the river as though someone had spilled a pitcher of milk. "O royal Sionna," said Brigid to the river, "I don't know that I believe in you any more than I do in the Christian gods, but you or holy Bridget or Mother Mary must make me control my tongue."

Sionna replied by hissing water through the reeds at Biddy's feet.

"It was bad enough when I had to keep my feelings well bound; now I have to worry about his too. I'm nothing but a worthless little *cuhmal*," she added piously. "I don't look like much and I'm a coward, and now I find that my only weapon can be as dangerous as a carelessly carried knife. What am I to do?"

Sionna offered no comment beyond her usual unencouraging hiss.

Biddy knew she was not telling the whole truth to the sacred river. A coward she surely was; but she had somehow turned attractive, much to her own surprise. It was a very complicated problem. She threw a stone at the river—*there, you old pagan hag, that's what I think of you—and I'd throw a rock at Mother Mary too—*

Superstitiously Brigid looked around to make sure no one heard her thoughts. Why offend both old and new religions? There was no sound, no thunderbolt from the sky, no horned stallion racing through the woods.

Well, she added, *I would if she were no more help than you are—*

Only a disgruntled owl protested the noise disturbing his meditations. Mother Mary did not seem ready to negotiate a new treaty for the sake of a single convert. The sacred river hissed derisively at her.

You be quiet! And she threw another rock at the sacred waters. Mother Mary was safer. She didn't identify with rivers. Just with saints named Brigid.

—Poor stupid man. He makes a fool out of himself—now I'm going to have to go back and tell him I'm sorry.

That would be bitter medicine. She never apologized to Cormac for anything. It would be like a warrior discarding his shield—*there are some things that are just too cruel even for me—*

So now she had to worry about hurting Cormac's feelings. If she were not careful she'd lose her shield completely—then what would happen?—and why did the smell of spring flowers have to be delicately sweet when he had sung of her skin in the moonlight? There was a noise, close to her feet; Biddy jumped in fright—only a tiny rabbit.

"You run fast too, don't you, little friend?" she asked bitterly, "especially when you're terrified—"

She bent over the river waters and pulled some rushes up. Skillfully she twisted them in the sun cross that was the symbol of Brigid—both the goddess and the saint. It did no harm to have such protection in the woods at night.

The fight had started while they were eating the fish she had fried at their camp on the bank of the river. Cormac had seen horsemen riding in the forest on the other side earlier in the day. Fearing that they might be Finnabair's warriors, he had pushed on farther into the dark oak forest, stopping only at twilight. She was hungry, tired, and ill-tempered to begin with. The fish, which she had learned to hold over the fire for just the right length of time, restored Cormac's good humor but not hers. Sipping some of the mead they had been given at Athlone, he reclined against an oak tree, strumming on his new harp, self-consciously striking the pose of a handsome young bard.

"What will the magic princess look like, Lady Brigid?" he asked wearily.

Instead of feeling compassion for the poor oaf, Biddy lost her temper again. "She will be fat and old and well used," was her prompt and bitter answer.

"And pleasant to open and enter?" He was now as provoking as she was, fingering his cursed harp again.

Brigid dropped the bracken at the other side of the fire. It was so dark now that she couldn't see the tilt to his head.

"Who could resist the assault of a High King?" She threw his crudity back at him.

The unpredictable Expected One laughed again. "Biddy, Biddy, Biddy—no one will ever win a duel of words with you. I think you're wrong about Delvcaem though. Let me sing of her—"

The curious moon poked its saffron head above the horizon, bathing the oak trees across the river in golden light. Moonrise at Beltaine time—a dangerous interlude. Biddy held her breath, fearing the mixture of song and magic. Cormac must have consumed more of the mead than she realized. He described her as though she were the magic princess. Biddy reflected in the waters of the Shannon. It was a clever, tempting, flattering song.

Her brown hair turning sunset gold
Eyes as wide as the surging western sea
Lips warm to kiss, in taunting bold—
The magic princess who waits for me

So lithe her clever woman shape
At first she seems a lovely child
Then I see beneath the purple cape
Deft body to drive a lover wild

Cream white skin trembling to my touch
Heart beating like an eager doe
Naked to inflame my weary lust
Bathed in soft silver moonlight glow

Waist slender like a yearling oak
For strong fingers a belly firm
Sweet buttocks my harsh hands provoke
And smooth thighs make my fingers squirm

Breasts as fair as roses new and white
Shaped like the subtle Wicklow hills
Stiff nipples, ravishing delight,
More lovely than blooming daffodils—

"Please stop." She almost choked on the words. She had heard bards praise women many times; this was the first time one praised her. Cormac meant no harm, she tried to tell herself; it was customary to compare a legendary goddess or heroine to someone in the hall during a feast. Still, he should not have—

He seemed to be waiting expectantly for her reaction. What should she say? She was paralyzed, her face flaming as brightly as the campfire, her breath coming in gulps the way a stream swirls around big rocks. How dare he think about her that way? How cruel of him to compare her with Delvcaem—

The water lapped against the rushes. The moon, eager to see what Biddy would do, was now peeking over the trees; she wanted to cry, she wanted to shout with rage—words would not come from her lips. Her insides were melting with pleasure at his song. How like an Irish poet to say outrageous things in a way that left him safe.

Ordering strength back into her legs, she walked down to the boat to get the bread and cheese that would be their hasty breakfast.

"You don't like my song?"—a tired voice in the dark.

She had to answer him and then escape from the camp before the traitor moon could illumine her confusions. "Irish poets never tire of comparing women's breasts to hills, do they, royal minstrel?" she finally managed.

"Not when they are as soft and as lovely as the shapely hills of Ireland for which the weary pilgrim longs wherever his sins force him to roam," he continued in rhapsody, carried away by his own poetry.

That is really bad, Cormac; the song was lovely if out of place; I know you've had too much mead when you become that common.

Aloud she said, "Yet, is it not true that some pilgrims yearn for high mountains instead of soft hills?"

"And more for a soft tongue than a chariot rider's whip?" he replied irritably, rising from his poet's pose by the oak tree.

Brigid was terrified. "You can easily ridicule a defenseless slave girl, O brave and noble High King," she stammered, "but someday you will use your inferior poetic skills on someone who is strong enough to fight back. Then you will be forced to eat the mud that is your proper food."

She stormed unsteadily out of the camp, blundering against an oak tree and bruising her shin in the dark. Is it only the Irish, she wondered, who flee when they become angry and afraid?

"Biddy," pleaded the High King in alarm.

She ignored his cry. Since he didn't send Podraig after her, he must feel that she needed time to cool her temper.

Now with the moon high in the sky, she was stumbling back towards the camp, embarrassed and afraid—not of Cormac but of the dangers in the forest and the riders of Queen Finnabair whom, in her fury, she had forgotten. *Still such a terrible coward, Biddy.*

She could not tell him she was sorry; how can you admit that you are pleased to have your breasts compared to the hills of Wicklow without destroying a carefully cultivated manner of dealing with a man who has the power of life and death over you?

How dare he torment me, she demanded of the moon which had heard and seen it all. How dare he forget that I'm a slave and a foster daughter, not a woman to flatter? Doesn't he know how dangerous it is?

The moon didn't reply. Biddy threw a stone at it, and then felt very foolish as she heard it splash far out in the river. *Poor Sionna, you get hit even when I'm not aiming at you.*

It was the time before Beltaine. Yes, that was it—the first full moon, the changing of the seasons, the change in the great forests. The Many-Colored Land was opening—anything can happen—

Biddy knew that there were two worlds, the ordinary land in which humans lived and the Many-Colored Land in which dwelt the gods and goddesses, the demons, the fairies, and all the other strange creatures which occasionally intruded into the lives of humans. The two worlds were not distinct but flowed alongside one another like a river passing its banks. Sometimes they blended together and humans went on adventures into the Many-Colored Land, and other times the inhabitants of that world, not necessarily unfriendly, blundered into human lives.

Humans were better off if they had nothing to do with the inhabitants of the Many-Colored Land; even those who meant no evil, like the fairies, could be dangerous through inattention or mistake; sometimes even the fairies, who were the godlike folk that had ruled Ireland before the present inhabitants came, would take a fancy to a human and imprison him or her forever in their land of endless and pointless merriment.

Biddy shivered and clutched the cross of her patroness. She did not want to join those people, not if she could avoid it. They would not want one as plain as her anyway. She thought of Cormac's song about her body and held the cross even more tightly.

The most dangerous times, the times when the two worlds were most likely to blunder into one another, were times of change—twilight, the transition from winter to summer, the principal events in a life like marriage or childbirth or death, the time of a woman's monthly flow of blood. The powers of the other world were especially likely to burst in upon you at such a time.

Beltaine was not as dangerous as its counterpart, Samain, when the spirits of the dead were out in the world. Still, it could be very dangerous if you were not careful. It was the part of the year when the world might come apart, when a king would sing love songs to a slave.

Or, she told herself ironically, *when a slave could dare to love a king.*

Brigid was frightened. She must hurry back and explain it all to Cormac; they must take precautions; the dangers were far worse than Finnabair's riders. He must pray to his King Jesus to do something. Did King Jesus live in the Many-Colored Land or did he live elsewhere?

Fear turned to terror. Dangers were lurking everywhere now. She had insulted the Powers only a little while ago. At least her blood was not flowing; that would make the dangers worse. Her arms were turning cold, as they had been in the mountains, though it was a warm night. Picking up her skirts, she began to run along the river bank towards the fire she could see glowing, a mere hundred yards away. Her feet seemed to be weighted, the fire wasn't getting closer. She tripped over a rock and fell headlong against a young tree. All the lights of heaven dropped from the sky and raced through her skull.

Dazed but still conscious, she pushed unsteadily to her feet, leaning on the tree for support. "You have a stronger head than I do, brother tree," she said, and then became afraid again. Talking to a tree—

The campfire was close now—why had it seemed so far? She must tell Cormac all the things she had discovered during her angry walk—embarrassment at her foolish behavior was obliterated in eagerness to protect him from new dangers.

Cormac was not in the camp. The fire had burned low, their baggage was untouched. Podraig was contentedly asleep. But Cormac was gone—so was his harp.

She put a dry branch into the fire to make a torch. No sign of him. No, wait—his *leine* and *brat* by the oak tree—could he have been a fool enough to try to swim in the Shannon by moonlight? Podraig—wake up—

She screamed at the wolfhound and then kicked the poor beast. He slept on. "What have they done to you, poor Podraig—? where have they taken our Cormac—?" she wailed.

Podraig continued to sleep.

She fought back hysterics. She must be calm. Cormac needed help. She must keep her wits. She must not go blundering off into the woods again—what was the smell—?

She sank in exhaustion, gasping for breath, on a log. There seemed to be sweet perfume at the end of the log; illuminating the ground with her torch, Biddy found a small trail of powder; following it like a hound trailing a rabbit, she discovered that the powder made a complete circle around the fire, enclosing Podraig, Cormac's garments, and the bracken on which he'd been sleeping. Magic—the folk from the Many-Colored Land had come and gone. She wanted to weep the way a drowning person wants air—but there was no time for weeping—she had to get him back—she could remember no remedies—her Brigid cross—the sun that drove away darkness—King Jesus, the light of the world—she must find them first—where would they take him—a meadow, of course—that's where fairy folk danced till the light of dawn and then rushed back into their own world—she must find a meadow—the fairy folk were lazy—they wouldn't go far.

With a stealth that would have impressed Podraig, had he been awake, she crept through the woods though she knew that she didn't have to be careful. If Lug MacEithlenn and his troop were indeed frolicking in a meadow they would post no guard and not care about protection. The fairy folk had been driven into the night but they had never been defeated.

She searched for hours, hoping the sun would rise to chase the demons of the forest night and fearing its appearance because it would mean the end of her effort to save Cormac. At last, so weary she could no longer walk, she collapsed to the soft fern-covered forest floor and wept in sorrow and rage.

Then she felt the ground moving beneath her. Silencing her grief, she listened carefully—she was imagining it—no, the sound of music was real—wild music—drums and pipes—her own feet began to move in eager rhythm—

Her strength renewed, Biddy sprang up and dashed through the woods in the direction of the music. Now there was light, more light than from the bonfires of Beltaine, more light than from the sun—the Troop of Danann was near—she rushed to the edge of the trees and into the glittering meadow—

Not even Tara, in its most brilliant festivals, was as

bright, as merry as the sight that momentarily blinded her astonished eyes. Tall, handsome men and women, in dazzling white and saffron and pink garments, spun around in flowing rhythms like a spinning rainbow. The pipes and drums were beating a wild frenzy like a river sweeping over its bank at floodtide; the dancers kept pace with the beat effortlessly, elegantly, almost as though it were hardly a challenge to them. Their supple bodies bent gracefully to the rhythms like birds taking wing on a summer day; laughter spilled across the meadow, the laughter of those for whom existence was nothing but pleasure—

It was hot in the meadow; Biddy cast off her mantle; her pilgrim's robe was sticking to her body. How did they remain so cool?—then she saw that their gowns were transparent, mere wisps of cloth which emphasized rather than hid their splendid bodies. She knew then that it was dangerous—that she should flee—too late—her feet were now moving with the rhythm of the fairy music—

She saw Cormac, asleep at the edge of the meadow—poor foolish Christian king, his magic no match for the Tuatha Dé Danann. She wanted to help him—it was too late—dawn would come soon and he would go forever into the Many-Colored Land. She envied him—to dance forever with these graceful and beautiful beings—

Two of them spun up to her, elegantly dancing their bows and respectful greeting—the two most gorgeous creatures she had ever seen—lithe, strong, perfectly proportioned—long blond hair flowing easily in the warm breezes—Lug and Erihu, the king and queen of the fairy folk—the leaders of the Tuatha Dé Danann. She bowed respectfully in return.

"Welcome, Mistress Brigid," said Lug MacEithlenn in a clear, bell-like voice, his pale blue eyes twinkling expectantly. "We knew you'd come; we prefer you to your sluggish master; you are the one who dances as lightly as a snowflake on the air; we've watched you all the times you've danced secretly; you were born to be one of the troupe to dance happily forever; come with us!"

How had they known about her love of dancing?—she'd told no one. Awkwardly she took his outstretched hand—the magic rhythms surged up through her feet and took possession of her whole body. A deep, musky scent swept into her head, sweet, powerful, abandoned, inviting her to reckless and violent pleasure.

"You can never dance in that robe, my dear," said Erihu playfully. "Here, let us take it away—among our folk there is no fear of beautiful bodies."

Biddy felt no shame as she was stripped; rather, she exulted in her own loveliness. Cormac's poetry had been not nearly strong enough—nor was she embarrassed as the other gentry swept by and exclaimed at her beauty. Truly she belonged with them—why had she never seen this before? The aroma grew stronger—stupifying and yet exhilarating—was this the smell of beautiful bodies in ecstasy? She and Lug whirled across the meadow; the music was louder, the beat more frantic, sweat poured from her skin, she seemed to be falling, she pleaded with her partner to let her go—he only laughed and twirled even more recklessly. The world whirled drunkenly around her—she wanted to collapse in dizziness—he would not let her.

"Do not be afraid, Princess Brigid," he shouted above the sound, "you will soon be the best dancer of any of us—your poor, slow-footed master will become your humble slave—give yourself over to the dance—"

Captured by his grace and charm and the torrid pounding of her own restless feet, Biddy surrendered to the dance. She and Lug were in the middle of the meadow, with the other dancers forming a circle around them. The music now was faster than humans could possibly endure; yet Biddy knew she could go faster and faster and faster still—the others were clapping their approval—even Lug seemed impressed. She had gone beyond dizziness now, and entered a world of shining clarity—was she already in the Many-Colored Land? Then she saw a woman in white at the edge of the meadow—not one of the troop—her hair was black, her skin brown, her face troubled. The woman in the dream—the woman who had told her she would be Queen of Ireland—what was she doing here?—it did not matter—her prediction was wrong. Biddy would be the queen of the Many-Colored Land—Lug would be her king— The woman vanished back into the trees—had none of the troupe noticed her?

Lug was not her king—Cormac MacDermot was! A longing deep inside Biddy, a terrible hunger which ripped at her spirit broke through the music. She must get to him before the sun rose—she had to outwit the fairy folk—caught up in their dances, they were reputed to be easy to fool. Biddy let her legs collapse under her and fell to the ground—

Only Lug MacEithlenn even noticed. "Too much for the first time, eh, lovely little raspberry?" He laughed and with consummate courtesy helped her to stand.

"Thank you, kind lord," she lied. "It will take practice to dance as long as you without growing weary—if only I may rest for a few moments—"

The fairy king helped her to the edge of the meadow, bowed ceremoniously, and spun off again into the frenzied dance of his troupe. Only then did Brigid realize how hollow and weary his eyes were.

There seemed to be light already in the sky, a cold, gray light more mundane and more dangerous than the fairy mist. Her throat on fire with fear, she dodged around the edge of the meadow searching for her clothes; the mantle she found quickly, but that was not what she wanted—the light in the sky seemed to be getting brighter—the troupe could dance till dawn, even to sunrise, though not a second after the great lamp ascended the eastern sky—she must hurry—so little time—

When first dawn light broke the heavens, there was an anguished and disappointed moan from the dancers. Time was running out—the music became even more stormy—who was playing it?—she had seen no musicians. Did Lug and Erihu know what she was doing?—they were probably too caught up in their pleasure to care—only a few more minutes and all would be lost—they would take her as well as Cormac. Then she found her tattered pilgrim's *leine* and *crios.* Summoning all the strength in her legs, she dashed recklessly across the meadow, weaving her way among the lunatic dancers—only a few seconds before the dance ended—she had to get to Cormac before they did—to save herself and lose him would be worthless—

The eastern sky was white now—almost time. She still couldn't find him—then she tripped and stumbled to the ground—what had tripped her?—no tree roots here as in the forest. Oh, my poor dear Cormac, I fell over you—

Lug and Erihu were there beside her as she huddled over the naked body of her poor defenseless king. "Come now, Queen Brigid," exclaimed the goddess, "the sun will soon be with us—take our hands and the hand of your new slave and come with us to sleep in the Many-Colored Land until tomorrow's festival—"

She held the rush cross of her patroness in front of her. "The sun is already with us, fairy folk, depart from this sacred king of Ireland—he is mine, not yours—" Her voice wavered and her hand shook. She plunged on. "Leave us now in the name of the light of the world—"

Lug was not angry, only mildly disappointed. "You are such a fine dancer, princess, what do you have to do with Christian prayers?—why, you are not even a Christian," he smiled ingratiatingly.

"This cross was the light of the world even before Podraig came," she countered, her voice still quivering. She thought about explaining the difference between the dog and the saint and then realized that she was almost as mad as Lug.

"Dear child," pouted Erihu, "you will never have him as yours in this world; come with us to the multicolored land and he will be yours for all eternity."

Brigid hesitated. The troupe did not lie; they might trick you, but when they made promises that bald, they meant them.

Lug sensed her hesitation. "Only a few seconds, princess; we keep our promises, you know." His splendid smile again. "King Cormac will be yours forever in the Land of Splendor."

Brigid decided to join them and began to lower the cross; then from the innermost center of her spirit the last defiant words poured out: "Better he be mine in the land of humans for a few moments than forever in the land of hollow shades—back to hell, you demons!"

She rose from the ground, oblivious to her nakedness, and pushed the sun of her patroness in their faces. The two shades faded away and with them, the whole troupe. The sun rose peacefully on a quiet meadow. *For a moment,* Biddy told herself, *I sounded almost like the Holy Abbot Colum.*

She knelt by the motionless body of her king. *How beautiful he is. I saw him so quickly that night we got rid of Finnabair—now I can look at him longer*—She touched his chest with her fingers, felt the smooth velvet skin of his belly, kissed his passive lips—*Biddy, you have the heart of a wanton, even though you don't have the skills.*

She searched the meadow, much smaller in daylight than during the fairy dance, and found her discarded garments. She covered Cormac with her *brat* and put on her own *leine. Naked dancing in the forest, Biddy, you're mad,* she told herself disconsolately. —*So tired and weary, must wake him up—get him back to the river—on the boat, Finnabair's riders—I'm falling asleep—wake up, you stupid king*—

"Gently, Princess Brigid," said a musical voice behind her. "The whole of Ireland expects you to care for him."

She whirled around in terror expecting the troupe had returned; it was only the dark-skinned woman in white. She wore a glowing saffron *brat.*

"You shouldn't be out in the sunlight," Biddy said reprovingly.

The woman's face lit up with a merry smile—it was, Biddy decided, the most beautiful face she had ever seen. "Light is just fine for me, Princess Brigid."

She was young, not much older than Biddy actually. "I'm not a princess, only a slave," she muttered petulantly.

"Sometimes it's hard to tell the difference, isn't it?"

The woman was laughing now. She was a thousand times more beautiful than Erihu.

"I know who you are," complained Biddy querulously, "and I don't believe in you. Besides, if you know so much, why don't you help me to awaken this great oaf of a king and get him back to the Shannon?"

"Poor Shannon—you threw so many rocks at her last night." The girl was still making fun of her. "Did you ever think that if you put your light on him, the poor man might wake up?"

"Light—" The rushes were still in her hand. "—this?" She touched Cormac's forehead, he seemed to stir, and then Brigid, the slave girl, fell asleep.

"Biddy—" It was the voice of a small boy with a minor injury seeking his mother's help. She would not open her eyes. Had she put on her gown?

"The sun is already high in the sky," the hurt child's voice went on. "I have such a terrible headache—did I drink that much mead last night—?"

"Flagon after flagon, noble and abstemious lord," she replied and forced her eyes open. They both were modestly clothed again. The sun was indeed high in the sky. Cormac held his hands to his head as though he had been hit with a hurling club. Podraig was struggling to waken too.

"Shouldn't sleep so long—too big a chance," muttered the king groggily. "We'll have to eat breakfast in the boat—even Podraig seems to have had too much mead—"

Cormac was hopelessly confused. She wasn't much better. Her head hurt terribly from her collision with brother tree. She felt the lump; strange it had not bothered her in the fairy meadow. —Why, brother tree was the oak against which Cormac had leaned when he was singing—strange, last night it had seemed so far from the camp—

The two of them blundered around the camp, loading the boat as though they were in a fog. Munching on cheese, they steered an erratic course into the river. It was already an unbearably hot day.

Cormac rubbed his aching forehead. "You've had even more mead than I, gentle foster daughter." He clumsily avoided a drifting log. "Never have I seen the Lady Brigid with her *crios* unknotted."

She blushed furiously and knotted her belt. Maybe she had danced without her gown. He had forgotten everything. Did the fairy drive it from his head?—or the woman in white—or did it happen—? Had the fairy meadow happened—or had she only hit her head against a tree?—what hit his head?—and Podraig's?—was there fairy powder in the camp?—she had not thought to look— Had she fallen over him after she'd hit the tree and knocked the two of them out?—and why was Podraig so sleepy? Had it all been another dream—?

"Clouds coming up the river, Biddy," Cormac called from behind her. "We will have rain before nightfall."

The rain, Biddy told herself, would be soft and cooling. She did not want to face sister moon tonight.

Chapter 13

"*Cormac!" The voice* shattered his dream like the monastery bell in the morning. He struggled to fight it off, to slip back into the sweet depths of sleep.

"Cormac!" The voice was insistent, terrified. Someone was shaking him. Where was he? In the hills above Ravenna? No, it was Ireland. Who was the woman? He peered at the shape in the darkness. Who? Biddy— Unaccountably his heart sank.

"Wake up, wake up! There's a terrible thing here!"

A terrible "thing." Now he remembered—they were on a small reed-encompassed island in the Shannon. They had camped here despite Biddy's superstitious reluctance. The girl was having nightmares again. He rolled away from her, pulling his cowl over his head to keep out the rain. Then, suddenly, he was wide awake. There was something terrible at the edge of the tiny clearing where they were sleeping.

Instantly he was on his feet, sword in hand. The rain was falling hard, blinding his eyes. A strong wind was wailing around their island refuge. Despite the wind and the rain, a sick, rotting stench filled the air. The thing had angry red eyes that glowered at them through the darkness; its breathing came in deep, agonized gulps. It seemed to be angrily pawing the earth.

Biddy clung to him in terror. Podraig, who feared no creature that walked the earth, cowered to the ground, his great ears flat against his head, his teeth exposed in an anxious snarl.

It was a nightmare apparition, a monster from his dreams. Only he was not dreaming. Biddy's clutching fingers dug into his arms. They were not of the stuff from which dreams were made. The thing pawed the earth more vigorously as if it would charge. A bear? Too big. A dragon? There were no such things. He would not be frightened by night creatures. If it lived, it could be killed. The High King of Ireland would not be overawed by those raw red eyes. He pushed his slave woman aside, gripped his sword tightly, and began to advance on the creature.

Biddy threw herself in his way, hugging him fiercely. "Cormac, don't do it, don't be a stupid Irish fool! Let us leave this island. Don't kill yourself needlessly. What will Podraig and I do without you?"

He shoved her away again. The woman wanted to make a coward of him. She clung to his sword arm, holding him back. "You'll not find the magic cup on this evil island, Cormac. Please, please, let us go."

The magic cup—the rain dimmed his eyes again. The creature was not going to charge, it was waiting for him to attack. He would not be so foolish as to walk into the trap. "Get our things into the boat," he snapped at the girl. "Podraig, the boat."

Neither the girl nor the wolfhound needed any urging. Podraig bounded into the boat with a single leap. "Yes, all-wise master," said Brigid fervently, as she quickly loaded the curragh. So he was no longer "Cormac." He grinned. Scheming little wench.

He backed slowly towards the boat. The thing stared at him, unmoving, implacable. Would it make a leap at the last minute, or was it merely driving them from its island?

He eased the curragh into the river with one hand, his sword ready in the other. The Shannon current began to wrench at the craft. At the last possible second Cormac leapt into the boat, shoving it off from shore. The red eyes continued to glare at them, but the thing did not move.

"It was a dragon from hell," said Biddy with devout conviction.

"Christian hell or Druid hell, prudent foster daughter?" he asked ironically.

"Hell," Brigid insisted, "is hell."

The red eyes shone on the shore like twin angry campfires until they had drifted downstream and the island was lost in darkness and falling rain. Spring or not, it was cold. The wind cut at their faces, the rain drove down on them as if it had been unleashed by demons. What time was it? How long till sunrise? How long had he slept? Where were they on the Shannon? How close to the monastery of the holy Brendan? He must be careful not to fall back to sleep. The Shannon current was vexing going by these islands.

His head nodded and his hand became lazy on the tiller. The boat twisted out of his control, the tiller tugging away from his grip. He woke with a start. They were caught in a bed of reeds. He pulled the tiller back, but the boat turned dizzily. It was trapped in the thick reeds. He cursed to himself. The wind was worse, the rain still beating down on them, and now they were tangled in reeds. He let go of the oar and groped through the dark towards the bow, stumbling over Biddy, who was huddled in the center of the boat.

"Be careful, gentle master, do not tip us over," she warned him.

He'd had enough of her advice for one night. "I will worry about the boat, Biddy," he snapped at her as he leaned over the bow, pulling at the tenacious reeds. He freed the curragh from the grip of most of them; it began to straighten out. He reached for one last clump of reeds, the boat tilted to one side; the wind howled more loudly, he tugged at the weeds, there was a quick eddy of current, a strong gust of wind, and the boat broke free.

Cormac leaned precariously over the side. He struggled to right himself and not tilt the boat, then he lost his balance, straightened up, and fell over the other side into the numbing waters of the sacred Shannon. The bow rope of the boat had twisted around his ankle. It was caught on something. He fought to pull free from it. The icy Shannon waters poured into his lungs; the sacred river was trying to claim him for its own. He tried to swim. His leg could not move. He went under water again and clawed his way back to the surface, his chest nearly bursting. This would be the end. Already the peacefulness of death was taking possession of him. His thrashings were growing weaker. One or two more times under the cold waters and it would be the end.

There were white limbs near him in the darkness, a strong swimmer in the water, the swimmer diving as he went under again, his leg free from the rope, the swimmer tugging him by his hair, muddy riverbed beneath his feet, a wet river bank, aching lungs, miserable cold, the swimmer breathing heavily beside him.

"You will not laugh again at the knife on my thigh, agile master," gulped the swimmer.

"I may never laugh again at anything if I survive this night, savior woman." He put his fingers on the back of her neck, squeezing it affectionately. "I seem to be forcing you into water very often."

"Is not water the source of all life?" she responded primly.

"Unless you drown in it," he replied. "But come, Biddy, we must find Podraig and our boat. Please Jesus and Mary it will drift ashore on this side of the river."

"Also my cloak and tunic," she murmured in embarrassment.

The poor child. "Worse luck for the king," he laughed, "it is too dark to delight in your charms."

She sniffed indignantly and began to thrash through the reeds down the river.

Good God, how cold she must be. How many more times will that brave little wench save my life? Jesus and Mary, I do not deserve her devotion.

The search for the curragh was long. The first light of morning was beginning to stain the darkness on the other side of the river when they at last stumbled upon it wedged against a rock, a wet and mournful Podraig howling at the retreating darkness. His joy at the return of his friends was perfunctory compared to his delight when a warm fire finally began to blaze. Brigid, bedraggled, muddy, and weary, slumped against a tree modestly covered by her soaking gray cloak. "Next time you will listen when I tell you to be careful," she mumbled triumphantly as the sun pushed above the river bank and the rain fled to the south. It would, thought Cormac sleepily, take both the sun and the fire a long time to dry them out—if ever he were to be dry again. Soggy or not, he was too tired to worry about any more troubles. His lungs still hurt from their struggle with the sacred river. There would be no more trouble. He drifted off into a deep sleep.

But there was more trouble. Again the disturbing voice—but now tight and quiet. "Cormac, they're here."

He forced open his eyes. Four of the king's guards, one with a battle-axe, three with swords. His own sword was in the boat. Outnumbered—he could take care of one, Podraig another—Biddy's knife was on the ground—too far away. He must think quickly. There had to be a way—

The leader, a man whose name he remembered as Osian, grinned through his immense black beard. "Pardon us for disturbing your sleep, O High King," he said with mock politeness, "but we have come to collect a head."

"You will find it hard to take," he snapped back, struggling into a sitting position. He must think.

Osian laughed. "But it is not your head we want, O High King. We would not take a sacred head." They all joined in the laughter. "Queen Finnabair and King Dermot have promised us seventy head of cattle for the head of your slave woman. You will go free." He fingered his battle-axe lovingly. The man must be an executioner at Tara, delighting in his work.

Cormac was desperately trying to devise tactics. "Stay, Podraig," he ordered the fretful wolfhound. The four warriors seemed to relax. So that was it. They thought he would accept their offer of freedom. Well, why not accept it? He stood up.

"You are surely welcome to such a worthless head. I marvel that Royal Meath has so much surplus cattle in times of bad harvest. But that is of no consequence to me."

Roughly he grabbed Biddy's shoulder and pushed her to the ground in front of the axeman. "You heard him, worthless bondwoman, why do you hesitate to offer your head in exchange for the life of a sacred king?"

Osian approached the kneeling girl, rubbing the blade of his axe. "It does not hurt very much, small one, and it is over very quickly." He laughed, and his companions joined in. Brigid bowed her head silently, not a word of protest escaping her tightly pressed lips.

Cormac harshly pushed her head further towards the ground. "Bend over, foolish girl. Do not make good Osian's work more difficult for him."

A broad smile on his face, Osian lifted the axe full into the air above his head, paused a moment to take aim, and felt the impact of Cormac's head hard against his stomach.

Instantly the High King was on his feet. Snatching the axe from the surprised and gasping Osian's hands, he swung it deftly, slicing into the sword arm of another warrior who was thrusting towards his heart. Podraig, trained to perfection, sank his teeth into yet another sword arm. The odds were now even—Cormac with a battle-axe and one remaining warrior, hesitating with his sword.

"Think carefully, Finn," warned the king. "Two of your fellows will never lift a sword again, Osian has several broken ribs, to judge by his screaming. They all live. Drop your sword or you will die." He moved his axe into the air, preparing to swing. The four of them could still kill him if they wished. They were only surprised and frightened. If his bluff worked—

Finn dropped his sword, retreating towards the edge of the forest.

"Quick, costly slave girl," he barked, "get off your knees and get their swords. Do you think being worth seventy head of cattle excuses you from work?"

As though in a dream, Brigid scrambled to her feet, and under Podraig's watchful stare, gathered the three swords and put them into the boat.

"Now our own supplies, expensive maiden. Have you lost your powers of thought completely?"

Dutifully she loaded the boat. The wounded men were moaning with pain and watching Cormac in terror. The retreating Finn could run, but the other three might easily be killed if the king wished.

Cormac threw the war-axe far out into the river. "Count yourselves lucky that I am in a good mood this morning," he told them sternly as he launched the boat back into the river, "or you would all be sent to hell. Go tell Queen Finnabair that there is but one king in Ireland and he will return to take her head and put it to rot on the ramparts of Tara."

As soon as they were in midstream, Cormac threw the three swords into the river. Despite the drenching of the previous night he felt fine. He had struck back at his enemies and the morning sun was warm. He sighed in satisfaction.

"Were not the legends true, Brigid?" he asked proudly.

The shoulders of his hunched-over slave were shaking. Poor, frightened child. "Come here, Biddy," he said softly.

She shook her head. "I will not."

He took her into his arms anyhow, gently holding the quivering little frame. "For a foster daughter you seem to be in my arms a remarkable amount of the time," he laughed.

Biddy merely sniffed, her teeth still chattering. She did fit rather nicely into his arms at that. He kept one elbow crooked around the steering oar. "Did you really think I would trade your pretty head for merely seventy cattle?" he asked reprovingly.

She turned her face towards him, a quick look of almost animal shrewdness. "I was afraid, devious master, that you might ask for a hundred cattle." She either whimpered or giggled.

"I once thought you would bring only four head of cattle on the slave market. Someone thinks you are very valuable indeed, foster daughter. We must keep you alive a while longer to see why."

Brigid was silent. The sun grew warmer, the Shannon turned a peaceful blue. Cormac felt a softness in his heart for the girl he was holding. A man would travel many miles to find so fierce a woman. "Biddy—" he said gently.

But her eyes were closed. Sound asleep.

"Behold, good wolfhound, the High King is so attractive to women that they fall asleep in his arms," he muttered to Podraig.

There was no bark from the bow of the boat. Podraig, too, was asleep. If anyone was to praise the exploits of the High King he would have to do it himself. But before praise, a tough and mysterious question. Why did they want Biddy's head so badly? Why was she worth more than he?

Chapter 14

T*he early morning* sun forced open King Cormac's eyes. He had fallen asleep only a short time before. Beltaine was drawing near; the days grew longer, the nights shorter—bad for a man who could sleep only in the dark. The immense lake was already steaming in the sunlight.

The sacred Shannon broadened often into wide lakes, in which the flow of the river current was hard to find. For two days he and Biddy paddled slowly along the shore, awed by the great brown oak forests filled with wolves, bears, stags, and deer. They camped on the shore of the lake to get out of the boat and stretch their cramped limbs. With Podraig's protection they feared neither wolf nor bear. The leaves on the oak trees were budding; the forest rang with the song of birds celebrating the lacy green of spring.

Cormac could not sleep despite the comfortable layer of bracken that Biddy had dutifully spread on the forest floor for him. King Jesus' story about the steward who buried the coin fit him perfectly. His life was wasted. What use of talent was it to drift down the Shannon toward the great ocean chasing a foolish dream? Podraig and Biddy were still asleep. She was wearing her drab gray pilgrim's gown, having dutifully asked his permission. But her hair remained long—for vanity a small triumph. She had no trouble sleeping. He marveled at the look of innocence on her pretty face. He twisted away and tried to fix his eyes on the dull glow of the lake as it responded eagerly to the sun's rays.

Had she really grown so much more lovely, or was it merely the memory of the dark red gown molding her body in the village across from Clonmacnoise, the glow of the sun in her pale hair? Was she aware of the change? Was she at peace with it? Why was she so often silent? Cormac stretched. If only he could sleep.

He had begun to feel shameful lust for her. It was powerful and insistent. How long had it been since he desired a woman? The gentle wife of Enda, Finnabair, that terrible night at Tara. What would Biddy be like? Probably awkward and frightened. She was rigid every time he lifted her out of the boat; she must sense that he went out of his way now to pick her up in his arms. Such a slender and sweet woman form. He turned back to look in admiration; his gaze turned instantly into feverish desire. His famished eyes were consuming her, he reached out to touch her.

He rolled quickly away. Rising from the ground he leaned against an oak tree at the edge of the small lakeside clearing where they had camped, breathing heavily.

He must not surrender to his passion. What a graceful white neck. The birds were already singing a merry chorus; the air was filled with the sweet scent of spring flowers. Slight her body might be but delectable. He clenched his fists to control his fingers which ached to touch her.

Oh, King Jesus, you know I would not hurt her. Gentle strokes of the hand, soft sighs, a girl's body coming alive. There had to be great passion in her too. It would be a kindness to free such feelings. A few quick steps and he could claim her. She was a slave. What else were slave women for?

God in heaven, what was happening to him? He pushed his clenched fist against his beating head. Lusting after a slave girl whom he had proclaimed his foster daughter, a mere child who was not ready for lovemaking. He was turning even more foul. Cormac groaned. He had to get away from her. He would get some fish for the morning meal. Besides, the cold waters of the lake would—

Podraig opened one eye, then the other. Reluctantly the dog stirred himself to accompany his master on the fishing expedition. Was it wise to leave Biddy unguarded? They had not seen any humans in more than five days. No animals would come near a human camp at this time of the early morning. If there were noise, Podraig would hear it. With a last, lingering look at the peacefully sleeping body under its great cloak, he walked down the shore, spear in hand, toward a pool that looked like good fishing.

Cormac quickly speared five good-sized trout—enough food for a whole day. Then he pulled off his short *leine* and plunged into the cold waters of the lake. Podraig jumped in after him and just as quickly jumped out. The good hound did not have to worry about cooling his lusts. The painful cold of the lake was exhilarating.

His muscles tingled with vitality. His head cleared, he smiled at himself. Fierce, passionate High King and afraid to touch a fragile slave girl worth four head of cattle at the most. They were well matched. She would be in less danger from him than if she were in a convent full of nuns. MacDermot would keep his lusts raging only inside his head.

Refreshed, he climbed back on the shore. He let the sun soak up most of the moisture from his body before he put on his *leine,* then walked briskly back down the shore with his spear in one hand, the morning meal for his woman in the other.

When he and Podraig reached camp she was not there. The boat was untouched; but the food by the fire, his sword, and Biddy had disappeared. Cormac felt his heart twist with pain, his stomach knot with fear. Beside him Podraig uttered a menacing growl. Whoever had taken her could not have gone far.

"Find her, Podraig!" he shouted, his voice hoarse with worry.

The aroused wolfhound leaped into the forest, nosed around frantically until he found the trail and raced down through the trees on a narrow footpath. Cormac ran behind him.

In minutes, which seemed like years, they came to a small clearing filled with a band of men and a screaming Biddy pinned to the ground, her gray tunic ripped open. They were bending over her, fondling and tormenting her—culdees—dangerous wandering religious fanatics neither Christian nor pagan but something mad in between.

Podraig stopped running. Like a good war dog he stood tensely quiet. Cormac counted them—nine men armed with sticks and knives, one with his sword and shield. Three restrained Biddy while the others warily approached him, their eyes narrow with hatred, their muscles tense, their huge paws eager for battle. The one with Cormac's sword was a huge fellow with a coarse face and a long brown beard. Next to him were two shorter men, one with a wicked shillelagh, the other holding a glittering little knife.

They were fools, he thought, feeling the comfortable shaft of the spear blending smoothly with his taut fingers. They all should have attacked him at once. You do not attack an Irish warrior with only three men. His throat was dry with the beginnings of the blood lust.

The three culdees came closer. "Release the woman and give me back the food. You shall come to no harm," he warned, quietly holding the spear point down without threat.

They laughed. He could smell mead-soaked breath. They had been drinking. *God, poor Biddy.*

"Do you hear him? We will suffer no harm? He is a joker as well as a spearman," chortled the big man with the sword, now in striking distance.

Cormac kept the point of his spear toward the ground. "You still have a chance to live," he said softly.

"And you to die," screeched the big man, lifting his sword clumsily to strike.

The sword arm never came down. Knocking aside the shield as if it were paper, Cormac plunged his spear into the man's heart. Podraig leaped at the culdee with the knife, ripping his throat open. Before the survivor could lift his club the king retrieved his stolen sword and slashed his arm. He would never use it again. The other culdees quickly fled down the footpath.

Biddy, her gray *leine* in tatters, lay motionless on the

ground, sobbing hysterically. Podraig chased the culdees into the woods; then, sure they were on the run, trotted back to the now peaceful clearing where Cormac held his battered little bondwoman in his arms. The High King crooned soothing sounds into her ear. Slowly she calmed. He noticed a long, thin, white scar accenting the smooth, lovely curve of her back—an old wound. Someday he would have to ask her about it.

Rocking her gently back and forth, he explained sorrowfully, "I went fishing for our morning meal—I didn't think—"

Instantly she forgave him. "There is danger everywhere, good master. With protectors like you and Podraig a small girl child is always safe."

She was warm and soft in his arms. The lust began to return. To have lost her would have been— He lovingly tightened his grip. Was there a response to his hunger in her? Was her shiver something besides fright?

"Did you catch any fish?" she abruptly interrupted his thoughts.

"I've just saved you and you worry about fish. All the fish in Ireland would not be worth danger—" He choked.

"Have you not said, all-wise king, that it is a sin to waste good food? Should we not go back and eat our morning meal?" She spoke sensibly, though without effort to escape his arms.

Cormac picked her up and carried her carefully back to the lake shore.

"Ought you not return to bring the food those evil men took, and retrieve your arms?" she whispered serenely.

Giving orders again. "Will you not be afraid to be left alone again?" he asked, tenderly placing her against the trunk of a sturdy old oak.

"Not if you leave the brave Podraig with me."

When he returned from the clearing she was dressed in her blue gown, sewing together the tatters of her pilgrim's robe. The fish were on the fire; a jug of fresh water waited for him to refresh himself. He gulped it down and accepted the piece of fish and the thick crust of bread she respectfully handed him.

"You recover quickly, foster child," he said curtly, angry at her return to vitality.

"I am learning, my lord. I fear I was born a coward and will die one." The gleam of gratitude in her eyes, more silver than the lake in the sunlight, smothered his anger.

"We are all cowards, Biddy. The wise among us are brave enough to admit it." He was very weary, the battle lust fading into exhaustion.

After they had eaten, he was too sleepy to rise from the hard ground. "We will stay here today, good foster daughter. It is a pleasant place to rest after much time in the boat. Unless—"

He stretched out in the warm spring sunlight, his eyes closing. He yawned. Was she offended because he was yawning after her adventure? He forced his eyes open. "If you wish to swim in the lake, resolute one, there is a quiet pool in that direction. I'm sure the faithful wolfhound will go with you even if I don't tell him to—though I cannot promise he will stay in the water for long." *Go away, girl. If I can't have you, I must have quiet.* His heavy eyelids closed again.

She hesitated, embarrassed. He looked up at her. *Biddy blushing!* "I promise I will stay here." His eyes closed again. He was almost asleep.

"Has not my master the right to do anything he wishes?" she exclaimed, angry with herself for displaying modesty.

He didn't bother to answer. He heard their footsteps in the brush as she and Podraig walked down the shore towards the pool. The sun was now high in the sky, the air damp and hot. He wished he could go with them to frolic in the waters. That would be most unwise. He made no promises about his imagination. The pictures of Brigid's sleek white body parting the blue waters brought him peace. By the time she came back he was sound asleep. She let him sleep till the sun was low in the sky.

Two days later Brigid saved his life. As they huddled under a big oak tree on the bank of the Shannon while the rain beat down on them, Cormac devoutly thanked King Jesus and Mother Mary for sending this odd angel to protect him.

Earlier in the day they had fastened the boat to a tree on the bank of the river and eaten a full supper of venison, onions, and wild watercress, with fresh new raspberries. They had finally found the current and moved out of the big lake into the main course of the Shannon. The river was wide, and when the sky grew ominously dark, Cormac insisted on stopping. He had no wish to be on the river in a fierce spring storm. He opened one of the precious wineskins the disreputable Kiernan had left on boat.

"If you keep feeding me this way, generous cook, I will grow too fat to search for the magic cup," he sighed, spilling some of the wine he was drawing from the skin.

"The princess will be angry at me if I make you fat," she answered tartly, refusing his offer of the wineskin.

Cormac did not feel like fighting, not on a full stomach. He wiped the spilled wine off his mouth and took another long draught.

It was twilight—the long, caressing twilight of an Irish

day in spring. A storm threatened, but the rains would not come for a time yet.

"Would you wish to walk a way before it rains? We turn stale in the boat all day." He rose, a courtier inviting a great lady to walk in his garden. Obediently she followed.

He put several sticks of dry wood into her arms and took a lighted torch from their fire. They started off through the thick, silent forest. Podraig continued to sleep by the fire.

How long had it been since he walked through the woods with a girl on a spring evening with the smell of flowers in the air? He wanted to converse with her playfully and joyously; he did not know what to say. So he said nothing. Nor did she.

They came to one of the small round hills that lined the course of the river. This was larger than most of them; it seemed to rise suddenly out of the forest. At its base was a well-worn path. Along the side of the path there were upright stones marked with Druid signs. Colum's Christianizers had not yet converted them into symbols of the new religion. The air grew heavier still. The storm must be very near.

Biddy broke her silence. "I do not know the meaning of these signs, master, but I fear this path," she said anxiously, dropping some of her sticks of torchwood.

He laughed lightly at her fears and picked up the wood to carry himself.

They continued down the narrow path. Soon they came to a large rock with a grotesque human head carved on it. Biddy grabbed his hand in terror. "What does it mean?" he asked her. It was as he had noticed often before—a very nice hand to hold. He clung to it.

"I know little of the old religion, royal lord, but the gods Lug, Dagda, and Mennanin are holy; the women, like Erihu, are good most of the time. Yet in my bones I feel evil is here."

She did not pull her hand back. *Well, prudish wench, we have made some progress.*

Cormac circled the stone. Behind it there was a hole in the hill—an entrance to a cave. Reluctantly releasing her complaint fingers, he bent and crawled in with the dubious slave close behind him. He groped several yards though a short tunnel. Then the roof rose up suddenly. They entered the main chamber of the cave.

It was an awesome sight that Cormac saw when he raised his torch. They were in a stone basilica with high walls and long aisles made of gleaming green, red, and yellow rocks. At first he thought it was man-made, but it was a natural basilica carved out of the rock long ago. Behind him Biddy gasped in surprise. Slowly they walked the mysterious aisles of the vast chamber, exploring the little side chapels and listening to the sound of running water somewhere in the distance.

He lit another torch. They turned down a corridor and found a large underground pond, almost a lake, shining black in the glow of his fire. "There must be an underground river here that empties into the Shannon," he told her. "It is a lovely place, is it not? There is no sign that any of your Druid priests have been here in a long time. Perhaps it is the entry to their heaven."

"My lord knows much more than I. It could also be the entrance to hell." Her voice cracked. His poor superstitious little *cuhmal* was terrified.

As they edged their way against the wall around the lake, Cormac began to feel dizzy. A strange smell hung in the air—not the darkness of the cave but something deep and smoky. His head whirled. He thought of the sweet incense of the cathedral at Ravenna.

He heard slow, high-pitched chanting in a language he did not understand. Smoke drifted down the corridors of the cave and obscured his vision. He felt light-headed, began to laugh—a wild, keening, hysterical sound. Strange colored lights appeared all around him—bright red, green, yellow, and blue. Something was terribly wrong. He wanted to talk to Biddy, but his laughter made it impossible.

Then the monsters came—huge, green monsters with forked tongues, red eyes, and smoking nostrils—slimy, scaly dragons moving in a slithering rhythm around and around and around. Were they doing the singing? Was it their voices? Why could he not stop laughing? Who was that pounding on his chest, hitting his face, screaming at him? Who was it dragging him, pulling him, pleading with him? Who was trying to save him from the monsters? He did not want to be saved. They were nice monsters, friendly monsters, beautiful monsters. It was all so very funny. Why did he want to stop laughing? What was it that hit him on the head?

There was rain falling on his face—good, clean, fresh rain. Someone holding his hand pleading with him. Who was it? A girl? Which one of the girls that he had known? What was she saying? "Please wake up!" He was awake. Who was she?

"I'm awake, Biddy. Stop shouting," he pleaded. All the pagan demons of Ireland were pounding inside his head. "Why am I so sore?" There was a big lump on his head, his face was painfully tender. "Did I run into something?" His throat was thick, his words unsteady. He was lying on the ground, the rain pouring over him.

"You ran into your foster daughter Brigid. I slapped you and punched you and kicked you and hit you over the head."

He couldn't see her face in the dark. Was that laughter or terror? How dare she laugh at him. "Did you enjoy pounding me, fierce slave?" he asked, trying to be angry but sounding laughable even to himself.

She giggled. "Oh yes, master, I enjoyed it greatly. Then I was so worried. You wouldn't stop babbling about lights and voices and monsters. I'm sorry. You can hit me back if you want to," she added meekly.

Instead he took her hand in the dark and kissed it. She quickly pulled it away. "You saw nothing, Biddy? No lights, no smoke, no dragons?"

"You did not have that much wine, great king," she responded sternly.

"It was not the wine." Then terror took possession of the soul of King Cormac MacDermot. His body was shaking; he tried to stand and found that he could barely do so. "You strike heavy blows, little warrior," he sighed.

"Lean on me, my lord. I will help you back to the river."

"Nonsense, I can walk myself," he insisted irritably.

He could not. She had to lead him back to the river—a hard task in the darkness and the rain, though occasional lightning flashes gave bursts of light to help her find the way. With every clap of thunder Cormac jumped in fear.

"You see me as a coward, Brigid," he admitted, his voice wavering with shame.

"I had to drag you out. I hope that your back is not too badly scratched," she said penitently, ignoring his shame.

He wanted to sink into the bracken beside the path, pull his cloak around him and sleep for a week. She urged him on until they stumbled back into their camp. Podraig barked a grumpy protest at the interruption of his nap.

On the dry side of the big oak tree he slept. In the middle of the night he awakened. He felt as if he had been drinking for a week. The journey was getting more dangerous. Were the magic cup and the magic princess worth it all? Could he risk the resourceful girl sleeping so soundly next to him? He bent over her and kissed her forehead. How many months had he wanted to do that? She did not stir in her sleep. He slipped back into unconsciousness.

The next morning when he awoke refreshed he could not remember whether he had really kissed her or whether it was only a very pleasant dream.

Chapter 15

F*lames from great* bonfires ate away the blackness of the night. The people of the kingdom of Limerick herded their cattle between the fires, praying that the mating season would be fertile. The strong green logs carved and bound together to look like a four-yard-tall man began to glow. They would last all night long in fires kept burning by frequent refuelings of dry wood. There would be plenty of light for the drinking of mead and the making of love.

Laughter, song, the twanging noise of the lyres, rhythmic clapping of hands—the Limerick folk were whipping themselves into a frenzy. The spring festival was much like the harvest festival—a ritual excuse for the excess which the Irish seemed to need periodically in their lives. Beltaine was a healthier orgy than Lugnasa, thought the High King. The fertility rites of midsummer were innocent enough. The life forces of human coupling were stronger than the death forces. It was a mark of his own perversity that the innocent joys of Beltaine offended him and the dark pleasures of Lugnasa appealed to him.

Cormac MacDermot stirred uneasily in the chair next to the old King of Limerick, who though the intermediary of the King of Cashel was theoretically his subject. King Leary of Limerick cared little for either the lordship or the rivalry of the higher kings of Cashel and Tara, but he was a courteous host.

Cormac was angry in the depths of his spirit. He hated Limerick, he despised the lascivious old king, he was affronted by the Beltaine merriment; but he felt an even deeper rage that was like an old wound reopened. In the twisted darkness of his angry soul he groped for the cause of his fury and could not find it.

They were no closer to the magic cup. Brendan was not at Clonfert. The abbot and a band of younger men had gone to the ocean to build a new curragh for their pilgrimage to the Promised Land of the West. He and Biddy continued down the river, hoping to find some trace of Brendan or a hint of where the pirate islands were.

As the Shannon widened, Cormac felt sea breezes sting his face. When they passed by a large rath on a river island, he decided to visit the lord of the fort and discovered that it was Leary of Limerick. Since he needed Leary's help, Cormac accepted the invitation to spend the spring festival of Beltaine with the king, his family, and vassals.

"She's a great beauty, that woman of yours," said the old man drunkenly.

Biddy was leading the young women of Limerick in the twirling spring dances. Where had she learned to dance like that—and sing too? She was a stranger here. Where did she find the power to take command of the Beltaine dancing and singing? She was in the midst of the girls, clad in a short green smock, clapping the beat with her hands, and, solemn-faced as always, singing the old pagan tunes. A provoking slave woman who deserved to be punished, he told himself.

"Nothing like a young girl to pep up a king in bed, is there?" continued the old man, nudging him with his elbow.

"No indeed." He paid little attention to Leary's maunderings.

"Is she as good in bed as she is in the reels?" the old buzzard persisted.

Did he want an invitation to try Biddy? It would serve the wretched girl right. "Even better," Cormac lied. He eased away from Leary as much as he could without rising from his chair.

"Not a man in Limerick who won't envy you for what you will do to her when the fires die out," the king cackled, poking Cormac with an obscene thumb.

They would be sadly disappointed, thought Cormac ruefully to himself.

The king didn't want to talk about pirates; they were enemies whose raids on his land must be resisted, not objects for mystical pilgrimages. He had heard of a queen named Morrigan somewhere to the north—"Wicked bitch, let me tell you, Cormac, my boy, but the kind of woman you'd like to get on top of if you ever had the chance," he said with a vile wink.

Beyond that lewd advice there was no information. He was no closer to the magic cup than when he left Tara.

Cormac did not like his Brigid dancing pagan fertility

rites. He wondered why. They were done at Tara still, she was a pagan herself, and the dances were relatively harmless. Did he wish he could dance with her?

The pipers began to play again, their mournful sounds following the flames up to the towering vault of the night sky. The young women stopped dancing. Biddy came over to Cormac and the old king, who did not bother to hide his lecherous thoughts. Cormac was disturbed at the sight of her slender white legs. Why had he not observed before what nicely carved thighs she had? He gripped his wine goblet tightly. It tipped, spilling on his tunic and beard.

"Does my master wish me to stop dancing now?" she asked, ignoring his discomfiture with the spilled wine.

"Not if you find it pleasant to celebrate with the other young people," he replied curtly.

"I am grateful, honored and ancient master." There was anger in her voice too. What right did she have to be angry?

She bowed to him with deep respect, revealing beneath the thin smock the tops of her trim young breasts. *Very nice, my Brigid. I've watched you turn from girl to woman; yet you still surprise me. I should have left you in Slaine. Enda knew more about such things than the rest of us. You make a lovely spring goddess, little pagan slave. Would that I were not an autumn king.*

Brigid went back to the dances. Was the sway in her walk new, or had Beltaine made him notice it? *Thoroughly presentable backside too, little goddess. Are you deliberately stirring up my aging lusts? Our convent is getting unsafe again.* He sipped his wine. *Careful, Cormac, no more of it or you will be in an even deeper bog,* he told himself, gripping the carved side of his chair.

Long before the fires went out and the morning sun

rose, Cormac walked slowly to the small, conical-shaped hut which Leary had assigned to them. Podraig, who viewed all festivals as human foolishness, was long since asleep. Cormac's anger and depression were so deep he could not sleep. He was awake when Biddy came in, the morning sunlight shining briefly through the doorway as she gently opened the curtain.

She handed him a goblet of wine with the graceful charm of a mature woman. "I thought my master might be thirsty."

"Always the considerate servant," he snapped irritably. Why should her grace make him even more angry?

The girl was breathing heavily from her exertions; her body was covered with perspiration, which had soaked her short garment, causing it to cling to her in the most revealing ways. A strong spring smell emanated from her body. If you dress that way, woman, you might just as well wear nothing at all, he prudishly told himself.

She sat on the floor, her lovely legs close to him. For a girl who was ordinarily so modest, she now seemed quite reckless and abandoned. Was this an invitation?

"My master is angry because I danced with the pagans?" she asked tentatively, as though she were afraid of his mood.

"May not pagan dance with pagan?" he snarled, pulling back from those dangerous legs.

"May I bring you more wine?" Patient, obedient respect.

"No. That will not be necessary." He turned away from her and curled up to try to sleep again.

"I found out about your pirates." The words sounded quietly in the hut. He sat up suddenly and peered through the gloom at her, sitting against the mud wall, tense, expectant. Softly she went on, delicately trying to avoid his rage. "They don't like to talk about them. Queen Morrigan—that is her name—and her husband rule on an island fifteen days' journey north of here. They are terrifying folk who fear nothing. They make all the seas and coasts of the west of Ireland dangerous; they have even come down the Shannon to raid Limerick. The last time they almost captured it. Only in the land of the O'Donnals to the south are they not feared."

"And the Princess Delvcaem?" he asked.

"They had a daughter. My friends say there is a tradition of such princesses here in the west. Delvcaem died long ago. They did not know her."

Anger, despair, lust deprived him of words.

"I will sleep now, if it please you, master," she sighed.

"It does not matter." He dismissed her.

The softness went out of her voice. "If one is so proud as Cormac MacDermot, nothing matters," she thundered at him.

"What did you say?" He was very angry. His hand instinctively reached for his knife. He sighed and relaxed. Anger was useless. "Why do you hate me, Biddy?" he asked despondently. "Have I not been a good master and good foster father to you? What can I do that I have not done to escape your wrath?"

For a long time there was no reply. Then very slowly, "I do not hate you, King Cormac. If I fight you with my tongue it is because I am afraid." The music in her voice was very slow, the bells tolling in sorrow.

"My God, Brigid, what reason do you have to be afraid of me? What have I done to you?" he shouted, baffled and hurt. There was a heavy, dangerous silence. Finally he burst out, "You never smile at me!"

"I am afraid to smile, good master. If I smile, I have no more defenses," she said simply.

"Against me? You do not need defense against me." The provoking wench was trying to annoy him now, to deprive him of his well-merited sleep.

"The defenses are against my own longings," she whispered, terror clutching at her words.

The fever of Beltaine had destroyed the girl's sanity. How dare a bondwoman say anything like that to the High King of all Ireland! He pulled his cloak against the morning chill and strode out of the hut into the silent rath of Limerick. Rapidly he walked beyond the walls, curtly greeting the sleepy sentinels, then out into the bogs that stretched along the river on either side of the rath. He walked a long way before slowing his pace. Wearily he sat on a log overlooking the mighty Shannon. The bogs were covered with a carpet of white and yellow flowers, the bushes along the river bank had turned a deep purple. Birds were singing, the air was filled with rich, sweet smells. Bees buzzed frantically all around.

Why was he angry? Biddy had said she loved him. Small wonder. An innocent and sheltered slave girl wanders through the countryside for months with a legendary king. She was just at the stage in life when girls fall in love. Who else would she think she loved? Why should her love frighten him? She was not death; he feared her as death. They would both die eventually. Did that matter? It was absurd to fear someone you love—yes, he had said it to himself. He loved Biddy.

A good ten years older, much wiser and more experienced, he returned her love. He lusted after her sweet young body. He wanted her the way he wanted to breathe the spring air. He had never loved anyone before. He had not known even what this feeling for his tiny slave was. Now in the crisp, clear spring sunlight, he knew. Why did he love her? His own poems had said there was no explanation for love. She was pretty, she was brave, she was intelligent, she was clever. She was Biddy. Was that not enough reason? His heart was now beating rapidly. He wanted to embrace her, cover her with kisses, caress her hair, touch her breasts, stroke her thighs; he wanted to sing songs for her, dance dances for her, write poems for her. *You are a fool, Cormac MacDermot.*

He would be taking unfair advantage of her—a defenseless slave, an inexperienced child, a girl just barely become woman who could not know her own feelings. It did not matter. He would protect her, love her, make her happy. He would devote his whole life to her service. If Tara wanted him back, they would take the two of them together. If they didn't want him back, he and Biddy would roam the world, eating by campfires and frolicking in the streams. Who needed a kingdom when you had a woman like her?

He would hurry back to their hut in Limerick and proclaim his love. She would tell him he was daft. He would take her into his arms and begin to kiss her. She would protest in fright, resist pathetically, pleading with him. Then she would begin to melt, yielding to the passion they both had felt for so long. Gently he would remove the short dancing tunic and enjoy her womanliness without the guilt that had tormented him before. Then he would slowly and deftly release the fire that was inside of her. The two of them would be one, belonging to each other as long as God gave them life.

He rose and walked quickly back toward the ring fort, striding with the confident step of a man who knows precisely what he is doing.

When he drew near the outer walls, he saw a band of armed warriors on the bank of the river, old King Leary in the middle of them. One of the men saw him, the others turned in gloomy silence to watch him approach. He glanced up at the sky. The sun was sinking. Already late afternoon.

Leary came down the path to meet him, his expression grave. "I have sad news for you, Cormac MacDermot." Pain showed on the old profligate's face.

Cormac's heart turned icy. "What is this news?"

"Your girl was stolen by pirates," Leary said mournfully.

He did not believe it. The sky reeled.

The King of Limerick blundered on with his dreary news.

"This morning she and the dog left the walls of Limerick to look for you. They went down the river bank; no one has seen them since. An old peasant woman who lives in the bogs told us that she saw a curragh with many men in it take a dog and a girl. We have searched since midday and have found nothing. Our boats on the river can learn nothing about any curragh."

"How long ago?" The words choked him.

"Many hours," said the gloomy king.

Sobbing, Cormac MacDermot fell to the ground in front of the *rath* of Limerick and pounded the earth in bitter rage.

Chapter 16

The waters of the ocean lapped quietly on the Dingle beach. Behind the large headland the moon had already set. Stars stared implacably at Cormac MacDermot. Salt and fish smells permeated the air. In the little creek by the headland, the ocean-going curragh was ready. The mast was set, the sail furled. Tomorrow the pilgrimage of Brendan and his followers would begin.

Six months ago he had stumbled on Brendan and his band. He watched them curiously for a time, hard at work on the beach, tanning the dark leather and laying the framework for their craft; then, impulsively, he asked if he could join. With no questions the old man accepted him. The brutally hard work of building the boat was a drug that killed the pain in his heart. He did not think, did not question; he almost ceased to exist.

The Land of Promise in the West would never be

found. In Brendan's failing eyes, gleaming beneath the shaggy white hair, was the light of a man captured by a vision. As a sailor, Brendan was without equal in Ireland; as an abbot of monks, he was stern and wise; as a man with a mission to find paradise, he was mad. What did Cormac care about that? He, too, was mad. What better place to lose oneself completely than in the great ocean, free of thought, memories, regrets. The ocean was dark forgetfulness.

He had searched the Shannon to its mouth for traces of Biddy and Podraig. He journeyed above the river mouth and then below it, asking hopelessly for a girl with blond-streaked hair and a huge, friendly dog. Nothing. One day, walking down a beach in the land of Kerry, he faced the dreaded truth. They were both dead.

Poor Biddy. He could be coldly objective now. That was her destiny from the beginning. A pretty slave girl in Ireland was destined to be violated and destroyed. He had not caused her doom; it would have happened anyway. Ireland was profligate with wit and courage; her loss was just part of the pattern. A loyal wolfhound, a sharp tongued slave—what did they matter? No more than the grains of sand on the cold beach beneath his feet.

He could not pray for them. The love of King Jesus and the kindness of Mother Mary were for others. For Cormac MacDermot, one of the already damned, there was nothing but Brendan's sturdy leather boat and the great ocean.

He had heard of a land called Great Ireland beyond the seas. It was a vast and empty place where long ago there had been an Irish kingdom—not at all like the Land of Promise the demented Brendan sought. If he should survive the voyage, perhaps he could be reborn there—

Cormac closed his eyes and willed his hopes to go away. He slept, dreaming of a girl in a red dress with golden trim. Her round blue eyes and bright smile blessed him. By her side was a great shaggy gray dog. When he woke the next morning, he felt rested as if by dreamless sleep.

The abbot said mass; the fifteen crewmen boarded the little boat. Singing a hymn of thanksgiving, they energetically rowed their bobbing craft out of the creek onto the gentle swells of the ocean. The sky was cloudless, the breezes light; the great sea welcomed them graciously.

The final voyage of Holy Brendan the Sailor had begun.

For Cormac it was a dream—a succession of strange, colorful, unrelated images. He often did not know whether he was asleep or awake. He was seasick much of the time, then hungry and thirsty as rations diminished. A sip of water every day, a crust or two of bread, were all Brendan and the monks needed. There were times when he could not even keep that down.

The curragh bobbed up and down on waves that seemed as high as the Wicklow Mountains. Sometimes great sheets of water broke over the bow of the boat, soaking them all with a terrible coldness. He shivered in soggy wet clothes for days before they reached the first landfall, a craggy island with towering cliffs that made those of Ireland look small. Dimly Cormac remembered climbing out of the boat, pushing the craft up a freezing creek, then sinking to the ground, exhausted to the point of death. The abbot wouldn't permit him to die. He was fed, revived, given warm milk to drink, then put back on the boat for another attempt to reach the West.

Three times did Brendan try to break the hold of these

rugged islands; each time high winds drove him back to shore. Taking this as a sign that God wanted them to celebrate Easter on the islands, Brendan postponed further attempts until the Feast of the Lord's Resurrection had come and gone. Cormac did not speak either to the monks or to the kind, helpful sheepherders who made these terrible rocks their home. The Feast of the Resurrection—was it that long? Almost a year since Beltaine—

On the fourth attempt, Brendan broke from the islands with a strong wind at his back. For a long time they sailed to the southwest, sometimes with the wind, sometimes drifting with the current, sometimes feebly rowing. Almost all of their food and water were gone. They were weak with hunger and thirst and baked by the merciless sun. Cormac was sure that death would come now. Then a huge flock of birds flew overhead; another set of islands reared up on the horizon. Once more they dragged the boat ashore; once more he sank to the ground, hoping that it was over finally. Yet the sound of birds, the warmth of the sand, and the smell of flowers made him want to live a little bit longer.

Again friendly natives—this time dark, lovely women—gave them good fruit, warm baths in the thermal springs, and robes to cover themselves while their clothes were washed. Strength returned, and along with it the temptation to stay on the island. The call from the holy sailor came inevitably; they must raise sail and point for the Land of Promise.

He had fallen under the spell of the saintly madman. There was *something* in the west. Why not sail after it? What was there better to do in life than seek the Land of Promise?

So the battered boat was launched again, away from

the island of flowers and the beautiful women with the dark, inviting eyes. The smell of flowers stayed with him for many days.

They sailed rapidly now, always westward, until they came to what Brendan called the Sea of the Dead. It was a flat, motionless patch of ocean, laced with thick seaweed, rubble of logs, and the remains of boats—a swamp in the middle of the ocean. The light curragh bobbed over most of the treacherous, clinging growth. Still, the oarsmen had to fight to keep the oars from being pulled out of their hands. They moved very slowly. It was hotter than Cormac thought it could be outside of hell.

One night he stood at the boat's rudder next to the abbot, who seemed never to sleep. The clear-eyed, erect old man was reading the sky the way another monk would read a book. Brendan was trying to teach him navigation. Cormac listened, heard what was said, absorbed some of it—if only to keep the dreams, the images, the thoughts at bay.

"Brother Connor," said the abbot briskly, "you are not a sailor from a family of sailors, nor are you a farmer from a family of farmers, like these boys who sometimes believe more in an old man's dream than he believes it himself. You are not searching for the Land of Promise; you are running from something. Who are you?"

"May I not continue to search with you?" he asked meekly, surprised at his anxiety. It was so hard to banish thought and feeling. The cursed holy man was opening wounds. He eased his body to the plank next to the steering oar. He was trembling. What was trying to come up from inside him?

"You have more strength than any of them and more intelligence. If I should die, you are the one to bring them home. You may continue to search. Still, I must know whether you are of the devil or not." The abbot was uneasy, worried. He took his eyes off the stars and fixed them on Cormac's face while deftly adjusting the steering oar.

"I do not want to be of the devil. Often I seem to do the devil's work."

"I am not a scholar, boy. I know only that you cannot be of the devil unless you want to. Who are you?"

Cormac hesitated. What would the old man do? He had to tell him. There would be no peace, no sinking back into oblivion for him unless he did. The cold stars glared at him from the distant sky.

"I am Cormac MacDermot."

"The Expected High King?" The sainted navigator made three rapid signs of the cross. "Well, then, you are certainly not of the devil," he exclaimed in delight. "The anointed one is of God—and also of the Holy Abbot Colum, of course. Our voyage is blessed. We will find the Land of Promise and return to Ireland." His voice was exultant. "You know, King Cormac, I want to be buried in Ireland." Seeing in the starlight glow the puzzled expression on Cormac's face, the old man continued, "Do you not know the prophecies about yourself? Has no one told you? You would be the only one in Ireland then."

"I know of no prophecies, good father. I do not think I would believe them."

"After you left Tara the Holy Abbess Finvolva, the wisest seeress in the land, foretold that you would return with a queen whose hair was brown and yellow to rule for many, many years. During that time Ireland would be at peace and become Christian." Shifting the steering oar to his left hand, he crossed himself again.

Finnabair had heard the ravings of the demented old woman and thought of Biddy. She knew that when the girl's hair grew long it turned blond. If she killed Biddy, the prophecy would be frustrated. Biddy was dead anyway. So much for superstition. The Abbess Finvolva made Brendan and Kevin look as sane and sensible as Kiernan.

"I think, wise abbot, that if we do return to Ireland, it will be more because of your skilled navigation than because of my destiny."

The old man's delight was not to be denied him. "Destiny is destiny, King Cormac. You will bring us all back."

The next day they broke out of the Sea of the Dead. With their tattered sail billowing in the stiff breeze, the band of Brendan sailed again toward the west. Fifteen days later found them drifting toward a lovely island that gleamed in the warm sunlight. Wide beaches, green hills, and huge white breakers made them think of Dingle. Yet never on that shore had the sun shone so hot nor such sweet perfume ever tantalized mariners.

Cormac hardly noticed the heat of the sun. For many days he had been sick with a fever, his strength fading. The monks nursed him gently, tenderly, keeping wet linen on him through day and night.

Brendan steered the boat away from the dangeous reefs on the seaward side to beach behind the island where the waters were calm. They hauled down the sail and rowed to shore, singing the *Gloria* in gratitude as they dipped into the water with their oars. The wisdom of their holy abbot had brought them to safety once again.

The feverish Cormac was lifted off the boat and carried to shade. He was dimly aware of gentle hands and cooling liquid. He wanted to die. The conversation with

Brendan on the Sea of the Dead had stirred haunting memories that tormented him through his sickness.

Then the fever broke; there was delicious coolness in the night on the new island. He heard Brendan saying farewell and promising to return.

Chapter 17

G*ulls screeched over* her head like the lost souls who were freed from hell at Samaintide. Far beneath, the foaming white waves smashed against the base of the cliffs. The sky was angry, the sea morose. How long, wondered the Princess Delvcaem, would it take to fall? What would the moment of impact feel like? How long would the pain last? Her body shook with fear. She drew the woolly, purple mantle more tightly around her. She was still cold. Would the mantle pull her down as did the warm clothes of the fishermen—who did not learn to swim because it prolonged the agony of drowning? Unfortunately she had learned to swim. The fall alone would kill her; she need not worry about drowning. What would her body look like? Would it be broken and bloated when it washed up on the shore? Would it ever wash up? What about the *leine* she wore—white trimmed with gold?

What would the sea waters do to it? Why had she worn her best dress to die?

Would she really hurl her body over the side? She was not sure. Was it only a matter of courage? Was there lingering hope—foolishness if there ever had been any in the world?

There were two people with her, a man and a woman—both smiling and gentle. Who were they? Where had they come from? Why had she not heard them?

"Peace be to you, princess," they said, so softly she could just hear them above the howling wind.

"Lug and Erihu be with you," she said in return, making clear that she was still a pagan.

They laughed.

She knew who they were. "You cannot stop me," she told them fiercely, drawing the purple mantle even tighter.

"Yes, we can," said the woman with a most attractive smile. "We won't let you do it."

"I'm free to do what I want," the princess shouted defiantly.

"Most certainly," said the man in a resonant, tender voice. "But, gentle princess, you don't really want to jump. Just this minute you were thinking about hope." He was even more charming and persuasive than—

"I don't believe in hope. I don't believe in the two of you."

"Do you think, child, that it matters to us?" said the woman affectionately.

She wore a shining white cloak. The princess wondered where she got it.

"The Expected One will come," said the man. "You must wait for him. He needs your help. You must be here." He extended his hands as though he, too, were seeking her help.

"I am tired of waiting. He will never come." She was less certain now. Maybe these visitors *knew.*

"Waiting is praying, dear one," said the woman, "and praying will bring him. Now come away from this slippery and dangerous cliff." She put her hand gently on the princess's arm.

"I will not. You cannot make me." Her arguments were weakening. These folk were not fair. They put charms on you—such lovely charms.

"We will not make you do anything, dear princess," said the woman. "You want to go back and wait, so do what you want to do." She was a very confident woman standing strong and lovely in the wind.

Reluctantly the Princess Delvcaem turned her back on the angry sky and the morose ocean and walked slowly down the steep and rocky path, muttering at the suspicious goats who watched her.

Once she looked back. Her two friends were gone.

Chapter 18

Cormac sank his teeth into the last slice of the thick, sweet fruit. He wiped the juice off his beard. Smiling happily, the brown girl peeled another one for him and put a slice in his mouth, brushing her breasts against his chest. She kissed his ear as she drew back from him. Beneath them the tide was running out from the white beach back into the clear blue waters of the placid lagoon. The peaceful sun caressed him, bathing him in tranquil warmth. He had a lifetime of Irish cold to chase from his veins.

He dimly remembered the curragh of Brendan sailing across the smooth, rose-colored waters of the lagoon into the setting sun, its sail with the great Irish cross billowing in the fresh east wind. In his sickness he was angry because the Holy Sailor abandoned him. Now he realized that he had been too ill to continue the voyage. Brendan left him in the care of friendly natives, planning to return. After months of waiting he decided that the abbot's good luck finally had run out. Brendan had found his Land of Promise, though not in this life.

Soon he and the girl would climb down the rocky path to the warm sands of the beach to frolic in its waters. They would make love on the sand, then climb back up, eat a supper of fish and fruit as they watched the sun go down, playfully huddle in each other's arms, and make love again by moonlight. Not quite the Land of Promise Brendan had in mind, but satisfactory enough for a man who had forgotten almost everything from his past. He put his arm around the girl's thighs and drew her close.

Brendan and the other sailors were dead by now, Biddy and Podraig were dead. God alone knew whether anyone still lived in Tara. As punishment for his many sins, Cormac MacDermot had been sent into exile for the rest of his life. God in his mercy had made the exile pleasant.

The brown girl kissed him again, lingeringly this time. Perhaps he would not wait until after the evening meal. He patted her affectionately.

The sun cut a different path in the sky here than in northern lands. He guessed it was spring in Ireland. The weather was always pleasant; he had been here for most of autumn and winter. Close to Beltaine—two years since— He did not want to think about it.

Sun, warmth, good food, and the softness of her body dulled any desire to think. He had been a vegetable while he struggled back to strength; now he was an animal—well fed, comfortable, well loved. Guilt, fear, anger from the past were gone; he would not permit them to return. There were still dreams; but next to him each night was a quick cure for the pain of a dream. How had he gone so long without a woman? As long as he could not speak their language he had no responsibilities. He had worried, worked, and wondered long enough for one lifetime.

The girl read his thoughts. She unwound the wrap around her marvelous body, took his head in her hands, and moved his mouth against her. He enjoyed her, played with her in the lagoon, and then enjoyed her again.

His peace was destroyed the next morning. Offshore, in the light of the rising sun, the curragh of Brendan the Sailor sped briskly toward the beach, dipping oars sprinkling the bright water, the boat's slender wake slicing across the table-smooth sea. The brown girl ran out of their hut sobbing. She clung to him, her naked body tense with fear. He hugged her reassuringly. Why did not God leave him alone? He would not go back on that boat. He had found his Land of Promise; he would stay on it.

One of the men of the tribe came later in the morning, a question on his face. Cormac made signs he should tell the monks the castaway was dead. The man nodded, giving no hint of what he thought. These simple folk did not make moral judgments the way an Irishman would.

Cormac stayed in the hut, fearful of being seen by one of the monks. Brendan would remain several days to take on supplies for the trip home—if he was going home. Twice Cormac thought to seek him out, twice he changed his mind. The second time he was halfway down the side of the jungle-covered hill to the path on the other side of the beach. Grimly he had turned around.

The decision left him restless. The girl's anxious affection would not calm him. Returning to Ireland would accomplish nothing for him or for the country. Why did all the guilts and fears return at the sight of the old man's boat?

If he returned to Ireland, the brown girl would find another man—the islanders had no problem with such things. She would quickly forget him. Still, she cared for him more than anyone in Ireland did. It was foolish to think of going back. Did not the very sands, warm beneath his toes, plead with him to stay?

Their love was violent after sundown, the girl sensing that such was his mood and adjusting herself to it. His sleep was troubled—as it used to be when he was still King Cormac. His nightmares were formless, the green dragons with the red eyes from the cave on the Shannon bank returned, their frenzied, pounding chants in his ears. He was laughing uncontrollably again.

Then Biddy came to him—not the vague, hazy Biddy of other dreams but a clear, vivid young woman as solid and real as the rocks of Ireland. Her face was solemn, her eyes sad.

"Will you not come back to me, faithless master?" she asked him mournfully.

"Biddy, I cannot come back to you. You're dead. You died at Beltaine two years ago."

"If my royal master wishes me dead, then I must be dead." She bent her head, her long golden hair falling across her shoulders.

"It was my fault you died. I left you alone in Limerick," he replied sadly.

"If my cruel master wishes me to be alive, I will be alive." She smiled and extended her arms to him. "O Cormac, my beloved, please come back to me!" she pleaded.

He woke with a start. Biddy never smiled. Yet in this dream she did. Was it just a dream? He hurried out of the hut and down to the beach. He could see a figure there, the moonlight reflected on the yellow hair and red *leine.*

Biddy? He rushed toward her, wanting to fling himself into her outstretched arms. Then he could see her no more.

It was more than a dream. He was awake, he had seen her. A vision? A trick? A spell? His peace was gone. Again the brown girl attended to him, tried to comfort him. She knew his agony. Cormac wept—whether for the woman he would leave or the woman who called him home he did not know. Already the feel of the chill rain of an Irish winter was in him.

Cormac quickly sank back into the misty trance that had numbed his feelings and clouded his thoughts on the voyage two years before. There was little joy in seeing his old comrades despite their joyous welcome. Poor Brendan had aged greatly; the rest had been worn down by their journey like disabled veterans of a long war. Yet they were cheerful and he, in the full vigor of his youthful health, was as gray as Ireland before a summer rainstorm. They did not seem to notice.

Brendan turned over the steering oar to him. The old skills came back at once. He hardly had to think about them. He guided the boat from swell to swell on the fast moving current with the same inattention with which he used to ride his horse through the dark oak forests. He ached for the body of the brown girl and the luscious golden fruit, so like her willing breasts. There could be no return to her. Ireland was his fate, his destiny, his doom.

As they bounced over the purple waters so clear that they could see the fish swimming beneath them, he thought little of the vision of Biddy on the beach. It was a trick, a phantom from the Many-Colored Land come to trick him into returning to his doom. Brigid was dead.

Yet, on the starry nights, when the rest of the crew

slept, he dreamed of his pleasure as if she still lived, even smiling at memories of her witty tongue and her tiny clenched fists. A frail little rabbit she was, though rounding nicely into a woman, her pert buttocks so small that he could hold them with a single hand—not as soft and easy a conquest as the brown girl—still, a pleasant woman's body to have as your own—

Foolish, foolish thoughts, he told himself, keeping the prow of the swaying curragh pointed at the star Brendan had chosen. He drove off the thoughts as though they were a swarm of annoying flies. They did not vanish completely, however, but continued to buzz at the very back of his skull.

The ocean current on which they rode passed over shallow banks, sometimes seemingly only a few yards deep. Large fish played around the curragh, seeming to dance in the water as the monks chanted their hymns. The monks were afraid of some of the fish, thinking them to be so human as to be either damned souls or haunts from the Many-Colored Land. Brendan gently chided them for their foolish fears. Had not God brought them safely thus far? Would he now abandon them and turn them over to the powers of hell?

Yet, there had been one terrifying moment as they slipped over the brown and golden banks that raced beneath the sparkling waters. Cormac skillfully avoided the reefs in which the waters abounded; he had learned to detect the innocent rippling bubbles representing a sharp rock that might put a dangerous hole in the side of their craft. Yet without warning, he suddenly felt the whisper of sand under the boat. They had run onto a reef. Slowly the boat stopped, becalmed on what seemed to be a small island.

Cormac was baffled. No island should be there, surely not one this small. The white clouds drifted over their heads, and they did not move. Some of the monks wanted to get out and push the boat. Brendan ruled against it. At high tide they would float free if it were God's will. Cormac rubbed the smooth oak of the steering oar nervously. He did not like the island.

Suddenly the island leapt out of the water—the tide should not be changing that quickly. Then it dropped forward and dug into the ocean like a plow cutting into soft land; the curragh began to slide dizzily off the island, and then hung for a moment as though in an invisible hand above the now foaming water. Cormac desperately swung the steering oar in empty air and then was tugged away from his post by a crashing wave. Consciousness ebbed from his brain as waters poured into his lungs. Strange, he thought to himself, it is neither Biddy nor the brown girl I remember, but Queen Ethne—

Death released her icy grip and Cormac was conscious again, choking on seawater. The curragh wallowed in the light waves, listing badly to one side, half-filled with water. Brendan and a couple of the monks were already frantically working with wooden buckets, trying to return the ocean to its rightful place. A hundred yards away the great gray sea beast was swimming in a lazy circle around them.

They labored the rest of the day and into the full moonlit night. The poor old abbot had no strength left for such effort. Cormac took charge, though his body, soft from the pleasures of the island, demanded that he pause. Several times the beast charged the boat; the monks dropped their buckets and shouted frantic prayers for mercy at the end of their lives. Curtly Cormac ordered them back to work, while the ancient abbot laughed merrily about the marvelous jokes God's fair creatures play upon us.

Joke indeed, thought Cormac grimly to himself. The old man is no longer fit to command this boat. I'm going to have to bring it back to Ireland despite him. He shrugged his weary shoulders and dipped the bucket back into the waters in the bottom of the curragh. It was his destiny. There was no other choice.

They sailed on for many days. The air grew colder, the waves bigger. They left the banks behind and passed a great cloud-shrouded area where Cormac thought there might be a vast land. No time to explore. He had to get them home while the abbot still lived. Then they were on the open sea; the current and the wind, keeping their tattered sail still and taut against the mast, drove them ever to the northeast—closer to Ireland, he told himself. His actions were mechanical, the routines of an accomplished navigator. They must keep sailing; he'd forgotten the reason why, sometimes even where they were going. Often it seemed to him that his fate was to sail forever to the northeast. Then, as the light of the sun cracked the sky towards which they were racing, he remembered streaks of gold on brown hair—and vast blue eyes and an insidious little body whose tiny sweetness was so different from her harsh words—strange he could no longer even remember the words—

Then one morning there was more on the horizon than memories of Biddy—a great crystal column that reached to heaven itself, shimmering in the sunlight and rising out of the ocean like a mysterious city, sheathed in veils and mists. It took three days to come even with it—the column seemed to be moving in the same direction they were—a floating city—and then several more days until they were close enough to touch it; even, at the crazy old monk's insistence, to row their way into one of its small harbors.

It was not a city, but some rocklike floating mountain, made of jewels it seemed or perhaps one vast jewel. The monks were in superstitious terror of it; Brendan, now fully himself again, like a child with a new-found toy, was fascinated by it. Cormac merely wanted to continue the trip.

Finally, on one of its cold and rocky ledges they found a loose piece of the substance, shaped like a chalice. Brendan, turning pious and childish, announced that it was a chalice left there by King Jesus as a sign of his continued protection. Time now to go on to the green hills of Ireland. Cormac thought of the hills of Wicklow—he'd sung a song about them once—couldn't remember what it had been about—

Brendan yielded the command of the curragh back to Cormac, but getting out of the little harbor was more difficult than getting in—parts of the great column had cracked off and were blocking the entrance to the cove—a strange kind of crystal rock that floated. The crew had to push the floating rocks, some of them as big as a man's body, aside with their oars. As it was, Cormac thought they were lucky to get away. The rocks seemed bent on forming a fence that would contain them in the cove as though in a jeweled prison. Brendan called it a veil, which the powers of darkness were spinning to blind them. Always respectful of the abbot, Cormac resisted the urge to murmur that it was a veil made out of very solid material. He thought momentarily of the veils on the women of Ravenna—but that was in another lifetime.

Finally, they were free of the rocks and at Cormac's

urgent insistence pulled wearily on their oars to put several hundred yards between them and the column. Then the abbot quietly took the steering oar as Cormac slipped into heavy and dreamless sleep. He woke only once to see the crystal chalice that Brendan had removed from the column glittering in the moonlight—like a drinking goblet made of frozen snow, he thought to himself—and then plunged back into the chasm of sleep.

The next morning they were buried under fog, as though they were moving through a dark gray cave. One of the monks discovered that the chalice was gone. There was momentary panic, but Brendan replied that it was doubtless the holy cup in which King Jesus had first offered his precious blood at the first Lord's Supper. It was destined to be with them for only one night.

The magic cup? Cormac wondered. Might it have been on the boat with him for a few hours? No—it was a pagan magic cup he was pursuing—why he could not quite remember. Then later he crept up the boat to the little shrine where the chalice had received its brief night of honor. The oak-wood shelf was covered with water. Frozen snow indeed—the cup had been made of ice—the whole column—a mighty crystal mountain of ice. He thought about telling Brendan and the others and gave up the idea. All of them were a little bit mad—they had been away too long—too many days pulling on the oars, too many nights bouncing on the swells, too many drenchings with ice water, too many meals of dried beef, too many wounds infected with salt. How long would it take before he was as mad as the rest of them?—seeing angels and demons, gods and devils in every accidental occurrence of the voyage—

They sailed on. Finally, the fog lifted and there was

no sign of the ice mountain. Cormac relaxed. He did not want to encounter that monster again in the middle of the night, especially with the old man blathering about veils. Then eight days later they encountered another island which struck terror into even his heart.

The first sign of it was a thick greasy cloud, like an immense fire of animal fat, hanging ominously on the eastern horizon. Then there was a noise as of hammers pounding on a gigantic anvil. The air grew warm, then hot; the monks cast off the torn and battered cloaks they had been wearing. Finally, through the smoke they could see the island itself, shrouded in its huge mushroom-shaped cloud, belching fire like an angry dragon. A thick acrid odor, like a burning garbage heap, fouled the air.

"We must not land there," the sainted abbot screamed. "It is the devil's workshop; hear the bellows and the hammers on the anvil—it sounds like thunder—it is the devil's own thunder."

That was all that was needed to send the monks into new panic. Actually, the wind and the current were likely to carry them by the island without much chance to land on it even if they had pulled with all their might on their oars. Calmly Cormac urged the crew back to their work, reckoning that rowing would reduce their panic.

Then the island began to hurl fiery rocks at them. The fire at the center of the cloud leaped skyward and great pieces of the island came vomiting up with the fire and spread out over the ocean like a rainstorm of blazing rocks. For the first time since leaving the island Cormac was frightened. He remembered the legends he heard at Ravenna about what a fire-belching mountain had done to a Roman city years before. His voice under tense control, he ordered the monks to row for their lives.

Brendan was as frightened as anyone else.

"The devil's workers are throwing rocks at us, my brothers," he wailed. "See them running down to the shore with the rocks in great tongs. They want to sink us into the fiery depths of hell—strike out into the deep, raise the sail—Brother Connor, raise the sail—see the wind is coming—O Jesus Christ, free us from this island—"

Cormac ordered the sail up. There was no wind, yet something had to be done to calm the old man—the rocks were falling close, some only a score of yards away—one huge fiery mass, many times the size of the boat, less than a hundred yards away. The curragh swayed sickeningly, as it had done on the back of the sea beast, but this time it did not take on water. The rocks screeched through the air, like birds of prey diving on a defenseless victim. One of them is going to get us, Cormac thought helplessly.

Then the wind came—how did the old man know it would? and they pulled away from the devil's workshop—it did sound like a forge with thousands of giant blacksmiths at work—

The abbot was calm again. "Soldiers of Christ," he said expansively, "we are strengthened by the real faith and by spiritual arms because we are leaving the confines of hell. Be on your guard and act manfully."

It was as though he were preaching at the Lord's Supper back in his chapel at Conflert. Still, he knew the wind was coming when Cormac could see not the smallest hint of a breeze—

They sailed on, stopping for a day at a tiny rock jutting out of the sea where a solitary Irish monk lived. His name was Paul. Both Abbot Paul (as Brendan called him) and Brendan seemed persuaded that he was the Apostle Paul.

Cormac did not mention that the Apostle Paul had been beheaded outside the walls of the city of Rome—or so he had been told by the successor of Peter the Fisherman. Neither of the mad abbots would have cared about the successor to the Fisherman. Paul was more demented than Brendan and Kevin combined. He yearned for sane monks—Kiernan or even his lordly cousin Colum—how long had it been since he thought of Colum?—they must be getting close to Ireland. They sailed on.

It was a cold, rainy day at Lugnasa time when the curragh, the west wind blowing strongly at its back, sailed up the misty waters of the Shannon by Limerick and on to Clonfert. In the tiny stone chapel among the mud huts and wooden walls of the monastery, Cormac celebrated the feast of Mother Mary in Harvest with the old man and the rejoicing monks.

The voyage had been almost easy despite the terrors of the flaming mountain and the pillar of ice. He was weak from hunger and dizzy from the motion of the sea, but after a few days at Clonfert he was ready to travel again. He had thought that once he saw the rocky shores and the drab skies of Ireland he would forget the lovely paradise he left behind. The images of the blue sky and the sunny beach, the thick green forest, and the naked brown body of the girl would not leave him. Nor would the taste of the fruit, the warmth of the sun, and the feel of the girl's lips. Ireland was easier to forget than his paradise island.

Not a day passed that he did not curse himself for his folly. He knew in the depths of his soul that Biddy was dead. One night's guilty vision had brought him back to the land that he hated. Well enough for the monks to celebrate their return home; Ireland was no longer home for Cormac. He could not stay at Clonfert. If he was destined to wander about Ireland searching for magic goblets and princesses that did not exist, then he must begin to fulfill his destiny. It would not last forever; life did not last forever.

At Clonfert the monks knew little of Tara. King Dermot still reigned, they said; the white-haired witch still controlled him. There were wars and battles throughout the land. Outlaws, pirates, and fanatical culdees roamed at will. The harvests were bad this year—the worst of all. There was deep fear of famine.

Old Brendan gripped his arm affectionately as they walked slowly toward the gate of the mud walls of Clonfert. "Did I not tell you I would return to die in Ireland, O King of Tara? Did I not say that you would bring us back?"

The old man had visibly weakened since their return. He leaned on his walking stick like a cripple. Cormac helped him over a rock.

"Did I not say that it would be your skills which would bring us back? You will doubtless die in Ireland, holy monk, but I think God wants you to make many more voyages before that happens." Though Cormac was anxious to leave, he did not want to say farewell to Brendan, whom he would never see again in this world—and probably not in the next either.

Brendan laughed. "No, no, my boy. My time will soon be over. My destiny is finished. God will call me to the Land of Promise by another route this last time. I will voyage on the sea no more. Your destiny is already foretold by the Holy Abbess Finvolva. You must now find the queen with the brown and yellow hair."

"Where am I to find her, wise Brendan?" he pleaded, gripping his thick shillelagh like a sword instead of a walking stick.

"Ah, how can an old sailor tell a young king where to find his wife? Surely you will find her." He raised his hand in a frail benediction.

So Cormac, already mourning the dying Brendan, took his leave of the crude little monastery of Clonfert in a driving August rain. He walked slowly down the path through the newly harvested fields toward the gray waters of the Shannon, where a tiny curragh waited for him. He would begin again the hopeless search for his queen with the brown and yellow hair. Was she a magic princess or just a slave girl? The cold, stern rocks of the west of Ireland mocked his foolishness as he pushed his boat into the sluggish river current, heading back toward the gray ocean.

Chapter 19

P*ain and fear* spread through Cormac's body like a wasting disease. He was ready to die quickly and cleanly in battle, a noble Celtic warrior, but his nobility had been taken from him. He was a slave, not a warrior; he would die a slow, humiliating death, maddened by the agony of his suffering, pleading till the last minute with his tormentors for mercy.

He tried to move his wrists once more. The ropes were tight. The smallest movement of his pain-wrenched body was terrible agony. His wounds opened again, the soreness in his back and legs was like a devouring fire.

The final moments of agony the next day, the fear in this dank, cramped underground room where he was bound, were passing moments, he told himself. Soon the folly of his life would be finished. A thought of the western island and the brown woman flared briefly and then died. It was his destiny to leave that paradise behind, just as it was his destiny to wait in the ground underneath this pirate's rath to die on the morrow. One was a fool to fight one's destiny. Still the fear persisted. He was caught in its power, trembling in its sick embrace.

He prayed for the help of King Jesus to die bravely. He had not been brave during these weeks of slavery. You cannot be brave when you are hungry, sick, humiliated. For generations the pirates on these islands had perfected the art of breaking the spirit of their captives.

The island was a rocky hell where Hogshead, the grotesque pirate king, and his satanically beautiful wife Morrigan had made themselves god and goddess. Queen Morrigan's witchcraft was not the worst evil. The pirates would beat you almost to death, then come back to beat you again the next day. Today the beating had not been nearly as bad as when he first had tried to escape. Then he had hung in their torture room while men and woman tormented him with knives and whips. He prayed for death, but they knew how to keep a dying man alive. His wracked, bleeding body was a warning to prisoners and slaves not to try to flee their captors.

He would have been killed if the Princess Delvcaem, an evil daughter of an evil mother, had not suggested that he be kept alive to be humiliated more. "He was a great man in Ireland," she said. "Might it not be amusing to watch a great man grovel for food like a dog? There is no need for him to die now."

The queen and the pirate captains were delighted. He was turned over to the treacherous princess and her guards to be degraded to the state of a starving rat foraging garbage dumps. How easy it was to break the spirit of a king, to reduce a brave warrior to a sniveling animal. If only he would lose consciousness, then the fear shaking his body would leave him.

The princess did not tell her parents he was a king. Was there no one in Ireland who would pay a ransom for him? She desired vengeance for her own humiliation. What folly to think that it was his destiny to free her.

He was captured on a gray and rainy day on a beach in Mayo. He walked along the shore, weary of the search for his fellow pilgrims, his gray heart burdened with guilty memories. He did not hear the pirates behind him. His arms were pinned and the rope was around his neck before he knew what happened. He tried to struggle, but they were strong men and had the advantage of surprise and long experience in taking prisoners. He was soon as powerless as a pig prepared for slaughter. They threw him into the bottom of their curragh.

Two other prisoners were girls—gorgeous, red-haired twins. They had been pampered house slaves all their lives, used to gentility and comfort. The pirates knew that no physical force was necessary to restrain them. Threatening words kept them bound in terror; there would be no scars to mark the skins of slaves to be sold at a fine price. In his warrior's pride, Cormac wanted to defend them. He soon learned that on a pirate island a warrior's strength and pride were little good.

So he was turned over to the pirate princess and her two giant young bodyguards. She knew he was High King of Tara and could enjoy his humiliation to a base slave who cleaned latrines and hauled garbage from which he was permitted to steal his food.

"You were never humiliated this way," he said once, as she laughed at his searching desperately in the garbage for a crust of bread to eat.

"There are different kinds of humiliation," was her haughty reply.

She spoke rarely to him. The two guards untied him each morning in the underground room, damp, cold, and dark, and bound him again at night. They were not bad fellows—strong young men who had been pressed into service as part of the tribute Morrigan and Hogshead exacted from the mainland villages near the island. They put salve on his wounds and gave him potions which eased his pain. They also brought him food at night. Slowly his strength returned. He continued to eat garbage. If the young men were found out, his supply of food would be cut off.

The pirate queen and her captains thought his spirit was broken. They grew tired of watching him. The discipline in the pirate rath was slipping. Too much success, too much plunder, too much torture. With a few stouthearted warriors he could destroy this nest of devils. The legend of their invincibility had terrorized the shores of Connaught, but at the center of their power they were overconfident and vulnerable.

In his first attempt he did not know about the sentinels who guarded the small beach that was the only place on the craggy island where a boat could land. This time, with a sword and a shield, under cover of night, he would be a match for them. He didn't trust himself. Prolonged humiliation had broken his confidence, the long period of semistarvation had sapped his strength. He must strike the fine balance between his slowly returning physical strength and more rapidly declining spirit.

Now it didn't matter. He had neither strength nor spirit. The daylong beating left him bleeding, weak; he would not be untied until the test. No one survived the test.

When the pirate guards dragged him to Morrigan's bathing chamber, the sight of her as she sat naked in the copper tub attended by the terrified red-haired twins infuriated him.

"So, worthless slave, you seem to have grown fat on our garbage. Perhaps now you are strong enough to provide other services for us, services that ought to be more pleasant than cleaning latrines."

She grinned lewdly and arched her body out of the water in his direction.

Her hair was still jet black, her lips full; her smooth-skinned body was well kept and beautifully shaped with large breasts, a slender waist, and trim legs. Cormac felt a stab of lust; then revolted by disgust he spat on her face and paid for what was left of his warrior honor with a day of terrible pain. He was sure that this time they would kill him.

Morrigan intervened. "Gentle friends, if we continue our entertainment, this wretch will soon be dead. That would be a shame, would it not? It has been a long time since we've had the test. Would not this honorable warrior be an excellent prospect for that supreme entertainment?"

Her evil laugh tore at his spirit the way the whips and clubs had torn at his flesh.

The four pirate captains—one from each of the large boats—shouted with delight. The test was something they enjoyed. Morrigan was their commander, the gross old Hogshead only a figurehead king. Her amusements were their amusements.

Cormac was fainting from the pain of his bleeding body. He cared not about their amusements or their tests. Then there was blackness.

He woke up in his underground prison. Cathal and Connor, the friendly guards, were carrying him down the narrow steps, trying to avoid hurting him more.

"We cannot untie you, slave Cormac," said one of the black-bearded boys timidly. "The captains will notice it, and we too will be beaten."

"What is the test I am to face?" he asked weakly as they laid him on the stone floor. His teeth were clenched with pain, his voice strained with it.

"It is with the magic cup." Cathal hesitated. "You eat dinner with the king and queen and the pirate captains. They offer you a choice of two wine cups. If you choose the magic cup you may have whatever you demand on the island; if you sip from the wrong cup, you die from its poison. Men take days to die but they always die."

"An even chance then?"

"No one wins. She puts a spell on the prisoner. He thinks he chooses right, but he always gets the wrong one. His surprise provides much amusement."

He lost consciousness again. When he awoke much later he was hot with fever. Hell could be no worse.

"You are a fool, Cormac MacDermot," said a familiar voice. "Could you not have flattered an old woman's vanity? Would it not have made our escape easier?"

"Make love to your mother?"

"She is not my mother. Queen Ethne is the only mother I knew.

"Drink this potion," she went on. "It will ease the pain. I do not know why I bother with you, King Cormac. I had everything ready to escape. Cathal and Connor are loyal to me. I have promised them the two red-haired maidens. Poor children, they need brave protectors. Why did you have to ruin it? Was it not clear to you that I conspired to free us? Did you think I meant those terrible things I said? Have you no more faith in me than that?"

She forced the drink down his throat.

"If I ever escape, I promise you the punishment of a runaway slave. I will flay every bit of skin off your body. You will be sorry you were ever born!" Rage drove off his fear for a moment.

"If that is what my master wishes to do, may he not do it?" She began to rub salve in his wounds. Her fingers were still gentle as the faint wind of a spring sunrise.

"Let me die in peace, evil woman," he begged. "Why keep me alive for more pain tomorrow?" He was losing consciousness again.

"It will not be tomorrow," she said impatiently. "I told them that you would die quickly from the poison if they did not give you a few days to recover from the beating. Fools. I need time to prepare a new escape." She probed another wound, pulling back quickly when he winced.

"Time to prolong my death agony," he said bitterly through teeth grinding in agony.

"Do be still, silly man. I'm not going to let you die. You must have strength by the time of the test. Besides, we will need you at the oar of the boat."

He tried to say something more hateful. Words would not come. Blackness fell over him.

Her voice again. There was a gray light coming down the narrow ladderway. It must be daytime. "If you will not open your mouth, I cannot get this broth in you. I promise you, King Cormac, I will not let you forget ever again how much trouble you made for me on this island. You think Biddy's tongue was sharp before—" She put her hand softly on his cheek.

He was too weak to move more than his mouth which

opened to receive nourishment, then opened again for more.

"That's better. You're beginning to show some of the intelligence of which the bards sing. Now listen to me carefully, darling one, because I may not be able to see you again. Eileen and Grainne are braver than I thought they could be, poor children. They will be with us at the feast tomorrow night. Before you come, the evil woman will pour the poison into the false goblet and give it to one of them. The magic cup—remember the magic cup you have sought so long, poor, dear Cormac?—will be given to the other one. Before the test the witch will ask you what you want if you are victorious. You tell her that you want me and the red-haired maidens. When it comes time for the test, the maiden with the magic cup will have two fingers pointing upward on the front of it. The witch's spell will be strong; you will think you know with certainty that the other maiden holds the magic cup. Believe me, not her. Take the cup with the two fingers on it. If the spell is too strong, I will have to stop her at the last second. You must be prepared to fight. She will not give up easily. If there is a battle, we will flee to the boats and wait for the morning tide. With three men we can fight the sentinels. Remember, the cup with the two fingers. Then you'll have the cup and the princess—you can do with them whatever is your pleasure."

"It is all a fiendish trick," he snarled.

The spoon stopped short of his mouth. "Damn you, Cormac MacDermot, will you ever cease to be a proud fool?"

He wanted to strangle her. He pulled with all his strength. The girl jumped back in alarm.

"That's very wise, learned king. Injure your wrists

again. It will be even harder to swing your sword against these demons. For nothing did I make them change the ropes."

Her voice was tight with rage. He fought against her challenging him back to life. "You are the devil reborn, you worthless slut. I'll pull you apart limb from limb!"

"Yesterday you were sick; you did not know what you were saying. Today you do. I shall forget none of these words. —It does not matter, you will still do what I want. You always have, dear one." Her voice softened. Again he felt a touch on his face. Something old and deep stirred in his soul. He groaned in agony.

"Be still, I'm going to kiss you. I've waited long enough; I'll wait no longer. Know, you seeker of the magic cup, that you are a proud, arrogant, cruel, worthless man; and Biddy loves you."

It was the kiss of an inexperienced woman—hesitant and tentative. Her hand on his face was like the first light of dawn after a long, dark night. His anger ebbed. The pain was still great, but what had happened to his fear? Damn the girl, she always won.

"That was nice. I think I'll do it again." Her lips this time were warmer, open, seeking his with passion. Was the little wench capable of lust? He must not respond. He did not want to hope, he did not want the pain of returning life.

"I'm getting better, don't you think?" she said brightly. "I will take advantage of having you captive to do it once more. Next time you will have to be the brave one." This time she was fierce and hungry, demanding a response. Cormac's lips answered without his willing them to. Hunger leaped to hunger, passion to passion. "Wicked, lustful master," she said playfully, laying her head on his breast. "Oh, my sweet, wonderful Cormac, what a sad place to exchange our love. We will tell our grandchildren about it as though it was a great adventure."

A brisk kiss on the forehead and she was gone. Cormac sank back into unconsciousness.

He awoke to the darkness of pain and fear. Somewhere in his brain there was a tiny light shining, a pinpoint of hope. He strove to blow it out. He did not want the extra suffering. The light did not flicker. He blew harder. The light was unwavering. It seemed to grow brighter. Something broke inside him. It hurt to smile.

Chapter 20

Cormac *was enjoying* himself immensely. His woman was frowning. She was worried because he was too much the charming courtier at Morrigan's feast. The pirates might be suspicious. *Fear not, little one. I won't endanger your clever scheme. If I could only get my hands on one of those swords, we'd see how much cleverness is needed.* His throat was already dry.

The pirates were drinking lustily. They expected no battle tonight. The hall was built of thin wood, now very dry from the lack of rain. The walls would burn like straw. Across the table Hogshead was getting very drunk; his obese body and ugly, bloated face made him look like one of the wild boars whose heads and tusks adorned the wall behind him. The red-haired twins sat on stools by the same wall in thin gowns, shivering from the cold wind that blew through holes in the walls. He hoped their voluptuous beauty would inflame the two young giants lurking at the edge of the chamber. Morrigan was in black, looking like a sleek, black panther he had seen in Rome. Tonight made dinner with the Roman nobility seem like a meeting of pious monks.

They had dressed him in a saffron tunic with a blue *crios* and cloak. He was cleaned and anointed—and bandaged—as if he were the honored guest. Blue and saffron—kingly colors.

Outside, the wind howled ominously. The banshees were abroad tonight. There would be a thunderstorm, prelude to a mighty storm that would come in a day or two. They would have to get to land before the storm was upon Ireland.

"So frown if you will, gentle pagan maid," he thought. "I know I am wounded and weak. There is still pain in my body, but I have a strength you have never seen before, you lovely little wench."

Lovely she was. Her hair was long and very blond now. Her pale green dress sheathed a body that was lithe and trim, softly round and inviting. There were not enough demons in Ireland to keep her from his arms tonight.

He sang, told stories, paid compliments to Morrigan. Hogshead sniffled and mumbled, wallowing in drink. His heavy sword was near, but he would have to get to it to use it. The pirate captains were growing nervous; they had never seen a test candidate so confident. Morrigan responded to compliments with compliments of her own—a cat toying with a mouse.

Cormac mentioned the evening's entertainment first. "Do I understand that I am permitted to choose whatever I want on this island before we begin?" She nodded. "Will you swear that it will be mine if I choose the right goblet?"

The noise in the room stopped. Grainne, the twin on the right, cautiously lifted two fingers, Eileen raised only one. Good enough, the cup on the right was the magic cup.

The cat-woman smiled. "You seem certain that you will win, brave warrior."

Cormac feigned drinking another draught of wine. He was sure it was drugged. He carefully poured it on the straw-covered floor when no one was looking. "The odds are better than in most wagers," he said ingratiatingly to the queen. "One must be prepared. If it is true that I get whatever I want, I want the three most beautiful women here, saving yourself, of course, to leave the island with me."

Morrigan's green eyes clouded. She knew he meant Biddy. Was there any love at all for one who might be her daughter? Was Delvcaem part of her demonic vanity?

"What will you do with the princess?" she asked anxiously.

"To answer that question is not part of the test. Will you not swear to give me what is mine if I win?" His mouth was now very dry, the battle fever was on him. He must wait till just the right moment.

She smiled slyly. "Of course. I swear by Lug and Erihu that you will have the three maidens—if you win the test." She had regained most of her confidence, though for a moment she had feared him.

"And your husband the king, does he swear too?" Cormac insisted.

She nudged the fat old man. He mumbled something that might have been an oath. Smiling up at him, her voice venomous, she said, "Do you wish the test now, O lustful warrior?"

"Now? If it is the proper time. I thought it would occur only when the meal is over."

Her eyes clouded. He had shaken her once more. He looked at Biddy. Her frown was gone. "Thank you, darling," he thought. "I have done something on my own of which you approve—finally."

He deliberately delayed the end of the meal. It was a battle of wills to determine whether he or Morrigan would call for the test.

Impatiently she rapped on the table. "It is time, loudmouthed fool, for you to meet your destiny."

The room fell silent, the silence of death. Morrigan rose from her elaborately carved throne—stolen, no doubt.

"We continue, brave friends, a custom as old as this island. One of these fat wenches holds the sacred cup of our island, which promises to all who find it whatever happiness they desire in this world; the other opens to them the happiness of the Land of Promise in the West—"

A pirate captain giggled.

"—Our honored visitor has pleaded for an opportunity to test which happiness will be his. We have acceded to his humble plea. If he chooses the magic cup, he will receive the three most beautiful maidens on our island and is free to leave our company. If he chooses the other cup—we will console him as he voyages to the Land of Promise."

Her eyes locked on Cormac's. A cold chill swept his body, reawakening his pains and fears. He looked away, seeking the great blue lights in the face of his beloved. God, it was good to have a woman so proud of you. He turned back to Morrigan. She still stared, but some of the power was gone.

He remained seated at the table, playing with a ham bone. "I am grateful, O wise king and O so-beautiful queen, for the pleasant interlude I have had here on your lovely island and for the splendid entertainment of the evening. I agree that it is now time to bring the amusements to an end." He smiled.

The wind was louder; the candelabrum in front of him could turn the straw on the floor into a raging fire in a moment. Yes, it was time. He stood up.

"Come, lovely lasses, bring your wine cups."

The hall whirled around him. He was lightheaded. He knew that the cup on the left hand, the one held by the girl who supported its stem with one finger, was the cup he should take. He knew this with absolute certainty. If only the hall would hold still—

He glanced at the cupbearers. The wenches had marvelous bodies. Lust for one woman and you lust for all women. Who was the one woman? Brigid. She had lied to him. She said the cup on the right was the one he should take. It was filled with deadly poison. Where was that traitorous woman? He looked around for her.

She stood next to the king, watching Cormac intently. What was it she had said? What was the light? Nothing important—but what was it? He remembered. The spell broke. He laughed. The intent gaze of Morrigan was broken. *Now, King Jesus, I must fight!*

She knew that the spell had been destroyed. "Who are you?" she screamed.

Again his most pleasant smile. "I am Cormac MacDermot O'Neill, Boaire of Royal Meath and High King of Ireland. I have come to destroy forever this hill fort of demons." He twisted the magic cup from the fingers of the cowering Grainne and drained its wine in a single swallow. He grabbed the other cup and with full battle lust upon him hurled it in the face of Queen Morrigan.

The pirate queen screamed with pain. Recoiling from the table, she impaled herself on a wild boar's tusk, which pierced her body and came out beneath her breast. Blood poured out as she shouted her death agony. Hogshead rose from a table, groping dully for his sword.

Cormac seized a weapon from a pirate near him and slashed the king's throat with a single mighty swing. The king's blood mingled with that of his wife, his death cry drowning out hers.

The pirates, over their first shock, were jumping to their feet. Cormac leaped on the table and knocked the candleholder to the straw. It clattered to the floor like a rock signaling a mountainslide. Instantly a sheet of fire rose up. Throwing more candles against the wall and still others at the advancing pirates, he looked anxiously around for Biddy. Where was she? He saw her fall to the floor, the magic goblet clutched in her tiny hand. Two pirate captains stood in his way. With quick thrusts they were finished. Pulling her to her feet and supporting her with one arm, he fought his way to the hall entrance. The place was turning into a Beltaine bonfire. Pirate women screamed, their men cursed—all struggled to get away through the thickening smoke. In the press of human bodies, Biddy stumbled. Roughly he dragged her on—he was not going to lose her now. Out of the corner of his eye he saw one black-bearded giant with a screaming maiden. "King Jesus, protect them!" he prayed.

Outside the building the wind screamed. Cormac pushed his sword into his belt, lifted Biddy in his arms, and ran toward the beach. The smell of burning wood was thick in his nose; mixed with it was the sick, sweet smell of burning flesh. He plunged into the small forest that separated the rath from the beach, the wind tearing at his tunic and his hair. Biddy was shouting. "What are you saying, woman?" he demanded fiercely.

"Put me down! Put me down!" she screamed. "Look out—!"

He collided with a tree. A jolt of pain shot through him. Briefly there was blackness. Biddy was shaking him. There was no need to run anymore. She helped him to stand. They were away from the fire, no one pursued them. He steadied himself against a tree. What was he supposed to do now?

"The others," cried Biddy.

"Did they get out?" He tried to clear the fog out of his head. The heat of the fire seemed very near them.

"I saw them near the door when we came out. They are to meet us in a cave by the beach—back in the rocks." She began to run down the hill. Groggily he staggered after her, pausing to look back at a giant pillar of fire reaching for the sky. Not many pirates would escape.

A white light slashed the sky. The storm was coming. A thunder roll announced the rain, which soaked the two of them. The torrent would put out the fire before it spread to the rest of the rath and killed the prisoners and servants.

Finally the beach. His breath came in great agonized gulps as he followed the lithe Biddy around the rocks into a tiny cave. He sank to the floor gasping for braath. Outside the rain fell in thick, heavy sheets; lightning illuminated the nearby islands and the distant shore of Ireland, sometimes only a thin black line above huge white walls of surf.

Gradually his breathing grew easier. The pain was still in his arms, legs, and back, driving the thought of what he must do next from his mind. What was it? Oh, yes. He seized the gasping shape next to him, held her very tightly. "I promised you punishment, wicked slave girl."

He kissed her as wildly as he had swung his sword in the flaming banquet hall—hair, eyes, lips, cheeks, throat, shoulders, arms, breasts. She was soft and submissive in his arms. Something sharp cut into his chest.

He stopped to catch his breath. Taking the magic cup from her hands, he set it down beside them. "You don't have to hold this just now."

"Surely I have been more wicked than my punishment so far," she sighed.

"I have only begun, woman. It will go on for many days."

He pushed the wet gown off her shoulders. His fingers delicately probed the soft skin of her breasts. She trembled beneath his touch, but did not pull away. The feel of her body made his fingers quiver. His eyes filled with tears. *Dearest Biddy, how sweet you are. I am your master and your slave. Your flesh is so soft and warm. I can never escape from the prison in which it holds me. Your body is my world. I will spend my life protecting this soft, yielding warmth. Oh, Biddy, my dearest one.*

"I was coming to Limerick two years ago to do this to you," he said through his tears.

"Am I worth waiting for?" she asked dubiously.

"Evil, sinful woman." He pulled the wet *leine* around her shoulders and put his arm around her waist. She was an inexperienced maiden. He could have her now; it would be better to wait until she was ready. She understood and hugged him in gratitude. The final conquest of Biddy must be slow and patient.

They clung to one another in happy silence, listening

to the pounding rain on water, the screaming wind, and the roar of thunder that accompanied the wild light flashes exploding over the bay.

"They were going to violate me, when they saw the scar on my back. Then they brought me here," she said simply. "I discovered that I was Delvcaem. It was funny at first, then terrible. I was to replace Morrigan as witch. I knew you'd come."

"You were right." He kissed her again. "Podraig?"

"They tried to strangle him, then threw him in the river. He was not dead, I think." She kissed him so tenderly he thought his heart would break with the fragility of her lips. Now she was crying too.

"Did you believe that I had betrayed you? I couldn't give you a hint because it would have been death for both of us if you blurted it out. You were very sick, my poor beaten darling. I told the two boys to take care of you. Did you think they would have done it without my order?"

What was there to say? He was tempted to lie. Life with Biddy would eventually require truth; better to begin with it. "I have been away from you so long, I had forgotten what a brave, loyal, shrewd woman you are."

"Ummmm, that is nice. You're forgiven." She snuggled close to him. "Cormac—I really do not want to be a shrew—but you are hurt—you've been through a night of battle. We must sail home to Ireland tomorrow, and—"

"How can I sleep at a time like this?" he protested.

"It will be very easy. You just put your poor tired head on me—now I put my arms around you and stroke your hair as though you were my little boy—" The bells in her voice were pealing joyously. She began to croon softly in his ear, kissing him between verses.

How could he sleep? He was soaking wet, a storm was raging outside, his blood was still hot from the fierce battle in the banquet hall, he had his woman back.

In a few moments he was asleep.

Chapter 21

"*Wake up, fierce,* sleepless lover." A gentle voice taunted him.

He opened his eyes.

Biddy was bedraggled from the rainstorm. Her hair hung in tangled strings. She held a slab of cheese in her graceful fingers, teasing him like a pet animal.

He took her firmly in his arms, pulled her against his reclining body, and kissed her. She drew back slowly. The wind was less noisy; he could see blue sky through the narrow cave entrance.

"We must find Cathal and Connor. I fear for them," she said anxiously, but resisted not the comfort of his arms.

She put the cheese in his mouth, since his hands were still around her waist. One could, after all, eat cheese and kiss a girl. He finished the cheese and reluctantly released his woman. "We will find them," he said, trying to sound confident. He knew the pirates could purchase a small herd of cattle with those two lovelies. How good were the young fishermen as fighters? He sat up, now wide awake. He wanted to kiss her again. No, there was work to do.

"There are dry clothes back there." She pointed to the back of the cave, eyes averted in embarrassment.

"Then give me that brown tunic, honored lady, and I will leave you in your chamber while you prepare for the day." He spanked her playfully, something he had wanted to do for a long time. She squealed and smiled, dimming the light of the sun which had chased off the thunderstorm as night ended.

"You never smiled at me before, Brigid. It is well that you didn't; I would not have been able to resist you."

Her smile vanished. The old grim solemnity reappeared. It battled the smile and lost. She kissed him and shoved him out into the morning sunlight. "You have no respect at all for a woman's privacy."

Their playfulness was forgotten by the end of morning after a grim search for the twins and their protectors.

The wind had diminished, the sea was quieting. Large white clouds sped across the sky toward the bay and the mainland in the distance. The silence of death and the smell of roasted human flesh hung over the island. Soon they would have to leave to escape the coming storm.

They scaled the steep path up the hill toward the pirate's rath. Cormac heard the sound of rocks falling above them and pulled his woman off the path. They climbed up through the thick woods to the edge of a clearing. The pain in his body made it hard for him to move. He knew that he would soon have to quit.

The clearing was less than twenty yards wide, the ledge of a small cliff. Connor and Cathal had taken refuge in a hollow at the base of the cliff wall—a good place to avoid the rain and to fight off attackers but a bad place for escape. Five pirates surrounded them. Hunger and thirst would drive the black-bearded giants out. The pirates threw rocks into the hollow, forcing them to move to avoid the deadly stones. The two girls looked like trapped rabbits, waiting for the mercy of death.

"Poor children," whispered Biddy.

"Be quiet, old woman."

Cormac knew he was not strong enough to fight five men. They didn't know that. He had destroyed their king and queen and stolen the princess and the magic cup. They were probably superstitious enough to think him some kind of divine being. He walked out of the woods.

"I thought I had persuaded you last night that you should not defy the High King of Ireland. Must I give you another lesson?" He put his hand to his sword.

The five pirates scurried up the hill.

"Indeed, you are the greatest soldier in Ireland!" Biddy exclaimed proudly.

"Be careful, woman, paying me compliments could become a habit." He kissed her brazenly. The four young people climbed hesitantly out of their trap, reluctant to disturb the romancing of the king.

"Are you truly the High King of all of Ireland?" asked Cathal fearfully.

"I am," said Cormac, quickly grabbing for his sword hilt the way a king should—but keeping his other hand on Biddy's backside.

"Will you then accept the service of two simple fishermen?" Both of them fell to their knees before him.

The Irish will turn anything into a solemn ceremony. He gripped the huge hands of the young men and said,

"Of two brave and stronghearted fishermen, a king has much need." He must do this ceremony right. What next? Oh, yes—He turned to the twins, who cowered shyly at the edge of the rocky clearing. The boys had had the decency to wrap them in cloaks. "You are bondwomen?" he asked sternly.

The shapely children were quaking with fright. "All our lives, master," said Grainne—or was it Eileen? No matter. "Our master was going to sell us when the pirates came."

How much misery in that simple explanation. "How can women remain slaves when their bravery has saved the life of the High King?"

"I don't know, my lord."

"Lovely girls should smile at their king, not tremble in his presence." He took a soft, graceful hand of each and kissed it. They were truly luscious beauties, especially when their oval faces colored to match their hair. "Then it must be that you are now free. Will you follow the gentle princess?" He smiled his most reassuring smile. These two full-bosomed wenches could adore him any day they wished.

"Oh, yes, master," they responded eagerly.

"You, Connor and Cathal, will you protect these young women in the free service of our magic princess?" He turned solemnly to the two lads.

"We will, O High King, gladly."

They sounded as though they would enjoy their work. Lucky boys. Cormac tried to keep a straight face. The ceremony was a farce, but the young people loved it. To keep from laughing, he kissed the twins on their flaming cheeks, then extended his arms over the four youths in blessing. "Be loyal to the princess and good to one another," he instructed them severely, trying to sound like Abbot Colum.

He glanced at Brigid. No frown. She approved.

They hurried back down the hill toward the beach. Biddy dropped back with him to whisper in his ear. "You have learned kindness, King Cormac." She dug her fingers into his arm. "It will not be necessary to kiss the twins again." She was grinning happily.

The three men quickly loaded food and water on one of the large boats. Cormac slashed the leather hide on the other with his sword. The escaped prisoners would be able to use the smaller craft. The three women were bundled into the curragh wrapped in warm cloaks, Biddy clutching the magic cup.

The men pushed the boat out onto the water, felt the sting of the cold ocean on their legs, and quickly heaved themselves into the craft. The salt water stabbed at Cormac's wounds. The young men grabbed the oars; he took the tiller. Deftly he steered them by a pile of jagged rocks.

"You steer well, O High King," said Cathal.

"King Cormac does all things well," answered Biddy, laughing merrily despite the swaying of the boat. Cormac felt his face turn red. What was he to do with the woman?

Already the wind was beginning to howl again. Gray clouds, which had driven the white ones out of the sky, opened. Ireland was lost in swirling fog and driving rain. Their tiny craft was driven back to sea.

For four long days they were battered by the fierce north wind. The two young oarsmen were skilled at keeping the boat's prow into the waves. From his long days with Brendan, Cormac knew what to do in a storm with the stern oar. But weariness took its toll. His own body was still weak; many of his wounds were caked with burning salt. Often the boat slipped to the side and icy water poured over them. The cold waters of the ocean drenched their mantles, seeped through their tunics, ate into the skin, penetrated to the depths of their bones with a chill that seemed destined to last till Judgment Day.

The women were sick; they could only weakly help bail out the sea. His poor Brigid was the sickest of them all, hardly able to keep down a swallow of water.

The days were only a little less dark than the nights. Roaring winds and pounding waves deafened them. Sometimes the fog was so thick they could see only a boat-length ahead. The others prayed; Cormac was too tired. It was all up to King Jesus anyhow. He just clung to his steering oar and waited for the end—whatever it might be.

The clouds vanished as quickly as they had come; the wind diminished. A roof of blue appeared again over their heads. The waves turned into huge, gentle swells. The curragh bobbed along, drifting slowly towards the land that beckoned to them under the morning sunlight.

Headlands, green fields, wide brown beaches—all looked familiar. Could it be Dingle, that land from which he had sailed with Brendan? He inspected his crew—much more attractive than Brendan's monks, no doubt, but not such good sailors. He wouldn't want to have to navigate the great ocean with them. He thought pleasantly of all the stories he could tell his Brigid about the great voyage. He would leave out a few things.

His poor little one smiled up at him from the bottom of the boat, a wan, brave smile. He would sail the great ocean again for such a smile.

Swells carried them toward a channel between a gigantic

headland and a small group of islands. He did not like the small beaches on the headland or the foaming waters that suggested deadly rocks beneath. He urged the two fishermen to one last effort. They cleared the headland and drifted into a large bay with sharp cliffs on one side and the tallest mountains Cormac had ever seen in Ireland on the other. Inside the bay the swells became gentle rollers sweeping toward the base of the bay. Cormac relaxed.

In the distance there was a line of surf glinting in the sun. Behind it was a low green meadow, stretching almost the width of the bay, a sandbar turned into beach.

"Only a little while longer, brave friends, and we will be on the sands of Ireland. King Jesus brings us home."

Cathal and Connor cheered weakly. The twins moaned with relief. Biddy's hand clutched his ankle. Lovely little hand.

They were almost upon the beach when the curragh hit something hard, pitched drunkenly to one side, and heeled over. There should be no rocks on a flat beach like this, he thought to himself as he was hurled through the air toward the water.

There was the chill of the water, the sting of salt again in his wounds, a brief glimpse of Biddy's face, a sharp blow on the back of his head, then nothing.

Beneath his fingers the sand seemed warm. He was cold and wet. Without opening his eyes he knew the sun was bright. Was he in the Land of Promise finally? Near him was the sound of a body being rent by retching. He tried to open his eyes but they would not move. He tried again. Slowly they opened. Sand, dune grass, water, gentle surf. Next to him a naked body writhing in pain. A woman's body.

"How many times must I drag you the last distance to

safety, clumsy king? You are strong until the end, then a poor, frail woman must save you." Another spasm interrupted her complaint. Even blue with cold and sick from the salt water, it was a delicious body.

"Cormac," this time it was a sob. "I have lost the magic cup. We must find it—Oh God, our friends—! We must find them first!"

Somewhere a dog barked.

They would begin to search—if only he could move.

The barking grew louder.

He opened his eyes.

A great, shaggy wolfhound bounded up, wagging his huge tail and howling with joy.

Podraig circled his two old friends, yapping, jumping, running. Biddy won the first embrace.

She snuggled up to the big dog. "Oh, you silly dog. Now King Cormac will think you love me more than him."

Podraig leaped on his master and began to lick his face enthusiastically.

"Slowly, faithless hound, I will not go away again." He hugged his dog. Podraig was healthy and well fed. He must have adopted some humans as foster masters. They would be near. Would they be friends? After his time with the pirates, Cormac expected enemies.

In the distance there was a flurry of sand. A horse galloped down the beach.

Cormac had only a tiny knife to defend himself and his woman. He pulled off his tunic and draped it over the prostrate Brigid. Knife in hand, the barking dog by his side, he waited for the single rider. Farther down the beach more sand stirred. Other riders. If he could get the sword of this one—

The rider was a young man, slender and fair. He reined in his splendid white horse. "Hail, O High King. Welcome to the kingdom of Kerry! I am Donal O'Donnal, ruler of these lands. We are honored that the King of Tara visits us." Then, as though embarrassed that he had so long ignored the nakedness of the sacred one, Donal bounded off his horse and hastily threw his cloak around Cormac's shoulders.

He shuddered at the sight of the wounds and welts. "Must the body of the High King suffer such hurts?"

Cormac clasped the extended hand of Kerry's king. "Small price to meet a new friend in time of need, Donal O'Donnal. This is Princess Brigid, also called Delvcaem."

The lump of soggy brown tunic rose from the beach with dignity and modesty. She smiled and extended her hand. "It was good of King Donal to come to welcome us." Cormac thought how lovely her bare shoulders were.

"Had we known that the magic princess was here, my wife Begha and all her women would have come."

Thank God he had a wife.

"How did you know it was I on the beach? You have never been in Tara."

"Does not the whole of the west know that you destroyed the pirate stronghold only a few days ago? And does not everyone know that Cormac's wolfhound had come to Kerry? When the good dog began to run toward Inch—the name of this poor beach—we knew you must be here."

The other riders approached and raised their spears in respectful salute. Now that he was a king again, Cormac tried to think what came next.

"The others," whispered Biddy.

"O graceful Donal, some of my band were on the boat before we were thrown out. They may be injured on the beach. Will you ask your men to search—?"

The men of Kerry spread out in all directions on the sand. Cormac and Donal helped Brigid to a flat, raised rock on the edge of the dune grass. Donal wrapped a warm cloak around her shoulders. She was still very sick. Her pride would not let her show any sign of it to the King of Kerry. She held her head high, her body gracefully erect. Not yet a queen but already acting like one, marveled Cormac proudly.

"I will gather wood for a fire to keep you warm until your friends are found." Already captivated by Biddy's charm, the king went off to search for driftwood.

As soon as he was gone, she was desperately sick again.

The warmth of Donal's fire brought color back to her face and strength to Cormac's body. Every muscle wanted to sleep.

A horseman rode up to the fire, his face lined with concern. The king leaped to his feet.

"We found your friends and their boat, King Cormac. They are alive, but one of the red-haired maidens is near death."

Donal jumped on his horse; Cormac replaced the messenger on the other animal. Brigid ordered him to lift her up beside him. They raced down the beach, wind blowing their hair, sand cutting at their faces. Podraig galloped along. At the very tip of the land called Inch they saw the wreckage of their boat, a group of Donal's men huddled around a fire. Cormac sprang from his horse, paused a moment to lift Biddy down, and pushed their way through the circle of Kerrymen. One of the maidens was on her back, her arms and legs quivering in tormented spasms, her lips trembling, her face purple. Her sister wept by her side. The two fishermen were trying to hold their cloaks on the girl's shaking limbs.

"Oh God," said Brigid, clutching Cormac's hand. "She is dying."

"The sickness, the cold, the water—all too much," mumbled Cathal, his voice choked with grief.

"Can you not do something, magic princess?" asked Donal.

Biddy was startled. "What can I do?"

"She does not want to live anymore," wailed the dying girl's sister. "She has suffered too much." Soon there would be another red-haired maiden who would not want to live.

"Pray to King Jesus for me as you never prayed before," whispered Biddy.

Cormac took the hand of the sick girl. It was as cold as the north wind. He tightened his grip. "Live, sweet child," he prayed.

Biddy pushed Cathal aside and knelt on the beach next to the shuddering girl. "What kind of a worthless servant are you, Grainne? Will you be leaving me with this useless sister of yours and these clumsy boys? What good will they be? If you are going to die, should you not take them along with you?"

She was shouting in the girl's ear. The circle of Kerrymen drew back. They had never seen magic like this before.

"Do not pretend you cannot hear me. I know you can. I forbid you to give up! You are going to live. You will take care of this big oaf here just as I have to take care of the big oaf who is High King. Do you think women can die whenever they want to? Do you hear me, girl? I command you to stop shivering! I order you to breathe slowly and deeply! I want to see some color in your face, too."

The red-haired maiden tried to fight off her insistent commands. She twisted desperately to escape the sound of Biddy's voice. The princess slapped her.

"Oh, disobedient and wilful child! Do what you are told now." She slapped her again.

The twitching stopped, the blue faded from the girl's face; her eyes opened slowly. A tear rolled down each cheek. She smiled up at Biddy. The princess put two fingers on her mouth to keep the smile in place, then, motherlike, drew the bedraggled red head against her breast.

Cormac gave Cathal charge of the girl's hand. The fisherman was weeping openly.

Biddy kissed her. "That is better, child. You will be all right now. Do not any of you Kerry louts have broth for this child?" she glared at them.

King Donal himself brought the warm liquid.

"It is time, laggard," said the princess. As she began to feed Grainne, she added, "You had better give some to the High King of Tara too."

Donal laughed. So did all the Killarney warriors. So did the band of Cormac. So, in truth, did Cormac himself. What else was he to do?

Later, when they were preparing to ride to Agadhoe, Brigid searched among the rubble from the broken curragh. After a few moments she found it. Her hair hanging limp, clutching her borrowed blue cloak with one hand, she held aloft in triumph for all to see a badly dented silver chalice with glittering jewels. "We must not forget the magic cup!"

Cormac did not know whether to laugh or cry, so he

took the cup from her hands, and despite the Kerrymen, kissed her. His guests unaccountably cheered for the High King and his woman.

The *rath* at Agadhoe was on a hill that towered over the lower lakes of Killarney. Queen Begha was a slender, black-haired lass with flashing eyes and a saucy walk, even younger than Biddy. She was friendly and gracious to her guests, although almost fearfully respectful of the princess.

"What would have happened to me if that stupid girl had died?" demanded Brigid.

They were walking along the ridge looking at the lake turn silver in the setting sun. It was still warm; they needed no cloaks.

Four days after rescue, the young members of Cormac's band were recovered from their ordeals. The rich-bodied twins and their bashful protectors were off somewhere walking in the woods, talking about whatever young lovers talk about.

Cormac wondered if he had ever been a young lover. Probably not. He didn't want to be walking in the woods or gazing foolishly at the lakes of Killarney. Even with the birds singing in the dark trees above them, even with Biddy holding his hand, he wanted to sleep.

"You cannot sleep the rest of your life away," Biddy insisted, as she dragged him out into the hot afternoon air.

Now they sat to watch the changing pattern of colors on the water.

"Cormac—" Her voice was soft. "What did you think of me?"

"I think that if I ever have to face a storm at sea again I would not want you with me till the end; then I would want you more than anyone else."

"I didn't mean that—I meant—did you like my body?" Eyes averted, head turned away.

"What are you talking about, woman! Have you gone mad?" Hands on his side in exasperation. Did she think he wasn't human?

Her eyes were fixed on the grass. "You saw it on the beach."

"Brigid, we were cold, sick, exhausted."

"Cormac, I'm serious. Please tell me the truth."

"The truth, magic princess, is that I'm sure you would keep a man's bed warm during the cold nights of winter."

Furious, she began to pound his chest, paying no attention to the healing wounds. "You are a terrible, cruel man. I hate you."

He spun her around, roughly pulled off the top of her red gown and kissed her shoulders and breasts. "Does that answer your question, evil-tempered slave girl?"

She was limp in his arms. "Every woman has breasts," she sighed. "The twins' are much bigger than mine."

The fears of a little girl. He must say the right thing. Tenderly he stroked her arm. "Lady Brigid, the good God made the world in many different kinds of beauty. When it comes to lovely women, I enjoy all the varieties. There are some kinds I like more than others. The one I enjoy the most is the trim, intense, willowy kind, with legs like delicate ivory pillars, a belly like a field of new-fallen snow, a waist as slender as a young oak tree, breasts like full wine cups, shoulders as smooth as a beach, a curving throat—"

"Like the Lady Ann?" She interrupted his poetic rhapsody with little respect for his images.

"Now how did you know that?" He went back to kissing her.

"I am not a fool, Cormac. You never took your eyes off her when we were in Slaine. I'm like her?"

"Isn't that what I've been telling you?" Her skin was soft and silky. He would have to stop now.

She was crying. "That's the nicest compliment I could have."

His half-naked woman was shivering. *So lovely yet so fearful. How much fear in your short life.*

"Are you going to marry me, Cormac?"

"I am not. I am going to use you as a slave. When I get tired of you, I'll throw you away." His head was throbbing—she was so soft to his fingers, so tasty to his lips. *Slowly, Cormac, she is terrified. Now is not the time.* "Of course I'm going to marry you, foolish girl. Do I not have to marry the magic princess?"

Holding her *leine* at the waist, she drew close to him, covering her shame with his body. She was a fragile wildflower to be honored and reverenced. He touched her back between the two tiny shoulder blades. Her head burrowed in his chest. Such a superb woman and such a small child. He caressed her hair, burnished by the pale rays of the setting sun. There was a night bird singing somewhere. In Brigid's mixture of terror and trust Cormac found peace. *Do not be afraid of me, little bondwoman. I will protect you from harm.* Gently he put the gown back on her shoulders.

"You did not have to stop," she said quietly, still shivering.

"It is better that I did, is it not?" *Ah, I will have to be so soft with you, my pretty queen. That will make our pleasure even sweeter.*

"You should marry me for a year and a day. It is the right of all Irish men and women."

"I am a Christian. Why should I claim a pagan right?"

"You won't need a magic princess for long."

"I'll need a Brigid all my life. I'll have no more talk about discarding you. Fine chance I would have to do it, even if I were foolish enough to do it, even if I were foolish enough to want to."

She giggled. "Then you are going to marry me?"

"Haven't I said it already?"

Chapter 22

The *full moon* rose over the top of the Magillicudy Reeks, its pale light casting a ghostly glow on the still waters of the lake. Samain, the most haunted of all Irish feasts, was at hand. There should be spirits abroad in the mountains, the water elves spinning beneath the surface of the lakes, the fairy people dancing on the meadows, air spirits hovering above the cranog. It was a night for demons, banshees, leprechauns, ghosts, and other misty creatures of the underworld.

He looked in all directions from the lookout platform a few yards above the crannog. The moonlight shimmered on the thatch cone above the hut where his queen lay sleeping. Where are you, mountain spirits? Are you afraid of my Brigid? Has her wonder driven you to other glens?

All were silent—the water motionless, the air quiet, the land peaceful. Perhaps their cow, tethered on the meadow where the underwater causeway from the crannog met the shore, was still awake. If she was, only she and Cormac MacDermot were present to greet the moon as it beamed down on the warm earth of Kerry. Summer heat had lingered long into autumn—the same heat that had ruined the harvest in much of Ireland now delayed the harshness of winter and perhaps averted great suffering in the country. Cormac mechanically prayed that it would be so. It was hard to worry about evil that might come when you were drowning in happiness already here. A small, gnat-like concern lodged in the back of his head.

He wrapped a light green tunic around his waist. So warm was the night air that he needed no other robe. A faint breeze touched his chest tenderly, like Biddy's hand. He shivered—not from cold but from pleasurable memories. It was wise and kind of Donal and Begha to offer them the small lake fort, which had been refurbished for their own wedding weeks. Mountains to climb, fields and woods in which to walk, a waterfall with cold water to sting naked bodies, a stream in which you could frolic, a lake from which you could catch fresh fish and into which you could throw your woman when she became difficult, autumn field flowers from which to make garlands for her hair, a narrow beach around the lake where you could chase her—ah, the Vale of Magillicudy was a wonderful place to have a new wife.

He smiled to himself. Life with Biddy required all of a man's attention. The months of pilgrimage with her had not given a hint of what marriage would be like. Her tongue was more tart, her complaints more furious, her temper more persistent, her moods more erratic. A terrible woman indeed. His smile turned into a broad grin.

But often her tongue was gentle, her voice soft and

warm, her hands tender. She would scream at him one moment, then plead with him for pardon; cry over her foolishness, stamp her pretty feet, then burst into ribald laughter. Once, after sobbing in his protective arms, she whimpered, "My poor, sweet darling, why do you tolerate me? I was bad as a slave; I am worse as a wife. Why don't you hold me under the lake until I am dead? You can claim it was an accident."

"Podraig wouldn't let me." He grinned.

She pounded his chest with furious little fists.

Their first night together went badly. Dizzy with wine and lust, Cormac forgot how stiff and inexperienced his maiden was. His intentions were gentle and good; he wanted to be tender, but Biddy lost her virginity without any pleasure.

Instead of being angry at him she furiously berated herself as a cold, frigid, useless woman, unworthy of any man. Quickly sober and contrite, Cormac grabbed her bare shoulders and shook her like a disobedient child.

"Evil woman, stop talking about my wife that way!" he thundered. "I'll not hear another word of such foolishness against the woman I love." He clamped his hand over her mouth.

Instead of hysterics he got laughter. He removed his hand.

"Oh, Cormac, what a fool the poor slave girl is—clever enough to seduce a king but not clever enough to enjoy him." Gratefully she stroked his beard.

There was fire beneath the ice, but the ice was thick. She was submissive when he wanted her, tender with him, open to his every wish. Try as she might—and she tried very hard—she was unable to escape from her terrors. Cormac marveled at how brave she was to give herself to him despite the terror that made her taut whenever his caresses became demanding.

"I'd like to say I was a stupid, worthless fool," she mourned one night. "You won't let me say that. What can I say?"

"That you're the magic queen." He cuddled her in his arms.

"I am hard work for you, Cormac. Not the kind of joy a bride ought to be." A tiny fist pounded their bed.

"It is a greater joy to work hard with you, Brigid, my love, than to be at ease with any other woman."

A hot, noonday sun finally melted the ice.

They had been running on the beach. He was surprised again at her fleetness. Panting and sweaty, they walked back to the crannog. Biddy stopped to pick flowers. Cormac was a few paces ahead of her. Suddenly his tunic was pulled from his back; a very naked woman was covering him with kisses.

"Do not speak, great lover. Make a woman out of me this minute."

"God has already done that," he said, wrestling her to the soft grass of the mountain meadow.

God had made her a tempestuous, wanton woman, too, a hollering, biting, scratching woman. He was sure they could hear her screams across the bay at Agadhoe. The pounding of her fists on the meadow would make the nearby mountains shake.

"Why didn't you tell me it was like that?" she sighed.

"Because I knew you would make me work hard." He laughed as he playfully spanked her.

"Beast, monster, demon, cruel king—oh, my poor dear Cormac, I've made you wait so long." Then tears and more love. "You would make a stone statue passionate."

She moaned as though her pleasure had been almost unbearable.

Her golden body in the autumn sunlight, glowing with sweat, satisfied, happy, serene. Cormac was proud of his manhood. The ice was gone; now only the fire remained. "You are not a statue, woman."

Just as Biddy suddenly turned from ice to fire, she turned from mountains and valleys to high, smooth plateau. He hardly noticed the change, so quiet was it.

"Brigid," he said, chewing casually on an apple at the door of their hut after one evening meal, "you have not screamed at me in three days. Is there something wrong?"

Big tears welled up in her eyes. "Oh, my wonderful one, was I so bad that you think I am ill when I stop shouting?" She threw her arms around his neck in a hug that used to be reserved for Podraig.

His face felt hot. He had made a mistake. "I did not mean to hurt you—" he stumbled, tossing away the apple core.

"Silly man, you cannot hurt me as much as I hurt myself." Her arms tightened around him. "I no longer shout because it no longer does any good."

He began to eat another apple to hide his puzzlement. She was nibbling at his ear, much as he was nibbling the apple. "You are now the best husband in Ireland."

That night when she was asleep, he thought to himself that he had been aware of no change in himself, yet the guilt and the anger and the black restlessness were gone. Where had he lost them? He was not the man who rode out of Tara in the rain with a soggy waif in his arms.

That thought required another apple and a draught of wine from the magic cup that stood in splendor on their plain, unpolished table. After a second draught he remembered that there were other pleasures to be had in the crannog. But his wife was sleeping so peacefully that the best husband in Ireland did not wake her.

Cormac gazed at the moon rising higher in the sky, growing smaller as it moved across the heavens. What would come next? Back to Tara? The thought made his stomach tighten. Could he take his contentment back there and keep it alive? Would Biddy's love for him survive the intrigue of that terrible place?

Dark unease slipped into his soul like a cloud passing over the moon. Before he could banish the dread there were footsteps behind him.

"Am I so worthless a lover that my husband deserts our marriage bed to stare at the moon? Was it not better when it was apples and wine that satisfied his lust? Does he now seek a lover in the sky?"

A sleepy-eyed Brigid was standing at the foot of the watchtower, clutching a white *leine* in front of her body, squinting at him with the same elflike expression he had seen on her face the day they rode out of Tara.

"No, I merely wanted my wife to seek me under the moonlight." Leaping lightly to the ground, he took the gown out of her hand. The moonlight turned her body silver, like a fish darting out of the black water. Modestly she lowered her eyes. "Look at me, woman."

She was perfection. Golden hair falling on silver body, shoulders erect with delicious embarrassment, hands obediently outstretched like a slave woman in the marketplace, big blue eyes filled with love, she stood before him motionless, balanced between shame from her nakedness and joy from her union with the peaceful spirits of night. He would keep her suspended just so until modesty finally demanded surcease.

"Is it your wish, good master, that I stand here like this till morning?" she asked meekly.

"And then through the day, wanton child. I want to drink you in with my eyes till I am intoxicated forever." His words were slurred, as though he were already intoxicated.

"Is it not better that a man stare at his woman than at the moon?" She drew a deep breath as shame and joy heightened within her.

"It surely is. And better that he drink in his wife than drink in wine." The moment could be stretched a little longer.

"It is good of you to say so. Oh, Cormac—" now serious and sensible, "—what if someone comes by and *sees* me like this?" The two of them were close to bursting with pleasure.

"They will see the most beautiful woman in Ireland," he said devoutly.

"Soon you will be weary of me without any clothes."

"Only if I stop breathing." It was enough for the night. He picked her up, carried her compliant body up the steps, and put her on the ledge of the crannog wall, wrapping his tunic around the two of them. She snuggled close. Her fingers dug into his buttocks, her lips touched his shoulder, her breasts pressed against his chest. "You are thinking of Tara," she mumbled into his skin.

"Not a very lustful thing to say, woman." He hesitated, the spell now broken. He caressed her back, marveling as always by how much of its smooth surface his hand covered.

"I'm not ready to go back yet, Biddy. Is it hard for you to wait for me to decide?"

"Mother Mary said waiting is praying."

"Yes, she did, didn't she? No, she did not say that. Those words are not in the scriptures, Biddy. You must have heard them elsewhere." He tightened his grip on her waist. His hands easily fit all the way around it. "It is a beautiful saying. Where did you hear it?" he demanded.

She hesitated. "Please, don't hurt me."

He relaxed his grip. "I'm sorry, I didn't mean to." He kissed her. "I love you."

"I know you do, Cormac. I don't think I should tell you. It's a secret. Mother Mary told me it was a secret. Are you angry with me, darling lover?" Her lips moved to his throat.

"Of course not. Just surprised. If Mother Mary said it is a secret, then it is a secret." How do you make love to a wife who talks to Mother Mary? He almost asked her whether Mother Mary said that he should return to Tara.

"I love you, Cormac."

It was not so hard after all to make love to her.

The next morning they were awakened long after the proper time for rising by the loud but friendly barking of Podraig. A strange horseman was on the shore of the lake.

"Who is it?" asked Biddy. "He is heavily armed."

"Is it not Rory MacFelan?"

They looked at each other anxiously. Tara had come to them.

Cormac climbed down the ladder from the crannog. Rory would not find his way on the underwater stones unless someone showed him the path.

"The daughter of Lorcan is called Fionna," she whispered primly.

The woman never forgot anything.

The young man was worried, his young face taut and grim. Cormac shook his hand warmly. "Welcome to the highest mountains of Ireland, good friend. How fares it with gracious black-haired Fionna?"

A broad smile lifted the worry from Rory's face. "Very well, thank you, O great king. She sends her respect to you. We have a son and another child to come soon."

"Then what are you doing in these mountains."

Rory's handsome face turned tense again. "King Dermot is dying. The witch Finnabair has lost her powers. The men of Leinster broke the truce and are laying siege to Tara. All wish for your return. They—they thought you might listen to me."

He guided the young man across the rocks to the crannog. "We must hurry, Brigid," he told his wife. "It is time to return to Tara."

Chapter 23

D*ismal black clouds* hung low over the Hill of Slaine. The bishop's wife felt she could almost reach up and touch them. Tara was invisible across the valley; so were the tents of the army of Aed MacSweeney, King of Leinster. It was no longer raining, but fog and moisture saturated the air. She wished that Enda would hurry back. Each day he rode over to the other hill to minister to the dying king. The Leinstermen were Christians of a sort. They would not harm a bishop. Still she feared for him.

Her children were playing in the yard happily. Perhaps they felt secure because the Holy Abbot Colum was in their house.

The saintly man himself was silent and sad. He knew that his dreams for Ireland were dying with Dermot MacFergus. Tara would soon fall to invaders for the first time in the memory of man. There was no need for

MacSweeney to attack. When King Dermot was dead, he would proclaim himself High King. There would be no one to accuse him of violating the pledged truce.

She picked up the bucket of milk. As she turned to go back into the house, she saw out of the corner of her eye a splash of color emerge from the fog at the bottom of the Hill of Slaine. Warriors!

Running quickly to the house, she shouted "Holy abbot!" Her voice choked with fear. "There are warriors coming up the hill!"

Jarred out of his reverie, Colum hurried to the wall of the bishop's rath. There were now scores of men in chariots and on horses, moving slowly toward the base of the hill. They wore crimson robes and carried a banner of saffron and blue. Their advance guard paused at the bottom of the hill.

"Kerrymen!" exclaimed Colum.

"Cashel is attacking us too?" Her body was shaking with fear. What would they do to her children? Where was Enda? "Are they Christians? Will they attack Slaine?" she asked breathlessly.

"They are pious Christians. I can't believe they have come all the way across Ireland for a war that is not theirs."

At the bottom of the hill a chariot detached itself from the main body of Kerrymen and sped up the path toward the top. Who drove it? He looked familiar—the long red beard hadn't been there before—"God in heaven, holy abbot, it's Cormac!"

Moments later the High King was in the rath, his face glowing with a broad grin. He embraced his cousin, kissed the bishop's wife with considerably more vigor than was necessary, and swung the little boy high in the air. "What is this fine young man called?" he demanded playfully.

She hesitated. "Cormac—" She was embarrassed.

With the young lad still above his head, the king turned to her in surprise. It was now his turn to be embarrassed. "So, too, is the son of Fionna and Rory," he said, as though surprised.

"There will be many Cormacs in Ireland," said the radiant yellow-haired girl who waited in the king's chariot, watching his homecoming with a tolerant smile.

"Biddy—!"

"No." He put the delighted little boy back on the ground and presented his wife formally. "This is my magic wife, the Princess Delvcaem. She only looks like Biddy."

Biddy embraced the Lady Ann and shyly took the hand of Colum. "We return, holy monk," she said gravely.

"I knew you should accompany him," he said with equal seriousness.

The wolfhound Podraig ran about in confusion. Which of his old friends to greet first? The little girls? The new child? The old monk? He put his great paws on the bishop's wife's shoulders and began to lick her face.

"The wise dog still pursues beautiful women," laughed Cormac. He had never laughed that way before.

"If anyone is still interested in me," said Cormac, "I also have the magic cup." The king held proudly in the sky a silver goblet covered with shimmering jewels.

"Silly man," said Biddy tolerantly. "Who needs a cup when they have a princess?"

Biddy was swung into the air just as little Cormac had been. "Goblets cannot talk back," she was told sternly.

Later, in the house, Enda, Colum, Rory, and young

Donal O'Donnal planned strategy. Queen Brigid—for now she must be called that—helped to cook the evening meal.

"You are truly Delvcaem?" the Lady Ann asked diffidently as she rolled out the bread dough.

"In a way. I think that matters no longer." Biddy's hands were white with flour.

"Since Finnabair's illness she has no more power. She only ministers to the dying king. No one cares about the *geis* she put on Cormac. Still, the search was not wasted, was it not?"

"You would have to ask Cormac whether he is pleased with his prizes." There was no doubt in the girl's voice. She playfully shook flour at Ann's face.

"He is a man transformed, Biddy," she said, trying to wipe the flour off her mouth.

"And I?" She smeared more flour on Ann's face. The child would not have been so playful three years ago.

"Even more." Ann tossed a whole measure of it at the young queen. The two of them were shaking with repressed laughter, since they did not want to disturb the serious deliberations going on in the next room. For a magic moment they were two female bear cubs. Then they hugged each other affectionately, wiped the flour from their faces, and pretended again to be serious and responsible matrons.

"Do not tell him I have been transformed. He will become very proud if he knows what he has done to me." She went back to rolling the dough.

"He is a good lover?" Ann said diffidently, not looking at Brigid and blushing at her own curiosity.

"Oh, yes. The Most High knows he had to be with such a dull wife," she said softly.

Ann cautiously inspected Brigid's face. There was a dreamy and satisfied look in the girl's eyes.

"He does not seem unhappy with his wife."

"Silly man." She sounded very satisfied with herself.

Meanwhile, at the conference table, Enda was calmly describing the situation in Tara. "There is no will to fight. The king is dying—he may be dead by morning. Aed has bribed most of the lesser kings. The nobles have no one to follow. The bards have fled, warriors have lost their discipline. Finnabair is no longer feared. Aed has promised to hang her head on the walls as soon as he enters Tara. When Dermot dies the slaves will flee. Aed will march in without a fight."

"When it is heard that Cormac is back with the army of the O'Donnals people will begin to remember that Aed violated his solemn pledge," argued young Rory. "It is a privilege for Kerrymen to fight for the High King," said the gallant crimson-robed king from the west.

"There will be no battle," said Cormac MacDermot flatly. He had left the table and was looking across the valley through a narrow window.

"Aed will challenge you to single combat?" asked the holy abbot, his face a mask of worry.

"What else can he do?" Cormac smoothed his saffron tunic and continued to gaze at Tara. "With the *Tanaise* alive and in front of Tara with an army, he has no choice."

"He could ride back to Leinster and live," observed Queen Brigid, exercising the Irishwoman's right to interrupt male conversation.

"What a fierce woman you have grown into, Lady Brigid," said the Abbot of Iona, wonder in his words.

"Have you ever seen Cormac MacDermot fight, holy cousin?" she asked pertly.

"I have not."

"I have."

"It may be, fierce wife, that we can negotiate. I have no desire for blood. Ways can be found for Aed to return to Leinster with his honor unstained. We must try. He is not a very bright man; he will soon see Tara slipping from his grasp. Like any trapped animal, he may feel he must fight. If necessary, I will fight; but I would rather be king with no blood on my sword." He walked back to the table from the window, his shoulders slumped with the weight of his new responsibilities.

"He will fight, Cormac," said Rory. "He could not live with the laughter of the bards if he does not."

"Then curse the laughter of the bards. A man who cannot bear to be laughed at should rule no one—" He paused, realizing how absurd such words must sound coming from his lips. There was an awkward silence around the table. Biddy's eyes sparkled.

"Noble Cormac, my virtue is not that great. Do not tempt me again." She smiled sweetly.

There was laughter all around the table.

When the laughter had died, the Bishop of Slaine, dear man, tapped his fingers lightly on the table. Something was worrying him. "I do not mean to challenge the warrior code," he began slowly, "but the old king may be dead by sunrise. Sometimes he is conscious—would it not ease his death to see his son for a last time?"

The old sullenness returned instantly to the *Tanaise's* face. "I will not see him," he responded harshly.

"As you please, royal lord. He asks for you often. Until today he was the only one in Tara who believed you would return to fight the Leinstermen." Enda picked up his cloak. His eyes would not meet those of the angry king.

Cormac was grim. "He preferred the body of a harlot to the love of his son."

Enda shrugged. "It is your decision, O High King. I will go back tonight to say the prayers for the dying."

Colum tried. "He was an old man, Cormac; he wanted to recapture his youth. Many old men do it."

"I will not." The king's voice was tight with anger, his massive arms coiled as though for a fight. Ann was afraid.

"I am sure you will not, but King Jesus wants us to forgive."

"I cannot forgive what he has done to me and to Ireland. It would be sinful to forgive that." He smote the table with his hand.

No one else was brave enough to question his interpretation of the Gospels.

"I have kinsmen among the Leinsterfolk," said Rory nervously. "I will ride to them under truce and propose bargaining tomorrow morning."

"And I will prepare my Kerrymen for battle—just in case," said a puzzled Donal.

The conference ended. Rory and Donal left. Enda drew his plain gray cloak around his shoulders. He smiled at his wife. Another night without him.

Brigid donned a gold cloak, arranging it carefully around her bright red dress. What a beauty she was! "I shall accompany you to Tara, faithful bishop." Her words were barely audible.

Cormac looked up angrily from the fire into which he had been staring. "What are you saying, woman? Have you gone mad?"

"Is not the High King dying alone? If no one else from his family is at his side, should not his worthless daughter-in-law be there at least?"

"I forbid you to go."

"Even when I was your slave, beloved husband, that did not stop me. Do you think it will now? Are we ready, Bishop Enda?"

She had humiliated him in the presence of others. Cormac's face was white with rage. He gripped his sword. Ann's heart thumped against her ribs. What would he do?

His color flowed back; he grinned sheepishly. He looked as foolish as he must have felt. "Bishop Enda, I cannot expect you to protect such a devilish woman by yourself in the darkness of Samaintide. I will come with you to ease your burden." He swung his cloak onto his shoulders.

Did he really wink at me? the bishop's wife wondered. *Poor, dear man.*

"You are still a pagan, Queen Brigid?" asked the Abbot of Iona.

"I fear that I am, holy monk," she replied respectfully.

"Yet if King Jesus should come to me tonight and say there was but one Christian in the whole of Ireland, I would know to whom he should be brought."

Biddy's face took on all its old solemnity.

"I am sure, Abbot Colum, that King Jesus would know that it would be improper to ask anyone but you."

Chapter 24

B*rigid breathed rapidly;* her mouth was dry, her hands clenched so tightly on Podraig's leash that her knuckles were white. Cormac should win the combat. He was the better fighter. Still, there might be an accident—he might be badly wounded—his reluctance to kill would give Aed MacSweeney an advantage. She was confident of her man. She was also afraid. A huge abyss yawned in front of her. Happiness could be snuffed out in a few sharp moments of swordplay.

Cormac's chariot sloshed through the mud to the place where Aed already waited. The Leinsterman was silent this gray and gloomy morning. His brave taunts of yesterday were forgotten; he could see death coming for him in the broad-shouldered, thick-armed, red-haired man in the dark blue tunic.

How tense those strong shoulders had been last night.

Cormac was quiet, withdrawn—a very different warrior from the man who had freed her on the pirate's island. She had learned since their marriage that the only time to fear her man was when he became silent. It was a rare mood. Biddy restrained her tongue at those times. Waiting is praying, she told herself.

The two armies formed into straggling lines of horsemen and charioteers on either side of the valley—more than a hundred warriors among the Leinstermen, a little less on the side of Tara. Their banners and robes were somber threads of color against the black ground and the dark sky, like the drawings of the Last Judgment in the books at Clonmacnoise. These would not fight, however; the two leaders would determine which man would rule in Tara by personal combat. Aed had wanted a battle of armies; but some of his warriors had gone home, the loyalty of others was uncertain. The King of Leinster was not popular with his tenants and lesser kings. They followed him when it appeared there would be no opposition in Tara. The appearance of Cormac caused many to melt away into the mists.

So he had to turn to personal combat. After the wretched body of Dermot was buried in the sacred soil of Tara, the leaders of the two armies bargained all the day on the Hill of Slaine in front of the bishop's house. Cormac wanted peace. He offered compromises so that Aed could go home to Leinster in honor. The giant, barrel-chested, black-bearded Leinsterman grew more angry with each proposal. He insulted Cormac, his father, his mother, and even his new wife.

Brigid's face flamed with outrage when the Leinster king said that half the men of Ireland had tasted her flesh and found it bitter. It was a typical Irish insult, wild and exaggerated, meaning nothing. She would have scratched the eyes out of MacSweeney if Donal had not held her back.

Cormac was unruffled. Politely he suggested yet another solution. The bargaining went on. Finally, at the end of the day, he sighed deeply. "We have found no solution to our conflict, O King of Leinster."

"I do not make solutions with bewitched cowards," snarled Aed. His hand moved to his sword hilt as though ready to fight Cormac.

"It is between you and me then?" The words were soft, almost gentle.

The faces of the men and women assembled on the top of the windswept Hill of Slaine turned solemn.

"I will feed your intestines to my dogs for their noonday meal!" bellowed Aed.

There was no sound on the Hill of Slaine. The High King's eyes were softer than his voice. "I do not want to take your life, Aed MacSweeney." He extended his hands in supplication, like a priest at mass.

The Leinster king spat in his face and rode off down the side of the hill.

"The man is a fool," said Rory MacFelan hotly. "He knows you are the better warrior. He has come to believe his own boasting. He is a prisoner of his pride."

"Are not we all? He does not listen to his wife. Her face tells him not to fight me."

"She knows how unpopular their family is. If he dies, it will go hard with her."

"No harm will befall her." Still the unearthly calm, like a monk lost in prayer.

Colum, Enda, Rory, Donal—none knew what to make of the High King's strange mood. Biddy found Donal in his tent later in the evening. "Be not afraid, O King of Kerry. My Cormac is the most dangerous when the most quiet," she said firmly.

Donal was worried. "The Leinster folk think his stillness means fear."

"They will know better tomorrow." She turned and left the tent of the King of Kerry, knowing that one more word would be too many.

She and Cormac said little that night. Before he rode out to meet MacSweeney the next morning, he kissed her. "I love you, magic princess."

She clung to him. "I love you, King of Tara. I am praying for you."

A flash of light in his blue eyes and a smile teased the corner of his mouth. "To whom, kind pagan?"

"To everyone."

"Even to King Jesus?"

"Of course. King Jesus will take care of you."

"So you have spoken with him too?" The smile turned wry. Cormac could never make up his mind about her meeting with King Jesus and Mother Mary.

"Like all good kings, he takes pity on slave girls."

He kissed her again and went off to battle. How much she loved him. The thought of him turned her bones to water. Sometimes when he was about to enter her the joy was so great she felt she would die. "King Jesus, I waited for him as you said. Now you protect him as I say."

She wondered if King Jesus could be talked to the way she talked to Cormac. If he is truly a king of love, she decided, he does not mind.

Now she stood on the hill, waiting for the battle to begin. On either side of her, helping to hold back the anxious Podraig, were Cathal and Connor. Foolish fisherboys, they had not yet bedded the twins. She would have to speak to Cormac about them. Eileen and Grainne were almost mad with hunger for their lovers. There were other things to worry about first.

Cormac leisurely dismounted from his chariot. Sword still in his belt, hands on his hips, he walked to the rise in the valley floor where Aed was already swinging his sword. Once more he offered peace. Aed's response was to leap at him with a savage downstroke. Cormac deftly dodged it and drew his own weapon. The constriction in her chest was so painful Biddy thought she would die. Podraig wailed mournfully like a stricken banshee.

The sound of blade on blade echoed across the valley. Aed was slashing for a quick victory, Cormac fighting carefully to avoid killing his opponent. Destroy him, you fool, Biddy thought. Will you take risks and leave me a widow? Then she was ashamed of her hatred.

Cormac slipped in the mud. The Leinsterman, with a wild bellow, leaped in for the kill. Cormac twisted away, but Aed's sword dug into his left arm. The blue tunic turned red with blood. Biddy's own blood froze. "King Jesus," she prayed, "save him."

Now anger had finally broken through the High King's calm. He was like a peaceful lake stirred to a frenzy by a sudden wind. Aed found himself on the defensive, barely able to fend off the merciless blows of his attacker. "Finish him," Biddy pleaded.

As if in response to her prayers, Cormac brushed away the Leinsterman's sword as if it were bog grass, pushed aside his leather shield, and struck him a terrible blow across the shoulder and chest that brought Aed to his knees, blood pouring out of his body. Biddy felt her stomach turn. She must not be sick.

Her man lowered his sword, giving Aed one more chance at life. "Please live," she prayed, "he does not want to kill you."

The Leinsterman did not hear her prayers. From his knees he made one last desperate lunge. Biddy's scream and Podraig's howl came at the same moment. Cormac raised his sword to ward off the blow. Aed ran onto it, impaling himself. He paused for a moment as if to regain strength for another charge, looked with surprise at the huge blade protruding from his chest, and then crumpled to earth.

The rain was falling again in great dense torrents. Brigid jumped into the chariot she had packed with bandages. With Podraig running beside her, she drove her horses to the place of combat, heedless of the dangers of the slippery mud.

Drenched with rain, Cormac stood bemused over the body of his enemy. "It is too late, magic one. He is dead."

"I will bind up your arm then." The ugliness of his wound made her stomach turn again.

"I did not want to kill him. He killed himself," Cormac mourned.

"Cormac, your arm is bleeding." Delicately she tore the tunic away from the wound. His blood was flowing rapidly, mixing with the driving rain. She must stop it.

"God forgive me, I did not want to kill him."

He was in a trance, numbed by the enormity of the death of one of Ireland's mightiest kings. He did not resist her efforts to bandage his wound. She staunched the river of blood; it was a deep gash that would hurt him for many days, but it was not dangerous.

Later the Leinstermen brought Aed's queen and her children. The warriors who had remained with Aed were now frightened by the enormity of their crime in breaking the pledged truce. They were also terrified by the powers of the High King. Giving him Aed's family to work vengeance on would perhaps dispel his wrath.

She was a tall, thin woman with a stony face, her garments soaking wet. A little boy and a girl walked behind her. In her arms she held a crying baby. Like her husband she was too proud to ask for pity. She shivered from the rain and the cold.

"What do you expect of me, woman of Leinster?" Cormac asked grimly.

"What any wife of a king who violates his oath expects." Her voice did not waver.

"What is that?" Still grim.

"You will take my children's heads, you will give me to your warriors for their amusement. When they weary of my body you will put out my eyes and send me out to wander the roads of Ireland as a worthless crone."

"Do you deserve these torments?"

"Did not Aed MacSweeney break the pledged truce—?" She impulsively thrust the baby at Cormac. "Spare this wee babe. She has done nothing wrong. Her life has only just begun. Give her a chance to live!"

Cormac took the child carefully and stroked its tiny face with his finger. He who used to be unaware of children had become very good with them.

Returning the baby to her mother, he said, "Take your children, woman, and go home to Kildare. Let it be said in Ireland that anyone who harms you or them will have to answer to Cormac MacDermot."

The queen's courage vanished. She fell to her knees in the mud sobbing her gratitude. He put his hand on her head in benediction. "May time ease the sorrow of your loss. Let there be no more war between our houses." He lifted his head and proclaimed, "Hear me, all you men of Leinster. Violate the truce again, and there will be much more Leinster blood shed than on this day."

The queen kissed Cormac's hands. Some of the men led her and the children away. Others carried the body of her husband back toward their camp. It would be a long journey home.

Behind them Biddy could hear the murmur of approval among Cormac's people. He had behaved bravely and mercifully—a true High King.

"Did I do well, Queen Brigid?" he asked dully. His eyes were glazed with pain and weariness.

"Could my Cormac do anything else?" The rain had eased, but the damp chill was eating at her bones.

"Biddy, mercy is harder than hatred," he whispered in her ear.

"Should it not be so, my lord?" she asked with a sigh.

They rode up the hill into the walls of Tara. Behind them the Kerrymen and Cormac's other allies were singing. The people of Tara were cheering. Pipes and drums were blaring a royal welcome, banners on the walls and buildings hung limply in the drizzling rain. Biddy drew her hood over her head. She knew that Cormac heard none of the sounds proclaiming his victory. Podraig trotted along behind them, happily accepting the cheers as though they were meant for him.

"A day like the one we left, magic princess."

"Have there been no changes, King of Ireland?"

He looked down at her, his eyes tender. "One or two, Biddy."

There was to be another and more terrible test of Cormac's mercy. At the gate of the middle ramparts Murtaugh MacMurtaugh and several of the royal guard brought the white witch Finnabair. The girl had avoided them at Dermot's deathbed and funeral. Now she was tightly bound, her torn white dress wet from the rain, her hair dripping water. Still lovely, though the ravages of her illness remained. Bedraggled and beaten, Finnabair kept her head high. She would die with resigned dignity.

"We have brought the evil woman Finnabair for your punishment," said old Murtaugh.

Cormac dismounted from the chariot, knife in hand.

"Will you take my head with a knife, Cormac MacDermot?" she asked, her eyes wide with terror.

Biddy was shocked by the exhaustion in her enemy's voice. Did Finnabair want to die?

Cormac tilted up her chin with the handle of his knife. "It is truly a lovely head, woman, and one would be blessed to have it as a trophy. Still it would lose much of its charm if detached from the rest of you. I will leave it where it is for the present. I only intend this knife to cut your bonds."

He cut the ropes off her body. Tara had grown silent again. Hundreds of eyes focused on the three figures at the entrance to the walls. He arranged her dress to cover her bare shoulder. Poor woman.

"Am I free to go?" Finnabair could not believe what was happening.

"Or to stay."

"You would permit me to stay?" She swayed as though she would collapse.

Cormac nodded his head gravely. He steadied her arm.

"I will go today." The defeated enemy turned to leave.

"That I cannot permit," insisted Cormac. "It will not be said that the king turned out a queen in the rain with no cloak to protect her and no guard to accompany her. On the morrow you can journey to Armagh."

"I am no queen, Cormac. I am an enfeebled witch who was your father's harlot." Her head, secure now, hung in shame.

"The one who ministered with kindness to my father in his dying days is a queen."

Conflicting emotions struggled on Finnabair's face. She tried to speak but could not. She turned away so that her old enemies would not see her weep.

"Murtaugh, take this woman back to her chamber," Cormac said casually. "See that she is guarded so no evil is done to her."

"God go with you, Queen Finnabair." Was that my voice? Biddy wondered.

"Which God, O great queen?" The poor woman's voice was hoarse.

"The God of mercy and love." Brigid wondered who had given her that answer.

So it was that the three pilgrims returned to Tara.

Many days later, at the rising sun, the High King of Ireland was walking the ramparts of Tara, as custom said he should. His wife, Queen Brigid, walked with him. About her presence the custom said nothing. Her husband was emerging from the shock of battle. She did not wish him to be alone. He might begin to brood again. Another rainy day could plunge him back into the gloom.

She clung to his arm. After the battle, Cormac could not love. She was gentle with him. His power returned slowly.

Last night she knew it was time. Using every allurement she knew—and some she had never tried—she freed his manhood. Cormac's passion had flared like a bonfire at Beltaine. Exhausted in her arms, he sighed, "You'd seduce a statue, woman."

She hugged him more fiercely. "You're no statue, Cormac MacDermot," she sighed, feeling very satisfied with her womanliness.

"I have happy news, beloved husband. I was—too busy to tell it to you last night."

"Busy, Brigid? Whatever with?" he grinned obscenely.

She ignored him. "My red-headed servants Eileen and Grainne have at last been deflowered."

"Very good news indeed. One cannot have lovely virgins in Tara."

"Not when they are in love with hesitant lovers."

"Irishmen hesitant lovers? Slander, young woman."

Thank God that his merry laugh was back. He was most lovable when he laughed that way. "Like other Irishmen, Cathal and Connor are very good lovers when they finally decide to act."

"So our friends are happy. We will have two weddings soon?"

"Today. You don't think I will let them escape their responsibilities? And, fierce lover, you may kiss them both—once, and for a proper length of time."

He spanked her playfully, a delectable act that made her tremble with desire. "You have no dignity, wicked king," she remonstrated.

Podraig bounded up to them, barking in protest that they had begun the rounds of the ramparts without him. She was now resigned to the wolfhound's presence when they made love. His only reaction to human coupling was to open a big eye in baleful complaint when her cries disturbed his sleep.

Both Cormac's hands were at her waist. "How is it

possible for a woman who is as wanton as you were last night to speak of dignity?" he asked, his eyes crackling with laughter, his hands growing tighter.

"Beast—" She pounded his chest in mock fury—a sure method of making him embrace her even more passionately. "Cormac, not on the walls of Tara!" she pleaded.

"Not in daylight anyhow." He grinned, loosening his grip on her.

Then he began to talk about all the things he would do in Tara. He had become serious and important about being High King. She must prevent him from becoming dull and pompous too. She would have to remind him that everyone had now heard about all his adventures with the holy Brendan at least twice. She sighed. It would be a bother.

But not too much of a bother, eh, Podraig, you silly dog?

The stubborn Irish sun rose over Tara for another day of its timeless struggle against the clouds and the rain.

NOTE

The Irish Grail Cycle

In *the prehistoric* Celtic lands a mythological cycle of tales about an old king, a wicked queen, a young king, and a quest for a magic vessel and/or a magic princess gradually developed and was passed on through the centuries; traces of this lost myth have come down to us in the story of Tristan and Isolde and in the Arthurian sagas. Scholars have recently discovered that certain Irish stories are cognate with the myth and help us fill in its outlines. I believe that these Irish stories are closer to the hidden meaning of the original myth than the others, which were influenced by the traditions of medieval France. An account of one of the Irish tales that led me to try to tell the legend is recorded by Markale*:

> *In the* Adventures of Art, Son of Conn, *which appears to be one of the versions of the Quest for the Grail, the theme of the perilous cup is interwoven with that of tasks to be overcome before reaching the goal of the journey, the chosen woman who represents sovereignty. Art also needs her to fight the influence of a* geis *that is*

---

*From Jean Markale, *Women of the Celts.* Translated by A. Mygind, C. Hauch, and P. Henry. (London, 1975), pp. 198–200, by permission of Gordon & Cremonesi Publishers. (First publushed as *Le Femme Celte,* Paris: Editions Payot, 1972.)

affecting the kingdom of Ireland and is clearly analogous to the spell affecting the desolate Land of the Grail. Since this version of the story is outside any Christian sphere, we are better able to analyse the different episodes in terms of their intrinsic value.

Ireland, The Adventures of Art, Son of Conn

Because King Conn of the Hundred Battles had taken as concubine Becuma Cneisgel, a woman of the Tuatha De Danann exiled from the Land of Promise for some mysterious crime, Ireland was struck by infertility. The people tried sacrificing a child, for which a cow was substituted. But because the king could not send away his concubine, for he was bound to her by a geis, *he still lacked a third of Ireland's harvest. One day, Becuna Cneisgel won a game of chess against Conn's son Art and forced him with another* geis *to bring back and marry a mysterious Delbchaen [Delvcaem], the daughter of Morgan, who was on a distant island. Art left and had to overcome fantastic trials in his search for the fortress in which Delbchaen had taken refuge. He was received by her mother, who made him drink the contents of a cup; he had to choose between two, one full of poison, the other of wine, each held by a woman. Forewarned by a fairy queen, Art chose the right cup, and then all he had to do was cut the head off his lady-love's mother, seize all the treasure in the castle, and take Delbchaen back to Ireland. Then Becuna Cneisgel gave up and left Ireland, which immediately returned to its former prosperity.*

Note that the pivot in every stage of this story is a woman. A woman imposes the tasks upon Art; another is the object of his search; yet another, a mysterious queen, comparable to Peredur's Empress, who might well be just another face of Delbchaen, helps Art in his ordeal. An evil *woman is responsible for Ireland's infertility through her relationship with the king; this had shaken the natural balance he controlled. . . . Finally, a woman holds the cup through which Art finds victory, for it contains the wine he drinks to give him the courage and strength to fulfill his quest. . . .*

So, from whatever angle one analyses the legend of the Grail and all its many versions, some permanent and fundamental themes emerge: vengeance by blood, *after some action that has shaken the balance of the world and led to the infertility of the kingdom;* the impotence of the king *who can no longer rule;* ritual sacrifice, whether human or animal or through simple substitution of the victim or offering; tasks *inflicted on those who set out on the Quest;* female characters *who belong to a fairy world and guide those who take part in the Quest; and the* queen, princess, or empress *who controls the drink of power and sovereignty, which is given only to the man who has overcome all the tasks (the name Galahad probably comes from the Celtic* gal, *meaning "power"). The Quest for the Grail is inextricable from the quest for woman. Whoever finds her finds the Grail; and she who, while her land was cursed, grieved alone and infertile in the depths of her hidden castle, can form part of the ideal and perfect couple with the man for whom she was waiting. The languishing and impotent Fisher-King will be succeeded by the new, young King of the Grail, who can restore fertility to the surrounding countryside and symbolically to the woman who holds the cup, the dish or the stone, the priestess of a cult whose true meaning we may never know.*

In the Irish version the Grail does not wait passively to be found; rather the Grail/girl cooperates actively in the quest—in the case of Princess Brigid, very actively indeed. The Irish myth seems to be revealing that ultimate reality, illumined by woman, not only attracts but seeks. If there is a specific Christian addition in my version of the legend, it is not that Cormac is a Christian king but that the object of the search is seeking the searcher as actively as it/she is being sought. The sacred vessel is, in fact, the Hound of Heaven. No accident, then, that Princess Brigid and the wolfhound Podraig are allies.

One does not go to a legend to learn history or archaeology. Most versions of the Arthurian cycle portray Camelot as a late medieval castle—sometimes a nineteenth-century version of a late medieval castle. One could just as easily portray Tara with the marble halls of the famous song. In fact, the historical Camelot (and there is reason to suppose that the historical Arthur did have a great fortress somewhere in the west of England) would be very much like the historical Tara—a fortress of earthworks with stockades and timber buildings. In my retelling, I am portraying as accurately as I can the social, cultural, political, and religious life of Ireland in the late sixth century A.D. I have done so not to teach history or archaeology, but mostly for the fun of it. Any reader who is interested in the serious study of that era can consult the reading list, which is appended.

I have asked some experts on Irish history to look over the manuscript to minimize egregious mistakes. Still, I have doubtless made a few. We know very little about the late sixth century in any European country. In fact, we may know more about Ireland in that period, the beginning of the "Dark Ages," than we do about most of the rest of Europe.

Markale and others have little doubt that the stories of Art MacConn and Arthur are first cousins, descended from the same Celtic cycle of which we have only faint hints in the literature available to us now. A prime example of the parallels between the stories is the occurrence of the wicked queen, the "white-skinned one," *Guinevere* in Welsh, and *Finnabair* in Irish, which is the name I chose to give her in my story.

Our tale begins, in all probability, a half-century after the time of the historical Arthur in England, an era in transition from paganism to Christianity. The Lady Ann in our version, the bishop's wife, provides a good illustration of this era: a daughter of the last flowering of West England Celtic culture before the completion of the Saxon Conquest. I have done approximately what those who first set down the Arthurian cycle did—moved the pagan tale into a Christian setting, though unlike Arthur, my King Cormac has no historical counterpart.

The legend as told in this book is truer to the ancient Celtic myth than is the legend of the Holy Grail as it has come down to us, filtered through the body-hating Manichaeism of medieval France. As Denis de Rougemont has shown, the Arthurian story has been colored by the Catharist heresy's rejection of human sexuality. Salvation in the quest for the Holy Grail comes through the denial of the flesh—a heresy against both Catholic Christian orthodoxy and the "orthodoxy" of the ancient Celtic myth. It is a shame that the flesh-hating version of the story has had so much influence on Western culture and the flesh-respecting version so little.

I have played loosely with some historical facts. There was a King Dermot, the last king to celebrate the pagan festival in Tara, but Cormac and Biddy and the battle with Aed of Leinster are purely imaginary. The O'Donnals came to Killarney only long centuries after the time of my story. There was surely a settlement on King's Island in the Shannon where Limerick is today, though it might not have been called Limerick at the time. It was probably Christian at the time of the story.

Although Cormac MacDermot is a creature of my imagination, in the years after Dermot's death Ireland did become definitively Christian without any battles, forced conversions, or martyrs. (The martyrs would come with the beginning of England's millennium-long attempt to dominate Ireland.) The transformation of the culture to Christianity was not complete, of course; no culture ever really becomes wholly Christian. Thus the custom of trial-marriages, the sort that Biddy—not very seriously—proposed to Cormac, would last for at least nine hundred more years. But the woman had as much right to terminate the marriage as did the man. The active, not to say dominant, role of women in Celtic society is history, not fiction.

Women's power in Celtic society probably had many of its roots in the ancient belief that the enormous power of procreative fertility reflects the creative fertility of the Divinity. And, as Markale notes in the passage cited earlier, all the magical power in the Irish story is possessed by women. Thus it is in my story: magic resources are possessed by Finnabair, Morrigan, Brigid, the twins, and Brigid's mysterious friend in the white dress. Merlin (or Myrddin, as he was called in his original Welsh manifestation) represents a different tradition of legends, which was joined with the Arthur tradition at a relatively late period, long after the original Celtic myth was told in pre-Christian times. Moreover, Merlin is not absent from this tale. C. S. Lewis in *That Hideous Strength* converts Merlin into a Christian wise man (*Merlinus sum et Christianus*). I push the conversion a step further and assign the Merlin role to a Christian saint, Colum of Iona. One may be excused for observing that the remarkable organizing ability of that descendant of Neill of the Nine Hostages had far greater impact on the development of western civilization than did the magical powers of Arthur's seer. The spiritual descendants of Merlin, such as they were, did not range as far as Fiesole, Vienna, Cologne, Bobbio, and Luxeuil, to say nothing of the even stranger places visited by later pilgrim missionaries from Ireland—Perth, Nairobi, Davao, Tucson, and Miami, to name but a few.

I have taken at least one geographical liberty in this story: Lough Derg is below Clonfert on the Shannon, and not above it. It is not the same Lough Derg where the cave called St. Patrick's Purgatory is to be found.

The personalities of the Irish saints Colum, Brendan, Kevin, and Kiernan, as depicted in my story, are compatible with their historical deeds; but they are based on my imagination more than on the inadequate data we have about what they were really like.* The inclusion of the voyage of St. Brendan is *not* false to the legend. Quite the contrary; a number of scholars have traced the connection between Brendan's story and the Arthurian cycle.

---

* Kiernan died at the age of thirty-four, long before Cormac and Biddy could have visited him. The famous illuminated manuscript called *The Book of the Dun Cow* was allegedly named after Kiernan's bovine pet.

The "voyage to the West" seems to have been very much a part of the original Celtic myth.* Even in the version of the *Morte d'Arthur* we have, it is to an island in the West (Avalon) that Arthur sails—and from which he will perhaps return someday. Whether Brendan ever reached North America is problematic, though Samuel Eliot Morison admits that he must have traveled far enough to encounter icebergs. (The gratuitous anti-Catholicism of Morison's comments on Brendan are a disgrace.)

I relied on the text of Brendan's voyage as assembled by Dr. Carl Selmer from ancient Latin manuscripts, translated by Reverend C. R. Collopy. S. M. Paul Chapman reconstructed the voyage in modern terms in his book *The Man Who Led Columbus to America* (Valley Forge, Pa.: Judson Press, 1973).

Chapman sees Barbados as Cormac's isle of promise. (In 1516 it was already called the Isle of St. Brendan.) The return voyage went through the Bahamia area, by the fog-shrouded Grand Banks of Newfoundland, through the iceberg areas south of Greenland, close to volcanic activity in Iceland, and then home to Ireland. The current of the Gulf Stream and favorable winds would have helped the voyage all the way. It is not unreasonable to suppose that such a trip could begin in May (shortly after Beltaine) and bring the voyagers home close to Lugnasa, or Lady Day in Harvest (August).

---

* Cormac's reference to "Great Ireland" is based on a brief line in the saga of Erik the Red (mostly Irish in his ancestry) several hundred years later. The reference to an Irish kingdom in the years before the coming of Patrick is a nod to Barry Fell's interesting thesis of a pre-Christian Celtic kingdom in New England, a possible explanation for the persistence in very ancient Gaelic folklore of the belief in the Promised Land in the West.

Whatever is to be said of the story of the voyage of Brendan, the monks who set it down on paper three centuries after it happened (around 900 A.D.) had a remarkably detailed map of the North Atlantic at hand—including the Faroes, the Azores, the Saragossa Sea, Barbados, Bahamia, Newfoundland, the icebergs, and Iceland. They also knew the direction of the prevailing winds and currents. Similar information was available to Columbus five centuries later. It is unnecessary to assume that Columbus knew the Brendan story—though he probably did—but it does seem almost certain that both the authors of the Brendan tale and Columbus had available the same kind of information about the nature of the North Atlantic. The events of the voyage described in Cormac's perceptions are taken from the text of the Brendan tale, including even some of the metaphors, of the original authors.

The religious symbols in the story are Celtic in origin, but exist in many other religions. Water, as a symbol of the source of life and death throughout the legend, is central to all ancient faiths, not merely the Celtic religion; it is also present, of course, in Christianity, as is erotic love, the symbol of divine love.

The form of courtly love in my version of the legend is not a projection on the past of medieval chivalry. It is, rather, a reflection of the kind of courtly love that can be found in the Irish sagas. In those stories there is no conflict between chivalry and sleeping together, as there is in the Arthurian cycle and in the culture of the troubadors. The concern about colorful clothes and frequent bathing that we find in the era of our story is consistent with the sagas and the archaeological evidence. The bantering between Cormac and Brigid is also faithful to the spirit of the sagas, although it is less explicitly erotic in this story than in some of the old stories.

In most cases I have used modern English spellings for Irish words—Dermot instead of Diarmuid, and Kerry instead of Ciarraige. Podraig seemed to deserve a special name. The major feast days mentioned in the text are Inbolc (February 1), Beltaine (May 1), Lugnasa (August 1), and Samain (November 1). They are roughly parallel in meaning to the Christian feasts of St. Brigid, Easter (Passover), Lady Day in Harvest, and All Hallows Eve.

If my version of the legend suggests that the Holy Grail/magic princess might really be the girl down the street, it is a contemporary Irish American addition—though not one false to the spirit of the legend.

I have not intended to suggest that the sacred personages of the Old Faith or the New Faith actually lurked in the meadows and rocks of early medieval Ireland, but merely that it was taken for granted by someone like Brigid that the Many-Colored Land intersected frequently with this world. For us it seems impossible to enter into dialogue with the brown-haired, Semitic-featured young woman, because we do not expect to meet her. In those days, in principle at any rate, the dialogue was possible because one did not think it completely impossible that one might meet her.

It may be objected that in the "modern sense" Cormac and Brigid are far too self-conscious in their relationship with one another. Such self-consciousness, it could be argued, is highly improbable in their sixth-century barbarian culture. But the Ardagh Chalice (and you can imagine the magic cup looking like it), the *Book of Kells,* the monastic poetry, and the sagas were not the work of barbarians. In the stories of the various Irish mythological cycles, there is a sophistication about human relationships that strongly challenges our modern temporal ethnocentrism.

Cormac and Brigid may not have had available the resources of post-Freudian vocabulary to talk about their relationship, but it is gratuitous to assert that such folk were less capable of self-reflection than we are.

Finally, I do not know if the diminutive "Biddy" was used in the sixth century. It does not matter; it is still an appropriate name for a prototypical Irish woman—the kind of hard-tongued, strong-willed, soft-hearted, tender woman who has been a burden to Irish males down through the centuries—a burden, that is, until we stop to consider the alternatives.

SELECTED BIBLIOGRAPHY

Chadwick, Nora. *The Celts.* New York: Penguin, 1971.

Cunliffe, Barry. *The Celtic World: Portrait of a Civilization.* New York: McGraw-Hill, 1979.

DePaor, Maire, and DePaor, Liam. *Early Christian Ireland.* London: Thames & Hudson, 1978.

Dillon, Myles, ed. *Early Irish Society.* Cork, Ireland: Mercier Press, 1969.

Dillon, Myles, and Chadwick, Nora. *The Celtic Realms.* New York: New American Library, 1967.

Hughes, Kathleen. *The Church of Early Irish Society.* Ithaca, N.Y.: Cornell University Press, 1967.

Lady Gregory. *The Voyage of St. Brendan the Navigator.* Buckinghamshire, England: Colin Smythe, 1973.

Laing, Lloyd. *The Archaeology of Late Celtic Britain and Ireland, C 400–1200 A.D.* New York: Barnes & Noble, 1975.

Macalister, Robert A. *Tara: A Pagan Sanctuary.* New York: Charles Scribner's Sons, 1931.

McNally, Robert. *Old Ireland.* New York: Fordham University Press, 1965.

Markale, Jean. *Women of the Celts.* London: Gordon & Cremonesi, 1975.

Mercier, Vivian. *The Irish Comic Tradition.* Oxford: Oxford University Press, 1969.

Rees, Alwyn, and Rees, Brinley *Celtic Heritage: Ancient Tradition in Ireland and Wales.* London: Thames & Hudson, 1977.

Ross, Ann. *Everyday Life of the Pagan Celts.* New York: G. P. Putnam's Sons, 1970.

Severin, Tim. *The Brendan Voyage.* New York: McGraw-Hill, 1978.

Sharkey, John. *Celtic Mysteries: The Ancient Religion.* New York: Avon, 1975.

Thomas, Charles. *Britain and Ireland in Early Christian Times A.D. 400–800.* New York: McGraw-Hill, 1971.